SLOW LIGHT

Michael Donovan was born in Yorkshire and now lives in Cumbria. A consultant engineer by profession, his first novel *Behind Closed Doors* won the 2012 Northern Crime competition.

By the same author

Praise for Michael Donovan's writing

'At a time when there seems more competition than ever in the crime-writing genre, Donovan's debut novel is a real winner...'
Lytham St Annes Express

'... a wonderful debut novel in a hugely competitive market ... an enthralling novel ... deliciously complex ... make(s) the readers hair stand on end. Donovan ... succeeds in breathing life into a host of warm, witty and realistic characters.'
Cuckoo Review

'Eddie Flynn is part Philip Marlowe, part Eddie Gumshoe, a likeable wisecracking guy but with a temper when roused ... humour ... violent confrontations ... well recommended.'
eurocrime

'... good old-fashioned detective work. A slick, dynamic mystery...'
Kirkus Reviews Recommended Book

'... one of the best novels I have read this year. Brilliantly absorbing ... escapism at its best.'
Postcard Reviews

'For many thriller fans, one read may not be enough.'
Best Thrillers

www.michaeldonovancrime.com

SLOW LIGHT

MICHAEL DONOVAN

HOUSE ON THE HILL
Publishing

First Published 2018 by **House On The Hill.**

ISBN-13: 9781729023891

Cover design by **House On The Hill** from Rob Mitchell and Shutterstock images.

p0001

Independently published.

For the nephew we still miss.
A fallen hero.

Christopher Davies
1st Battalion Irish Guards

Quis Separabit

CHAPTER ONE

A recent accident I'd suffered

Business was temporarily slow. It was that time of year. I'd been caged in my office for two days pushing paperwork and the phone had rung only twice. Both were marketing trolls. The first was a company scraping for PPI victims and the second was a law firm wanting to know about a recent accident I'd suffered. I'd had plenty of accidents this last year, few of them compensatable. When I gave the guy details he hung up. It was three days to Christmas.

The morning was settling in as another slow one. I took a moment and manoeuvred the desk round to get it out of the draft then repositioned the two-bar fire and sat back down to attack a client report that was taking longer to write than the investigation. I was snagged on grammar. Needed a word for "screwed" to go into the cover letter but an alternative wouldn't come. In the end I gave up and went with the hard truth.

"To summarise the situation," I wrote, "your actions have screwed you royally. Prosecution and jail are both probable. Please find our final invoice attached."

I sat back and re-read the page. Now that I'd written the words I couldn't imagine any others. My client would appreciate the concision.

I cut and pasted a sign-off: "Yours Faithfully, E. Flynn. Partner. The Eagle Eye Detective Agency." The paste included an ersatz signature to save time after printing. The agency was gradually modernising that way. Stand still and you're dead. I hit the button and across the room the inkjet spat and coughed like a cat bringing up hairballs. I didn't know whether the machine came that way or whether our tech guy Harry Green had put the sound effect in to remind us what we were posting out.

With clear evidence of progress I took a break and swivelled my Herman Miller executive chair to get a view over North London, at least the bit I could see through the spray-on snow Lucy had put in the windows when it was clear that the real stuff wasn't coming. The phoney snow and the tree in reception are an agency tradition. They make us more approachable. Clients know they've come to somewhere that cares. If they come.

It was just me and Lucy in. My partner Sean Shaughnessy had finished until the New Year, and our part-timer Harry was in the Canaries sinking rum and sodas on a beach. I was holding the fort, detection-wise. Keeping an eye on the world. When I'd kept an eye on the clouds for a while I swivelled back to face my desk. One more report and I'd be through. If I got into gear I might shut up shop a day early and beat the rush out of town. I leaned forward to concentrate.

Then my intercom interrupted in its usual style. The thing is an old Motorola I'd picked up in a cheapskate moment and its static was getting steadily worse. When I pressed the button the noise intensified. Lucy's voice was there somewhere beneath the din but it had no meaning. I stood up and went out.

Lucy looked up. 'You've got a call,' she told me. 'A Mrs Elland.'

I nodded and went back into my room. Sat down. Pressed the button.

'Put her through,' I said.

The device clicked and the static cleared and the caller came on nice and clear. The tremor in her voice was entirely hers. She sounded young and she sounded nervous.

'Mr Flynn?'

'Right here.'

She paused. I heard an intake of breath. Then:

'I'm not sure I should be calling you.'

'Sure you should. We're not the cheapest but we're the best.'

'I mean I'm not sure I should be calling any detective agency.'

'I know what you mean, Mrs Elland. Most of life's difficulties can be handled without private detectives. But we're like dentists. When you need us we're right here.'

That got a strained laugh, the same type she'd give if she was in a dentist's chair listening to a joke about detective agencies as the drill warmed.

'It's just that... it seems a little foolish, now I'm calling you.'

'Seventy-three percent of what we do is foolishness,' I said. 'The rest is pure insanity.'

Another pause.

'Maybe that was the wrong word. I meant drastic. Like I'm pushing things over the edge. I don't know if this is the right thing.'

'Do you have a first name, Mrs Elland?'

'Lisa.'

'Tell me about it, Lisa. What's going over the edge?'

She paused another moment, like she was reconsidering, then jumped.

'I need to find my husband.'

'You don't know where he is?'

'I think something's happened to him.'

'When did you last see him?'

'Three days ago. He was away on an overnight business trip. It's a regular thing he does. But he's not come back.'

I pushed the paperwork away and pulled the phone nearer and racked the Miller back to get my feet onto the desk.

'What's your husband's name, Lisa?'

'Ray.'

'Has Ray not called you?' I said.

'Just once. On Monday evening. To say he'd be away an extra night or so. But he's not contacted me since. And his phone has been off.'

'Do you have an itinerary for his trip? Locations? Hotel names?'

'Only his regular motel in Dartford. I called them but he didn't check in on Monday night and the people at his work don't know anything.'

'What does your husband do?'

'He's a communications executive for a local company.'

'And you say the trip's a regular thing?'

'Every week. He visits the firm's shops. They're a chain. London and the south east. He doesn't travel far but he stays overnight half way round.'

'And now he's missing.'

'Yes. And it's so unlike him. I'm frightened.'

'I understand,' I said.

I craned my neck to watch the sky over the Westway. Heavy grey clouds. A few gaps showing more grey higher up. It was nine-fifteen in the morning and this was as bright as it would get. London Decembers don't call for sun-screen. I pulled my attention back and watched the ceiling. Subconsciously checked for signs of the damp expanding.

'You've nothing to suggest why Ray might be missing, Lisa?'

'No. It's never happened before. I can't imagine what's happened.'

'I see.'

'I suppose I ought to ask about your rates.'

'No need,' I said.

'What do you mean?'

'We're going to pass on this,' I said. 'It's three days to Christmas and tomorrow afternoon – maybe *this* afternoon – we'd like to shut up shop. Which doesn't leave much time to get a result for a client who's holding back.'

I listened to silence on the other end whilst Lisa thought it through.

'What do you mean?' she said.

'Obscuring facts. Forcing us to untangle things before we can even start working for you.'

'I don't understand.'

'There you go again. But thanks for giving us a try, Lisa.'

'Wait. Please! What am I supposed to be holding back?'

'The fact that you believe that your husband's cheating on you. That maybe he's run off for a few days' Christmas bonus.'

'That's crazy. Why would I think that?'

'Beats me, Lisa, but why would you need a private investigator when your husband's been missing just three days? Technically not missing since he said he'd be away an extra day or so. If you thought something had happened to him you'd have gone to the police. But you haven't. So you're not worrying about his safety. You're just burning up with the need to know what he's up to. As if, for example, you thought he was cheating on you.'

Lisa went quiet again.

I switched back to watching the sky. The clouds continued to roll by beyond Lucy's fake snowdrifts. From outside it probably looked like we were snowed up in here. Ten seconds passed before Lisa finished turning things over and spoke again. Her voice was no steadier than before.

'He wouldn't do that to us,' she said. 'It's Christmas. He wouldn't leave me and the baby.'

'He wouldn't, but you think he has. So you need someone to track your husband down and see what he's up to, which is not the same thing as finding someone who's actually missing.'

'This is driving me crazy. Why has he not called? What does he get up to when he's away? It's been his routine for as long as I remember.'

'I understand. You're scared that your husband is cheating on you and here's Christmas coming right up with you and the baby all alone and you need an answer before it tears you apart. But when you get your answer it might be a black Christmas for both of you.'

'I'll take the chance,' she said. 'Anything's better than not knowing.'

'Maybe Ray will show up today.'

'What if he doesn't? Or if he does... I still need to know where he's been.'

'Okay. So now that we've got some common understanding we might be able to take a look. If we dig hard we might catch up with Ray before he gets home. But if he beats us to it we'll be hard pushed to get evidence of what he was up to whilst he was away. Maybe you'll still have to ask him yourself.'

'But what if he doesn't come home?' she repeated.

I thought about it. How long might her husband stay out? Another night? Two? Would he stay away over Christmas without letting his wife in on the bad news? Was there any chance I could dig him out before we shut up shop tomorrow? I'd plans for Christmas and they didn't involve staking out an errant spouse's love-nest, so the job would be limited. Was two days enough? Logic told me no. Logic said to give Lisa our apologies and put the phone down. Then I looked at the paperwork covering my desk and thought about that aspect. The paperwork said "go".

'Give me your address,' I said.

CHAPTER TWO
Communication stuff

I searched the tired end of Wandsworth and found a tiny fashion boutique called TomCat, which Lisa Elland owned with her husband. The place was jammed between fast-food takeaways and charity shops but it was painted freshly and brightly and had a colourful and imaginative display window that would look good on any up-market street. I went in and the doorbell chimed and a slim, dark-haired girl in her early twenties looked up from behind the counter where she was reading a magazine and rocking an old-fashioned pram of the kind you pay a fortune for nowadays. The rocking was delivering contented snuffling sounds from deep in the blankets. Lisa Elland pushed the magazine away and released the pram to shake my hand. A faint, dry, squeeze.

I looked round. The display rails had the decent fashion the window had promised but not much of it. The stock looked a little sparse. The boutique was at the wrong end of the street to make any real money. Probably saw most of its takings go out in rent. I turned back and smiled and got a nervous response. Lisa was still wondering if she'd jumped over the edge too hastily.

'He still not shown?' I said. It was twenty-three minutes since we'd talked but better to ask. Lisa shook her head.

I glanced round the shop again.

'I'd better say it,' I said. 'This could get a little expensive. Private investigation doesn't come cheap.'

She gave me a fragile smile. Her face was long and pale, the sort that looks better happy.

'We've saved for a holiday at the end of January,' she said. 'Tunisia. Our first trip away since our honeymoon. I'll borrow from there.'

'Ray's going to be all right with that? Using holiday funds?'

Her face tightened.

'What choice do I have? I need to find out what's happening.'

She diverted her gaze to look out through the display window.

'We'll save up again,' she said. But she said it like she wasn't sure that they would. Her face said she wasn't sure of anything any more and I was thinking that it was a great time of the year for her husband to have gone off playing games. Merry Christmas, darling.

'It's not just the cash,' I said. 'From what you've told me I'll need to locate Ray first and that means asking around, which he's likely to hear about. With that and the holiday money he'll know you've been checking him out, guilty or innocent. And when I do find him I may not see anything out of order. Not in two days. It's not as easy as in the movies. Usually it takes a little longer to catch a guy out and get the evidence. So when Ray comes home you might still be left asking him yourself unless you want us to continue after the New Year, which would take more than holiday funds.'

Lisa listened but was shaking her head distractedly all the while, still watching the street. Finally she forced a shrug and looked at me.

'I can't wait here, not knowing,' she said. 'I'm sure you'll find Ray. He's got to be *somewhere.*'

'You mean *with someone?*'

Her eyes glinted. 'I don't know what to think. Ray just wouldn't do that.'

Though many do. I waited.

'Ray's a great guy,' Lisa said. 'All he ever talks about is developing the shop and moving up to Oxford street. Having kids. He's not the sort to hurt me and Jessica like this. And he doesn't need anyone else. We're a perfect match. Everyone says it. So why would he ever cheat?'

'You tell me. But that's what you're thinking. It's why you called me.'

Her lips compressed again and she folded her arms. Kept herself together. I moved on.

'How has Ray been acting lately?'

'Just normal.'

'Nothing unusual? No sense that he's been distant with you? No suspicious calls or movements?'

'No. The first thing I knew was his call on Monday evening. He sounded tense, like he had something on his mind. And that was the last I heard.'

'What did he tell you?'

'Just that he had some extra jobs to do and he'd be another night away.'

'He didn't give any detail? What the jobs where? Where he was going?'

'No. But it would only be round the businesses. Just his regular route. The company is just local.'

'And he's never stayed away before? Planned or unplanned?'

'Never. That's why I'm scared.'

'How long have you been married, Lisa?'

'Four years. We were going together for two before that.'

'And you say Ray's a family kind of guy?'

'Totally. Ask anyone. Everyone's always telling me how lucky I am.'

'A one-woman guy?'

She smiled half-heartedly. 'I don't know what I'd call him exactly. He was always popular with the girls. Always fooling around. But I was the serious one. The one he always came back to.'

'Where do you live?'

'Here. Upstairs. The lease includes a flat.'

'And people round here know him?'

'People everywhere. Here, Streatham, Wimbledon. Ray likes to get around in the evenings. He's a socialiser. More than I am.'

'Even though you're married? With you and the baby here?'

'He's just not the sort to stay home. I knew that before we were married. But he's always got time for us. He's always home at night, even if it's late. He always puts us first. Does little things. Brings flowers if we've had a row. Last month I mentioned that the curtains were a mess upstairs. I'd seen some lovely ones over in Bermondsey and Ray got them to come and measure up without telling me, then one day I went up and we had new curtains hanging. That's what Ray's like. He loves to surprise me.'

'Sounds like a great guy.'

'He is.' She looked at me. 'That's why I don't understand what's happening.'

'Okay,' I said. 'One step at a time. First thing, we need to find Ray. Let's give it the two days and see what turns up. I'm going to need the first day funding up front. We'll bill the second in arrears if we pick Ray up. If we draw a blank, or if he shows up back here, we'll forget the second day and you can let us know whether you want us to continue after the New Year. Is that okay with you?'

The glisten in her eyes said it wasn't but she was toughing it out.

She opened the till and pretty much cleared out what was in there. I gave her a receipt and a form to sign and when the formalities were out of the way I asked her where Ray worked.

'He works for a bookmakers called Odds-On,' she said. 'They've ten shops in the area. Ray's based at their Mitcham branch.'

I knew the firm from passing their windows on low-rent streets south of the river. The places had never registered with me, just struggling retailers jammed between greengrocers and kebab houses, eking a profit just sufficient to stave off the landlord. But maybe I was underestimating. Chances were that they were raking it in.

'What's a communications executive?' I said.

The baby stirred. Lisa reached for the pram handle. Rocked it some more. Smiled sadly.

'I don't know, exactly. Ray keeps an eye on things around the branches. Checks everything's running smoothly. That sort of thing. Communication stuff.'

I was none the wiser.

'And Micham's his base?'

'Yes. He works there when he's not doing the rounds. Mondays and Tuesdays he goes out to visit the other branches.'

I logged the info. Ray's disappearance was probably unconnected to work but my first check would be to see whether he was still showing up nine till five. Maybe he was only staying out of *Lisa's* sight.

'Tell me about the weekly trips,' I said.

'It's a regular routine. He visits all of the branches every Monday and Tuesday. Some are in town but there's a few further out: Sevenoaks and Chatham, Dartford. Ray stays the night in Dartford to save driving back in halfway round. When he finishes the round he heads back to Mitcham on Tuesday afternoon.'

'Where does he stay in Dartford?'

'There's a Travelodge near the centre.'

'Does he have places he visits in the evening? Restaurants? Pubs?'

'I don't know. I guess he goes out to eat and have a drink, but he's never told me.'

'Could he have been meeting someone over there?'

I saw the pain in her face. The baby stirred in the pram. Worked up towards crying. Lisa bent and lifted her out and clutched the child to her. The child's grumbles wavered and subsided.

'He just wouldn't,' she said to the baby. 'Ray loves us.' She raised the baby and pressed its face to her neck then looked at me.

'Really: Ray's a good guy,' she said. 'The best.' Her face pleaded with me.

'You've never picked up hints of anything? Calls he's received? A name you don't know?'

'None. And I'm sure it's not that...'

I grinned. 'Let's not go back to the start,' I said. 'The clock's running and you're haemorrhaging vacation money based on a gut feeling. If you want to open the till we can clip the fee right back in there before the damage is done. Otherwise we need to face reality. I'm going to need all the help I can get. You need to stop holding back, Lisa.'

But Lisa didn't get the chance to answer. Because right then the shop door opened and two characters from Mafia central casting walked in.

CHAPTER THREE
The third guy

One was a big guy with a face like a misshapen potato topped by a wire brush hairdo. Gym-jock muscles tested the shoulders of his suede coat. The second guy was smaller, five-five, with an angular face and a small mouth missing the smile muscles. He reminded me of Franco Interlenghi whom I'd seen six months ago in an old Bogart and Gardner film. His skin was a faint olive, adding to the hint of Latin blood.

They stood holding the door open like they were waiting for a third guy but the third guy didn't show. The two of them were looking at me. The message clicked: I was the third guy. The door was for me. A nice gesture if I'd been leaving.

Spud tilted his head. I grinned and shook mine. Thanks anyway!

'Hey! Pal!' Spud said. He tilted his head a little further. Franco watched and chewed gum slowly. I held my grin and leaned against the counter to clarify things. Door not needed. But my discussion with Lisa was on hold while these two were in here, and the clock was ticking. Whatever these guys had come in for I needed them to be quick, though if they were looking for their clothing size they'd struggle.

Spud stayed cool. Held the door wider. 'Hey,' he shrugged. 'C'mon! Skedaddle!' His voice was like a diesel at low revs and I was starting to wonder what the hell was going on.

'It's fine,' I said. 'I'm not quite through.'

I remained where I was at the counter. Lisa put the baby back into its pram.

'Sure you're through,' Spud said. 'Let's go, pal.'

His face was still broadcasting calm patience but his shoulders were beginning to bob with an inner tension.

I looked at him. 'It's a little cold,' I pointed out, 'with the door open.'

The door stayed open. Then Franco spoke.

'Is there something you don't understand here?' he said.

'Yes,' I said. 'I don't understand how long we need to waste on this stupid conversation.'

Franco stopped chewing.

'You think this is a joke? You think we're playing around?' He had a small, strangled voice. The sort that had been mimicked at school before the other kids learned their lesson.

I shrugged. Kept my opinions to myself.

'Let me show you a joke,' Franco said. He made to come across the shop but Spud's hand grabbed his shoulder.

'Okay,' Spud said. 'We'll call back.'

Franco turned to look at him but Spud held his grip and eased the little man back out of the door. The guy wasn't happy. He turned to throw me a look with a message as he stepped onto the street. Then the door closed behind them and the bell tinkled and the shop was quiet and warm again.

I looked at Lisa.

'What was that about?' I said. She was even paler than before. Her eyes were wide, focused on the street. I thought she hadn't heard me but then she spoke.

'Nothing,' she said. 'Just some people we deal with.'

'Strange people to meet in the fashion business.'

She shook her head.

'They go round all the businesses,' she said. 'They run this area.'

'Protection?' I said. 'Those guys are extorting you?'

She let out a bitter, scared, laugh. Went back to watching the street.

'It's part of the tax system,' she said. 'We don't make much but they get their share.'

'How much?'

She hesitated. Her eyes darted, looked at me, looked out at the street, looked back again.

'Two hundred a week,' she said.

Which sounded like a serious skim on the place. They were taking maybe a quarter, even half, of the net profits.

'Are you up to date with the payments?' I said.

Lisa smiled. 'There's no arrears option,' she said. 'I pay them every week.'

I thought about it.

'They're not going to be happy at a missed collection,' I said.

She sighed. Shook her head.

'It's no problem,' she said. 'They'll be back.'

But it would be a problem, seeing as how I'd nearly cleaned out the till to pay for the first day chasing her husband. I pulled the cash back out of my pocket and separated out two hundred quid, which was half of the fee. Held the notes out.

'We'll add it back on tomorrow,' I said. 'Better keep the till stocked today.'

She looked at the notes. Looked at me.

'I don't expect you to work for free.'

'I'm not working for free. I've got my deposit and you can dig into the holiday savings for the balance.'

She was still inclined to resist but I planted the notes on top of the till and since she had no way of forcing them back onto me she hit the button and the tray slid open. She clipped the cash back in.

'Thank you,' she said.

'Thank me if everything comes back negative,' I said.

Which it wouldn't. I've investigated a hundred infidelity cases and not a single one has come back blank. The nearest I ever found to a faithful partner was when a client had me follow the guy she'd been living with for seven years who she suspected was cheating on her. She was right. He was two-timing on her with the wife she'd never heard of, which I guess is a fidelity of sorts.

'Okay,' I said. 'Let's find Ray. First, I'll need a few pointers. Names. Places. Friends who might be keeping something under wraps. You say Ray's a socialiser...'

Lisa smiled. 'He's out most nights. Pubs, clubs, friends of his.'

She gave me the names of a few of the friends. One ran an Army surplus store in Tooting and shared an interest with Ray in vintage firearms – Ray and he collected anything manufactured before the First World War and travelled to fairs and military exhibitions together. Another crony ran a garage in Croydon and shared another hobby: restored motor cars. Ray drove a seventy-six Capri, rebuilt and finished off in a tacky gold according to the photo Lisa showed me. Ray was leaning back against the car, arms crossed like he was posing on a road trip. Lisa also named a few pubs and clubs and a few more drinking buddies including a pal from his school days who was a cab driver over in Brixton. I scribbled a list with some half-cocked addresses that might or might not get me within shouting distance of Ray.

'I guess you're all sorted with passports for the holiday?' I said.

Lisa's face brightened again, jumping ahead to a future that probably no longer existed. She said that they'd both got passports.

'Can I see Ray's?'

It was the first thing to check. I wanted to know that we weren't searching for someone who'd skipped overseas, which would be way beyond our two-day commission. When the purpose of my question registered Lisa's face dropped again. She told me to hang on and she'd check upstairs. I asked her to check a few other things whilst she was there. Ray's formal documents. Bank books, driving licence. His wardrobe. Any prized belongings. Just in case he'd taken an even longer trip. She went out and I waited for five minutes. The baby co-operated. Didn't stir. Then Lisa came back down and handed me Ray's passport and reported that all his stuff was there. The only things missing were his overnight bag and the few things he usually took on his weekly trip.

Which suggested that the guy was still in the country and probably still in her life. Good to know. I checked the passport photo and handed it back. Asked if she had a spare photo of Ray. She went back up and rooted one out. It was of the two of them, heads together at a table by a hotel pool. Blue sky in the background. I stashed it in my wallet.

I had a few pointers. Ray's pals, his workplace, his social territory. But no known location since Monday morning, which was three days ago. It was now Thursday, ten-fifteen, and I was planning to shut up shop at five tomorrow evening, which now looked tight. Even if I found Ray today that would only be the start, unless I got lucky and collared him *in flagrante* with his love interest, something I could bring back to Lisa and close the job.

Lisa read my thoughts. 'Do you think you'll find him?' she said. Her eyes were just as scared as before.

'Let's see where it goes,' I said.

I snapped a card onto the counter, threw her an encouraging smile and went out.

In the street I looked up and down but the pavement was empty. Our extortion team was gone.

CHAPTER FOUR

A certain touch with the customers

I drove down to Mitcham. Parked the car and crossed the Green to a mixed commercial and residential block inside the one-way loop. The Odds-On fascia was displayed above a frosted shop window on the far side. Ray's workplace. The shop had told Lisa that Ray hadn't been in, and maybe he hadn't but this was the middle of the day in the middle of the week and if you're starting a wild goose chase the best place to start is the one your quarry should be at. When I'd confirmed that Ray was AWOL from his job I'd start the chase. I opened the door and went in.

Talk nowadays is all about the north-south divide but bookmakers balk the trend. London shops project the same sleaze as Wetherby and Harrogate. They wear respectability as a cracked veneer that fools only their clients, blind to the mess of defaced furniture and discarded tickets beneath their feet. In the image department Odds-On were market leaders. The shop was small and narrow and floored in cheap discoloured laminate, walled in the dirty yellow emulsion from the old retail unit. Up top, stained polystyrene ceiling panels testified to the leaks that had driven the old business out. When Odds-On moved in they just put up their fascia and opened the door. Revamping budget zero. You knew the place was a betting shop only by the row of fixed-odds machines against one wall and the security cage across the angle at the back. Live feeds were brought in to a single screen above the table where punters wrote out their tickets. It wasn't entirely clear how things worked since there were no prices on display. Maybe you handed the ticket in and took SP. Take it or leave it. The place screamed under-investment. No chairs at the table, not even stools to keep the fobty addicts comfortable whilst they donated their benefits. Maybe the absence of furniture was deliberate. Minimised throwables, which had to make sense when you were luring people in to fleece them. And the season of good cheer hadn't made it through the door. Not a Christmas tree or holly sprig in sight; not a single strand of tinsel even over the cashier's window. More good tactics: conditioned the clients for the

Christmas that was coming.

Eleven in the morning and the place was almost empty. The racing crowd wouldn't be in for three hours. Just a couple of punters working the fixed-odds machines in tracksuits and hoods, focused on their quest for gold. One of them was talking to the machine. Some kind of mantra: 'Geddin! Keep going. Geddin! Keep going. Easy! Easy! Geddin!' The guy bobbed and bowed to the machine, oblivious, and his mantra followed me to the cashier's booth where a gaunt woman in a bright red jacket fixed me in a stare as I stooped to the window. I asked for Ray. She held her stare and said that Ray wasn't in. Didn't elucidate.

'Try later,' she said.

'He'll be in later?'

'He might.'

'He's your boss?'

She lifted a lip. Stared out through the glass.

'One of them.'

'You've more than one boss?'

'Whoever's in. I do what I'm told. Are you placing a bet?'

'But Ray does work here? He's one of your bosses?'

'Try later,' she repeated.

Blood out of stone. I gripped the counter. Stooped lower.

'Has Ray been in today?'

'No.'

'Yesterday?'

'No.'

Not today. Not yesterday. Maybe not this year. End of discussion. The woman was the one who explained to punters why their horse had fallen at the first fence or why the roulette wheel jammed short. I guess her lines of conversation were limited. I tried specifics.

'Any idea where Ray is?'

'They tell me what I need to know,' Redcoat replied. She was beginning to tire of the interrogation. Went back to tapping at her keyboard. I changed tack again.

'Is the manager in?' I said. A security door alongside the booth led through to the back. The cashier booth had its own door going back there. No direct access to the till from the shop. Redcoat kept tapping, watching the screen.

'I'm not sure who's in right now,' she said.

'Can you tell them I need a chat?'

'They're in a meeting.'

'So the manager is there?'

She looked up. Fingers poised above her keyboard.

'They're busy, sir. Are you placing a bet?'

I grinned through the bars. Stood upright. I guess working in a place like this demanded a certain touch with the customers. I'd got all I was going to, but it was most of what I needed: Redcoat hadn't seen Ray the last few days and he wasn't here today. Maybe he'd extended his business trip just as he'd told Lisa and no-one had told Redcoat. But why hadn't Ray got back in touch with Lisa? Legit business or not it made sense to call her. Whoever was behind the Odds-On security door might give me a pointer but Redcoat wasn't letting me through and I didn't have a hacksaw. I stooped again.

'One last question,' I said. 'What's a communications executive?'

Redcoat didn't look up.

I stood there a moment then threw a smile she didn't see and went back out.

~~~~~

I crossed the river in slow traffic under a press of grey cloud. The forecast was giving a forty-five percent probability of snow overnight. I got back to Chase Street and left the car on a meter outside the building. Gambled that the wardens wouldn't get close enough to see that the dial was running on empty. I went up. The tree lights were still on and Lucy was still at her desk. Unlike the bookmakers' premises, which dispensed with phoney affectation, our own reception was decked out in tinsel and a tree to complement the snow in the windows. The tree was a seven-footer that Lucy assembled each year and draped with lights. It was topped by a ten inch figure of Sherlock Holmes complete with deerstalker and drooping calabash. Holmes gave me the once-over through an oversized magnifying glass but didn't deduce anything. A sign below Holmes assured clients that "We sleuth the truth" so they knew where their money was going.

Catching Ray Elland at his supposed extra-marital games meant first finding him, which would take a bit of sleuthing in the two days we had. An extra nose might help. I decided to recruit Lucy. She gave me a bright smile and jumped up from her desk and went to pour coffee, assuming the drink would make me talkative. I was planning on being talkative anyway. I perched on her desk and waited. Lucy was wearing the same red as the Odds-On cashier only she wore it nicer and complemented it with a bright red hairdo.

Christmas.

'How are you fixed this afternoon?' I said.

'Nothing I can't unfix. I was planning to help Uncle Umberto but he can manage.'

When she's not organising the agency Lucy puts her qualifications to work running her uncle's music shop over in Bethnal Green. I'd heard once that they paid her, which probably made the job more attractive than this one. Lucy and I had first met through a shared interest in jazz followed by a shared interest in the agency, which I run with my partner Sean Shaughnessy from our top floor offices in Westbourne Green. At one time Lucy and I had a shared interest in each other but that had come to an end when the fireworks threatened to blow up both our lives. Luckily Lucy had opted to stay with us and keep the firm out of trouble with creditors. What she really wanted, though, was to be a detective.

She proffered the coffee mug and I told her I had work for her. Detective work. Her face brightened further. She joined me on the desk and I sipped coffee and briefed her on our mission. The coffee was good.

'You've got to *find* the guy?' she said. 'That's a tall order by tomorrow, Eddie.'

'Do-able if he's not scarpered to some remote love nest. He's got friends, acquaintances. Lots of them. If he's still in town someone will have seen him.'

'You think that's what it is? He's staying out of sight for a few days playing around?'

'Funnier things have happened. And it's what Lisa suspects. Maybe Ray will turn up back home and they'll have it out, but right now she's counting the hours to a Christmas alone. She's frightened. She needs this sorting, fast.'

'Walking out, leaving her guessing is pretty cold if they're as close as you say.'

'As close as *she* says. Lisa's still living the dream. Maybe a different one from Ray's. But yeah, if Ray is running around with another woman then he's pretty blatant about it and that's a little odd. If playing around is his normal thing then why rock the boat this time? Why not give Lisa a credible excuse? Continue with the quiet life.'

'Maybe he's not interested in the quiet life,' Lucy said. 'Maybe it's over between them.'

'Then why not tell Lisa? And if he's moved out why not take his stuff?'

'You saying it's something else?'

'I'm wondering. You recall any time things were what they seemed in this business?'

She got the point. 'Not ever,' she said. She sipped coffee and kicked her heels. 'Ray's not really *missing* yet,' she pointed out.

'Officially, no. He told Lisa he'd be staying away an extra day or so. But the trip has stretched a little too far by now and he must know that he's burning bridges.'

'So what's the chance that this is something else?'

I gave her fifty-fifty. The same as the snow. And even if we *were* looking at just a cheating husband we were looking at a cheating husband second. First of all we were looking at a guy who'd dropped out of sight, and that was our problem.

I planted my coffee. Hopped off the desk and made a scan of Lisa's photo. Cropped it down to Ray's head and shoulders and blew the thing up to four times size. The inkjet spat out two copies. Good for waving under noses.

'We need to talk to everyone who knows him,' I said. 'We've names and places. Someone may have spotted Ray or may know more than Lisa about what he's up to. Are you in the buggy?'

Lucy drove an orange and black Smart Fortwo on the days she hadn't time for London Transport. She hefted a key fob.

'Fully mobile,' she said.

'Okay. I'll take the friends. A couple of the places Lisa gave me. You take the others: pubs and clubs. Any other likely spots you pass. Play the jilted woman. They're not likely to know where Ray is or to tell you, but if you barge around with attitude there'll be a barman or busybody somewhere who can't resist painting a picture. Maybe give you some pointers about Ray's habits.'

'Wilco,' Lucy said. 'Jilted it is. I'm feeling mad at Ray already.'

I pushed myself off the desk.

'Attagirl. Let's see if some knight in tarnished armour will throw a name your way just to stir things up.'

I finished my coffee and we shut up shop. Turned the door sign but left the Christmas lights twinkling to let visitors know we were still alive.

CHAPTER FIVE
I advised her against it

Lisa had named a friend of Ray's called Dominic Samuels who lived in Brixton but drove a mini-cab for a firm called CityKab based here in Paddington. I retrieved the car and drove round to park off Westbourne Grove and walk down to the firm's offices which comprised a tiny shop with three plastic chairs and a counter, located on the main drag. Behind the counter a woman was working reception and dispatch. I told her I was a friend of a friend and needed to talk to Samuels. She radioed him and bounced back questions. I replied that the friend was Ray Elland. More crackly messages passed back and forth then the dispatcher reported that Samuels was on his lunch break, parked up behind Brixton Station. If I got there inside half an hour he'd be waiting. I thanked her and went out.

Lunch sounded like a good concept so I dodged traffic and ran into the deli across the street and grabbed two bacon barms and a fizzy water. As I waited to cross back I spotted William, an old guy who'd been selling The Big Issue on a pitch outside Sainsbury's since summer. He'd sold me the Christmas edition already but he clocked me and gave me a wave and I wouldn't be seeing him before the New Year so I went over. His smile was wide despite the biting wind as he waved the same edition at me. I smiled back. Fished in my pocket. The sooner the old guy flogged his batch the sooner he'd be off the street. The scars of outdoor life made William's age difficult to determine but he looked well into his sixties, and standing in the street in two degrees above freezing was no kind of a retirement. The last of my change had gone in the deli so I handed him a twenty and told him to keep it. I'd handed a tenner across last Saturday. I doubted if he remembered but his smile stretched as wide as it did then. He handed a fresh copy of the paper across.

'Marry Chrissmas my fren,' he said. 'The marryest of Chrissmas.' His grin beat back the wind.

He had a mutt at his feet, a brindle Staffie called Herbie. Herbie grinned too but didn't speak. His eyes were on my sandwiches and everything he had to say was in the grin which was as bright as William's but a mile wider. I took a barm out of its wrapper and sneaked it down and Herbie demolished it and got his eyes back onto my remaining wrapper.

'Merry Christmas yourself,' I said. 'Do you have any use for this?' I held out the second sandwich and William said no, he couldn't deprive a man. But what the heck, I'd grab something later. I handed the barm across anyway and left them to it, dodged traffic back to the Frogeye. When I checked back at the corner William was handing the second sandwich down and Herbie's grin was now two miles wide.

I reached Brixton in twenty minutes and spotted a black C-Max with a CityKab logo in a street off Acre Lane. I nudged in behind it and walked round. Slid into the front and held my hand out to a biggish black guy sipping coke. Food wrappers were stuffed into the door pocket and the car was heavy with the lingering odour of grilled chicken. Samuels set his can down in a dashboard cup holder and turned to see who the hell had come running all the way from Paddington to talk to him.

I gave him a half-straight story that Ray was away on business and Lisa wasn't sure where but needed to get in touch but his phone was off. The baby had gone sick. Ray needed to know.

'Friend of the family?' Samuels said. 'Never heard of you, man.'

'On Lisa's side. Ray wouldn't mention me.'

'An' Ray's out of town?'

'And out of touch. I'm asking around. Someone must know where he is.'

'What's his work say? They not in touch?'

'He's not contacted them. That's the puzzle.'

'Yeah, that's a puzzle. And the baby being sick and all. Well I hope you find him mister but I don't know who the hell you are and I'm not gabbin' to strangers without ID.'

I pulled out my driving licence. He checked it. Handed it back.

'Well, man, that's good and kosher. But it doesn't say on here that you're not a cop.'

I gave him a weary smile. 'Do I look like a cop, Dominic?'

'Sure you do. And I ain't setting the law on Ray's ass.'

'Has Ray got something to hide?'

'We all got something to hide. But Ray's a regular guy. Just hustling for a living. Keeping his family fed.'

'Call Lisa,' I said. 'She'll confirm who I am.'

The suspicious bastard did just that. He called Ray first, which got the same voicemail I'd listened to thirty minutes back. Then he called Lisa. She picked up and confirmed that she'd hired me.

'A private *what!*' Samuels said. 'Yo! girl, what's going down?'

I waited whilst Lisa told him. Samuels listened then disconnected with a frown.

'A private friggin' detective,' he said. He turned to look at me. 'You're taking Lisa's money to chase Ray?'

'I advised her against it,' I told him. 'But you just heard her. She's alone and frightened and wants this to end. What the hell is Ray up to that's put her in that position?'

'I don't know what the hell he's up to. I didn't know he was dropped out of sight.'

'So now you do. Are you going to help me? The sooner we catch up with Ray the sooner Lisa stops paying me.'

Samuels shook his head. Stared out of the windscreen. 'Man,' he said, 'what's happening? I've known Ray since we was in school. Him and Lisa both. What's private detectives got to do with that?'

The standard question. Private detectives have nothing to do with most people until their world comes crashing down. I moved on.

'I hear Ray gets around,' I said. 'I hear he's a bit of a party animal.'

'Ray likes to live,' Samuels agreed, 'the same as the rest of us. Likes to have a good time. He's a fun guy. The life and soul. The drinks are always on him, know what I mean? Ray would do anything for anybody. Nothing wrong in that.'

'Depends whom he likes to have a good time with. Having a wife and baby at home.'

'We all got a wife and baby at home. Doesn't mean we're chained to the front door.'

'Lisa tells me Ray was always popular with the girls. Is he still popular?'

'Sure Ray's pop'lar. Like everyone. He's a fun guy. The ladies come on to him. But he knows his responsibilities.'

'So he's never fooled around? All those years you've known him?'

Samuels gripped the wheel. Stared through the windscreen.

'No way, man. I'm not talkin' about that. For Lisa or no-one.'

'So Ray *has* fooled around?'

'Forget it, man. I ain't mouthing off on Ray. We go back, the two of us. An' he's always done right by Lisa and the baby. I was his best man you know? They're a great couple.'

'Doesn't mean Ray never plays around.'

'It means I'm not talkin' to you about it.'

'Have you ever seen Ray with another woman?'

'Are you deaf, man? Ray's my bes' friend.'

'Okay, but let's think of Lisa too. Imagine how she's feeling, all alone with Christmas coming up, wondering if she and the baby still have a husband and father. Is Lisa not your friend too?'

Samuels stared at the traffic on Acre. Worked up a slow shrug.

'If Ray ain't in work I don't know where he is,' he said.

'Has he mentioned anything? Any trips he might be taking? Anyone he might be seeing?'

'Nothin'. He didn't say about going nowhere.'

'No-one?'

He kept quiet. His fingers gripped the wheel. He stared up at the main road.

'Man,' he said, 'this is so messed up. I don't know what that boy's up to.'

'No-one?'

Samuels watched the traffic for a while. Then shook his head.

'Forget it, mate. I ain't dishing the dirt. I don't know what Ray's up to but he'd better get back to Lisa and the baby double quick. He shouldn't be fooling around on her right before Christmas.'

But he wasn't denying anything. If you're not inclined to dish out dirt it's good if you can vouch that your friend is squeaky clean and Samuels wasn't vouching for anything.

'What does Ray do for Odds-On?' I asked. 'They gave me some bullshit title: Communications Executive. What does that mean?'

Samuels relaxed a little.

'I dunno what Ray does. He's a busy man. Keeps the shops in order. Keeps things running smooth, know what I mean?'

'He manages the Mitcham shop. Mainly works there, right?'

'Yeah, that's his HQ. But he's not the manager. He's above manager. Some kind of area job. He covers all the shops.'

'Got it. So what does Ray get up to when he's not working or socialising? If I was a cop would I be interested in him?'

'If you were you wouldn't hear it from me,' Samuels said. 'I ain't tellin' tales. Ray likes to hustle like we all do. But he works hard. He pays his taxes.'

'You pay your taxes?'

'Enough of the time to keep the tax man off my back. But we all hustle. An' maybe Ray has a little dabble to bring in some extra income. I don' know an' wouldn't tell you if I did.'

'But there's nothing that might take him away from home? Nothing that might get him into trouble. I don't mean with the police.'

The cab was stuffy. The grilled chicken had permeated. Samuels wound the windows down and we both breathed.

'Ray's always up to something,' he said. 'But it's small time. Nothin' like drugs or stuff. Nothin' that's gonna bring trouble. Ray doesn't look for no trouble.'

'Where does Ray hang out? Who are his pals?'

Samuels thought about it and gave me a few places and names to add to Lisa's list, including one name that was already on it. A guy called Stuart Barr who shared an interest in antique firearms. He and Ray got together most Wednesday nights with some like-minds at the Bay Horse pub over in Clapham. Samuels joined them for a drink from time to time but he wasn't into guns or antiques and there's only so long you can sit listening to anoraks.

'Ray was prob'ly there last night,' Samuels said. 'That's where I'd start. Someone might know what he's up to.'

I pulled out a card.

'If you hear anything let me know,' I said. 'I'm not out to stir up trouble between him and Lisa but if she can find out where he is, what he's up to, it will be a weight off her shoulders. Maybe help both of them.'

'If I see him I'll tell him you're asking.' He inspected the card. 'I just hope you're not wrecking things, no matter what you say.'

So did I. Lisa was kind of sweet and Ray sounded like a regular guy and they both had a baby girl who depended on them. But I was wondering whether something was already wrecked. It was hard to see the good side of leaving your wife and kid alone and scared three days before Christmas.

CHAPTER SIX
Weird was her actual word

I fired up the Frogeye and rolled out onto Brixton Hill with Lisa's list and a day and a half to turn it into a result. One thirty in the afternoon. Lunch was barely over but the solid grey cloud had already dropped the streets into an early dusk. The Christmas tree lights over the road stood out nicely as I made the turn.

I drove a quarter of a mile up, to a working men's club in a knocked-through Edwardian. I pushed through a huddle of smokers at the entrance and found the place busier that you'd expect on a weekday afternoon. Good news for a P.I. asking questions. I drifted between tables. Asked. Got nothing. Half the people knew Ray but none had seen him in the last few days.

I paused at the smokers on the way out. They hadn't seen Ray either, though their answers were shorter due to the freezing conditions. I slid back into the car and keyed up some music to ward off the chill. Jarrett's Tokyo album, the one he recorded before chronic fatigue beat him down in the nineties. Still energy to spare. I hooked the sound to my 'phones and turned the volume high, and his keyboard work parted the traffic and eased me back under the railway to circle towards Clapham.

At the top end of the High Street I pulled in at the Bay Horse pub. This was the place Ray hung out on Wednesday nights, gabbing with his antique gun pals. The pub was almost empty but the landlord knew Ray and confirmed that he hadn't been in yesterday. He was sure of this because Ray had promised to close his tab this week. The way the barman said it made it clear that tabs were a regular thing. He didn't seem overly concerned. His money would come. He didn't seem overly-keen to dispense information about Ray either, though he did concede that Ray's gun-collecting pal Stuart Barr *was* in yesterday. He asked how I knew Ray and I said 'Doesn't everyone?' He shrugged and pursed his lips and I headed back out.

I left the car where it was and walked up to the railway bridge. Dodged traffic and crossed to a side street running alongside the viaduct and walked twenty yards below the arches to stand opposite a wall. A South London train rattled overhead. The wall spanned a ten yard gap between the buildings on the far side of the street and hid a two storey cottage annex. The wall's street face was black rendering, broken at the centre by a rotting door. I checked Lisa's list. The list said "Black wall. Door". I walked across.

The door opened onto a yard barely four feet across, laid with ancient cobblestones slick with a black sheen. The cottage it served was a low, mean building in crumbling brickwork broken on the ground floor by a window and door, and upstairs by a single window. A soil pipe parting from rusted brackets ran down into the cobbles. The windows and door were in the same distressed wood and flaking paint as the street door. Up top, the moss-covered roof sagged impressively and might or might not stop the rain. A few planters, rotted to the point of collapse, and two toppled wheelie bins, completed the landscaping. It was the kind of place that fires up the London estate agent's imagination to pull out the word "quirky". Lisa's list told me that the cottage was inhabited by a guy called Kevin Kobert, who was a pal of Ray's and was also quirky. Weird was her actual word. Prone to mood swings and tantrums and name-calling. Into soft drugs and short-lasting jobs. His last known employment had been in the Amazon warehouse up at Milton Keynes, which was a hell of a daily ride even on his reported motorbike. His quirky side gave him a mohawk hairdo and nose-ring and had him playing bar piano to supplement his minimum wage. Apparently he drifted round the night spots and talked like he was hip and called Ray "Man" and "Daddy-O" and annoyed the hell out of Lisa but for some reason he got on with Ray. They hung out, she'd said, a little more than was healthy. Ray had been known to come home a little high. She hadn't a clue what the two of them got up to but thought that if anyone knew what Ray was doing right now it would be Kevin.

There was no sign of Kobert's bike in the yard but I pressed the doorbell anyway. Nothing. I rapped on the wood. Same result. Street noise made it impossible to hear whether anyone was moving about inside, but if Kevin Kobert was working a fifty-five hour Amazon week between playing club piano he'd either be in Milton Keynes or in bed.

Another time.

I went back out. Walked up to the main street and caught a gust under the bridge that nearly knocked me for six. Temperature was dropping into the negative. Traffic batted by with headlights blazing, casting freezing eddies that slapped my neck and cheeks. People moved fast, hunched down. I followed suit and hurried past shop-fronts ablaze with Christmas lights. Got back to the Frogeye. Folded myself in and checked the list and rolled out west to cut across the top of the Common. At the Common lights I made a last-second lane switch so that my turn was unannounced and confirmed that a black Toyota Avensis thirty yards behind me wasn't there by chance. My sudden move left it fighting to get into the feeder lane and when I made the turn my mirror caught it pulling across traffic to avoid being trapped by a red. It cut off a bus and attracted a horn symphony I could hear above the Jarrett. I continued watching as the car worked its way back up and stuck, still thirty yards back, as we descended the underpass into Wandsworth.

We drifted with the traffic through the top end of the town. Falling darkness and Christmas lights smeared the mix of shabby and new into an almost harmonious whole, though the area wasn't much up on Lisa and Ray's end of town. I cut away from the main street, following Lisa's list, and checked out a pool hall, two pubs and a social club in an hour. Picked up tittle-tattle but nothing to say where Ray was or what he was up to. The people who knew Ray all seemed to like him. He was a top guy. A diamond geezer. That was about all they knew. I went into a place called the Mason's Arms and a codger about a hundred and twenty years old smoking an illegal pipe misunderstood my question and thought Ray was coming in. He yelled to the barman to pour him a double whisky on the premise that it was covered. The barman was more astute. He gave me a suspicious look and asked what was up. He didn't know me from Adam and didn't buy the implication that I was one of Ray's pals. I grinned and slapped a tenner on the bar to cover the old guy's shot and the barman chilled out. Pointed me to a guy in a suit working a phone at the far end of the bar. A regular on extended lunch break. I walked across and the guy introduced himself as Jeffrey Wright and dropped the fact that he owned Frejus and Winters, whatever the hell Frejus and Winters was, though it was clearly a big enough concern to need no explanation. 'Wow,' I said. 'How's business?'

He shrugged and told me that business was okay. Made it sound like that was the only possible answer. I said that was great. Asked if Ray had been in there lately.

He looked at me.

'Ray?' he said. 'Why is Ray going to come into F and W?'

'Yeah,' I said. 'Not his thing.' Whatever the thing was. 'Do you see Ray much?'

'Now and then. What's happening?'

'Hell if I know. I'm running round trying to find him. The bugger's got his phone off.'

Jeffrey shrugged. 'You know Ray,' he said.

Sure I did.

'If he comes in,' I said, 'tell him to call Eddie.'

Since Ray and I were such pals.

'It won't be today,' Jeffrey said. 'You're better catching him at The Carousel.'

'You think he'll be in there?'

'It's Thursday, innit?' He looked at me.

'Is the place round here?'

'Bayswater.'

I filed the information.

'Have you seen Ray at all this week?' I said.

Jeffrey shook his head. 'The guy's a ghost,' he said.

His comment was offhand. Seemed Jeffrey didn't know just how ghostly Ray was.

'Does Ray ever come in with anyone?' I said.

'All the time.'

'I mean a woman friend.'

Jeffrey sharpened up. Planted his phone.

'What is this? Are you after him?' he asked.

I thanked him and headed back out.

Ray was fleshing out pretty much as Lisa had described, a guy who liked to party, knew a lot of people, was generous to most of them. Apart from Jeffrey's abrupt brush off, the other times I'd dug for a hint of Ray coming in "with" someone had drawn a blank. Ray was Ray. He was always with someone. But no hint that the someone was a female he shouldn't be with. Still, I was beginning to sense that Lisa spent a lot of evenings alone in the flat above the boutique whilst

29

Ray did his rounds.

I hit a social club a few doors down and another guy working on a wrong assumption said to say hello to Lisa, so maybe she wasn't entirely blocked out. There were no women in any of the places – none under sixty anyway – so I had no female viewpoint to colour the picture. All I got everywhere was that Ray was a diamond geezer. That he hadn't been seen this week. That he was a ghost. That no-one knew anything. By mid afternoon I'd covered all of Lisa's Wandsworth leads and hadn't picked up even the scent of a scent. I went back to the list and drove south towards Tooting.

Next stop: Stuart Barr. Ray's gun-collecting crony who'd been in the Bay Horse last night and might have an idea why Ray wasn't there. I spotted Barr's shop on Upper Tooting Road, a place called Army Outlet, dressed up to look like a regular Army and Navy except that Army and Navys are open weekdays. This one was closed, display windows dark. Maybe Thursday was Barr's day off. Closed doors and dead ends: a PI's constant companions. You turn away and move on. Swallow a few more indigestion tablets. I eased the Frogeye back into the traffic and moved on. Jarrett's Autumn Leaves drifted through my 'phones, skittered and laughed at the concept of stress and took me onwards with the clock ticking and dark closing. I spun the wheel, watched the mirror. The Toyota was still following. I asked myself how the vehicle might be related to my search for Ray Elland and found no answer. When it had appeared on my tail back in Brixton I'd been on the case for four hours and hadn't scratched a single surface, which argued that it *wasn't* related. But the agency had no other business running that might attract attention and there the car was, sticking with me at every turn. I watched the mirror and wondered.

I drove through Croydon and turned out of the traffic just before the railway bridge. Rolled down a side street and onto the tiny forecourt of a workshop entrance with the name Castle Motors above it. I pulled off the 'phones and slid the perspex back. Inside the doorway machinery screamed and crackled under bright fluorescents. The shop was sized lengthways for two cars. No width for passing. The front vehicle would have to be backed out to release the rear one from the ramp, and neither would go anywhere until I shifted the Frogeye. I climbed out and walked in.

The nearer of the two cars was a Nissan Micra awaiting pickup. A bread-and-butter servicing job. The car on the ramp behind it was what the place was about, a late-60s Spider Boat Tail that looked like it had just rolled off the production line. A stocky guy in his early thirties came out from under the lift with an air wrench and said Hi. I put him down as Ray's car restoration pal Dean Jones.

'Nice,' I said.

The guy nodded. 'One of ours,' he said. 'Italian registered. Left hand drive. We rebuilt it eight years ago. In for a spot of servicing then it'll be off the road until Easter. Not a winter car.'

He was looking past me at the Frogeye. I wasn't sure which car he was talking about. The Frogeye is a rebuild that doesn't share much of its guts with the original, but its heating is wholly vintage and the hood leaks gales if you get a crosswind. Frogeyes had been my winter and summer rides for eight years.

We gabbed a little and he confirmed that he was Jones. Told me to say hello to Ray. I told him that I was struggling to get hold of Ray. Hadn't a clue where the bastard was. Wondered if he knew. Dean shook his head and told me Ray should be in work and I told him that he wasn't and that was it. Dean had no suggestions.

'Hell, I never know where Ray is,' he said. 'He's all over. Have you spoken to Lisa?'

'Lisa called me. She's the one trying to get hold of Ray. Asked me to poke my nose in here.'

'Ray's not gonna be here in the middle of the afternoon,' Dean said. He looked at me, air wrench cocked, trailing a hose round the ramp.

'Got it,' I said. 'I'm just wondering where the hell else he might be.' I looked out of the shop. The street was dark beyond the fluorescents. Dean still had no ideas, or wasn't sharing them.

'Do you see Ray often?' I said.

'Pretty much.' Dean finally planted the air tool and walked out to check the Frogeye. 'He likes to see if I've anything special in. Sixties and seventies. Ford, mostly. He's in most Tuesdays, heading back from his trips.'

'His work trips?'

Dean squatted to check the Frogeye's dash.

'Regular as clockwork. We service over fifty vintage vehicles so there's usually something in.'

'Was he here this week?'

Dean stood back up. 'No. I guess he's got something on.'

'I heard something,' I said. 'Someone claims they saw Ray with a lady friend. Know what I mean?'

Dean came back into the shop. His face wasn't quite as friendly. 'No,' he said, 'I don't know. None of my business. Yours neither.' He retrieved his air wrench.

'Sure. But it's Lisa who's worrying,' I said. 'She can't find him anywhere and we don't know what the hell's going on. She's scared he's fooling around on her.'

Dean held the wrench. Gave me a neutral stare. 'I wouldn't know, mate. Me and Ray are just car freaks. We don't hang out. I don't pry into his personal life.'

'But you know he's a married guy?'

'I know Lisa, yes. She's been in a couple of times.'

'Has he ever been here with anyone else?'

'Like I say, it's none of my business.'

'Yeah,' I said. 'But I'm just trying to do Lisa a favour. They've got a kid, you know.'

Dean shrugged.

'Yeah, I know. But it's their affair. I don't want to get involved.'

'Their affair? You mean Ray *is* messing around?'

Dean hesitated. Unsure whether he should just tell me to get lost. But my dropping of Lisa's name made it just as uncomfortable to hide what he was thinking.

'All I know,' he said, 'is that Ray came in here a couple of weeks ago with a nice looking girl. He said she was interested in old cars. He was giving her a ride in the Capri.'

'You think that's all it was? A ride?'

Jones gave me a look.

'It's like I say. I don't know. I just thought, hey, man, that's a real cutie, know what I mean? Blonde. Tall. One of those figures. But bringing her here was kind of embarrassing.'

'No harm if he was just giving her a tour.'

'Yeah. No harm. And I don't know if anything was going on. I just kept my mouth shut. But she was a real looker. Ray attracts the girls, that's for sure.'

'You didn't catch her name?'

He thought about it.

'Molly or Milly or something. Something fancy. But Ray's got a family. He knows I know Lisa. So I don't know if he was messing around or just giving her a tour in the Capri like he said.'

The two sounded like the same thing to me. Then Dean realised he was talking too much to someone he didn't know and turned away to head back to the Spider.

'Don't say I told you anything,' he said. 'Ray will be mad as hell if he finds I've been feeding stuff back to his wife. And the woman may have been nothing. Ray's just a ladies' man. That's the way he is.'

I followed him round the ramp and asked what being a ladies' man meant. Asked about rumours. Stories. But Dean retreated under the car and adjusted the light and told me he knew nothing.

'Ask Ray when you see him,' he said.

I would. I just didn't know when I'd see him. I'd been wearing out tyres and shoe leather half the day and had spoken to twenty people who should have seen Ray around but hadn't. Ray had vanished off the face of the earth and might not be findable in the day and a half.

I left Jones to it and walked out. My phone rang.

Lucy.

'Hey, Eddie, we've got a result.'

The "we" was rhetorical. I'd got nothing. Seems Lucy's jilted woman act had brought a little more success.

'I talked to a guy in Streatham who ratted on him,' she said. 'The guy knows Ray. They play pool. He wanted to buy me a drink and take me back to show me his house, seeing as I was all alone and sad. I told him I didn't know if I *was* alone or whether Ray was just playing around on me and he told me that Ray's not playing. Ray's brought a woman into the place three or four times recently and everything says that the two of them are an item and that I should expect bad news. The guy bought me two drinks and downed four himself while he told me all about it.'

'You still sober?'

'The drinks stayed on the table. But I hung around long enough to make sure the guy was sure. Ray's been seeing a blond woman called Holly for four months.'

Holly. Blonde. Not so different from what I'd just heard in the workshop: Molly or Milly; blonde.

And four months made it more than just a tour in Ray's vintage Capri.

'Any clue who she is?'

'No. The guy didn't have a last name but he says she lives over in Orpington. Do you think she's the one, Eddie?'

I checked my notes. Ray's weekly round would take him over to Sevenoaks and Dartford. His route made a nice circle round Orpington. An easy commute in for his night away, or an easy trip out for Holly to his Dartford Travelodge.

'Keep talking to people,' I said. 'You may get someone who can confirm things. Maybe give you an ID or address.'

'Wilco. Am I getting paid for this?'

'You run the wages department, Luce.'

'That's true. I guess it's on the books.'

She killed the line.

I fired up the Frogeye and rolled off the forecourt but didn't turn towards the main road. Rolled fifty yards the other way instead, to where the black Toyota that had been following me was backed against an access gate whose clamping signs advertised hundred quid release fees. A guy was just getting into the vehicle but I pulled the Frogeye across the pavement and blocked his exit and he got out again and stood holding the car door, waiting for me to come round.

It was nearly dark and his face was in shadow. Then he stepped away from the car and the light caught him and I stopped dead.

I knew the guy.

And he was the last person I expected to see.

CHAPTER SEVEN
Damage limitation

A Croydon back street in the winter chill. Dark closing in. Two guys who'd not expected to meet again. Or at least one of us hadn't. I don't know what the other expected when he started tailing me through this hopeless chase. I watched him and searched for appropriate words while the traffic zipped by on the bridge ramp behind the buildings. A face out of time. Out of place here on this street. No connection. No meaning. A freezing wind hit my neck. I jabbed my hands in my coat pockets and hunched it tighter about me.

'Hello Peter,' I said.

'Eddie.' His smile might have been chagrin. 'Sharp as ever,' he said.

He was going from memory. He hadn't seen me for seven years unless I wasn't as *sharp* as he was making out.

I took a guess.

'Out?'

'Five years ago.' He looked up the street. 'The job no longer fit.'

I hadn't heard, but then I wouldn't. Peter Bonney and I weren't close. Office buddies. A shared building. A shared detective grade. Occasional drinks at job bashes but no shared investigations. No stories. Passing ships but for the single time our paths had collided. Bonney was ten years older than me and the street light brought all of them out. His face had aged.

'Good to know it's not the Met on my tail,' I said.

'Just me,' Bonney confirmed.

'Hobby or work?' I said. 'Better than Christmas shopping, either way.'

Bonney smiled. 'Let's say hobby. Not one that I'm enjoying. You're a tricky target in that Sprite. I thought I'd lost you back in Clapham.'

'Swerve-check,' I said. 'I wanted to know whether you were real.'

Bonney nodded. Smiled. Puffed a vapour cloud.

'I'm real,' he said. 'We'd better talk.'

~~~~~

We walked up to a corner pub on the main road. The place was decked out in holly and tinsel, and seasonal muzak was playing for the dozen or so locals in killing the afternoon. We drifted to one end of the bar and I toyed with a soft drink whilst Bonney downed a double whisky and ordered another. Then he turned to me, elbow on the top.

'How's things, Eddie? You look like you're busy.'

'Busier than I intended,' I said. 'But things are fine, all things considered.'

Bonney nodded. 'That's good,' he said.

And that was it. We were out of conversation until Bonney told me what he was up to because I'd no words of my own. Time was ticking and I was out of chit chat. Bonney picked up the vibes. Sighed. Looked for his refill. Turned back.

'So where is the bugger?' he said. He said it with a hint of frustration, like he'd been searching too and needn't bother with the formality of clarifying whom he was talking about. Though if he *was* looking for Ray Elland then following me was an odd approach to the job. I loosened my coat. Took a sip.

'I assume we're talking about the same thing,' I said.

He nodded. 'Yeah,' he said. 'We are.'

'Beats me, Peter,' I said. 'I'm chasing round without a clue. I don't know where the guy is or what he's up to or whom he's with. And if we really are talking about the same guy the question is: why are you on my tail?'

Bonney's refill arrived. He grabbed the tumbler and held it up to catch the light.

'Lisa's my daughter,' he said.

There you are. We *were* talking about the same thing. And that was the connection. The explanation. But like most explanations it needed more explanation.

'Lisa got your name off me,' Bonney said. 'Squeezed it out of me. I should have said no. Warned her off.'

'Off me?'

'Warned her off hiring any detective. Ray's got her scared to death but you don't sort out marital problems with private investigators.'

Though many do, even if our rates limit demand for our services to a certain financial bracket.

'Is there anything in it?' I said. 'Or is she worrying over nothing?'

Bonney sipped at his whisky.

'Yes, there's something in it,' he said. 'Ray's cheating on her. Has been for as long as I remember. His latest fling is a tart by the name of Holly Sharma. She's a dancer up the West End. He met her four months ago but she's not the first and won't be the last. I don't know how much Lisa has ever suspected but she's a tendency to hide her head in the sand. It's a habit she picked up with her wedding ring.'

Holly Sharma. Lucy's blonde woman. Things had just shifted from a blind search after a possible nothing to confirmation of Ray's antics and an ID for his co-player. But I was still waiting to hear why Peter Bonney was following me round. I thought about it whilst he fidgeted with his drink and stared into the tumbler's refractions.

'How do you know about Holly?' I said. 'And why didn't you tell Lisa? She'd wouldn't have needed a detective then.'

Bonney swirled his glass. Ice tinkled.

'Lisa knew Ray from way back,' he said. 'School days. Ray was three years older but they hitched up anyway and Lisa has never looked at anyone else since. Which is more than we can say for Ray. The guy has never stopped playing the field. But Lisa's never wanted to see that he isn't a one-woman guy and never will be. Ray told her that she was the one and she swallowed it even when her senses must have been telling her different. She also didn't want to hear that Ray was mixing with the wrong kind of people, drifting onto the wrong side of the law. He had money in his pocket right out of school and that impressed her. Sheryl and I couldn't get through to her.'

Bonney tilted his glass and drained it. He planted the empty tumbler. The ice chinked.

'We thought it wouldn't last,' he said. 'So we backed off and just hoped that Lisa didn't get into any trouble before she ditched the guy. But in '07 they announced that they were tying the knot and there was nothing we could do to dissuade Lisa. Ray Elland wasn't the guy Sheryl and I had ever pictured for our girl. Nothing like. But we saw the way it was and decided that a truce was best. We gave our approval and hoped things would work out, which was pure wishful thinking.'

The background music sprayed chorals and sleigh bells. Coloured lights twinkled in the optics behind the bar and the pub door opened and closed and new voices burst in with the blast of cold. Chairs and tables scraped. I was still waiting for Bonney's explanation, the reason he was following me round as I worked through his daughter's list. I toyed with my drink. Bonney raised his finger to the barman for a third shot.

'When Lisa told us they were getting married,' he said, 'I did some digging to see how far Ray was in with the bad guys. Ex-copper's instinct, I guess. Ray's own family were dodgy as hell so it was no big surprise that Ray had ended up knocking about with known criminals but I wanted to check that he wasn't one of the diehards. He wasn't, was never part of the firm, but he was right there on the periphery of bad business. Drugs. Extortion. Women. Loan sharking. You name it. So I had a quiet word with him. Said I'd paste him all over town if he dragged my daughter into the dirt. But it wasn't just his criminal activities. You only had to follow Ray for a week to see that he'd no intention of giving up on the good life. He and Lisa were out on the town the first couple of years after they married but he was playing around even then. And when Lisa dialled things back after she became pregnant Ray just carried on like he was single. Half the time he was out there with some woman on his arm.'

'Did you tell Lisa any of this?'

Bonney's third shot arrived. He fingered the glass and took a sip.

'Not directly,' he said. 'I couldn't tell her I was spying on Ray. But I gave her hints, passed on as second-hand rumours – though none of it was rumour – and suggested that she keep a close eye on Ray. But Lisa didn't want to hear. She accused Sheryl and me of interfering. Didn't want to hear the message.'

'The word I've been getting,' I said, 'is that Ray's still the dedicated husband and father. Despite his games.'

'Sure, the bastard's dedicated, the same as he's dedicated to having his fun away from home.'

'Is he seeing his dancer friend on his weekly trips?'

'You got it! Every week. He's over at hers whilst Lisa thinks he's watching TV in a Travelodge.'

'And you're still following Ray around after all this time? That's paternal dedication!'

'I keep tabs, that's all. I keep my ear to the ground. Sheryl and I agreed that Lisa and Ray will have to see this through themselves. If we interfere directly we'll just make things worse. Sheryl's a grandmother now. She doesn't want to tip the cart.'

'So back to my original question: why are you following me?'

'Damage limitation,' Bonney said. 'Ray's fling with the dancer is getting serious. It's going to tip the cart anyway and Lisa senses it even if she pretends she doesn't. She's scared, this time. Doesn't know which way to go. So she talked to me. She recalled that there was a copper who had done me a turn back in the job and was now a private investigator. Squeezed your name out of me. Told me that she wanted to know what Ray was up to. Finally! Progress, of sorts. But she'd no idea that I already knew the answer. And my problem was that if I educated her I'd have to admit to spying on them and it would go down badly. She'd turn on me and Sheryl just when she needed our support. But hiring a private investigator was going to bleed her dry, just for the privilege of finding out that she didn't have a husband any more.'

Bonney drained the glass and snapped it down.

'So that's the reason. I followed you to make sure you got her what she wanted. If you didn't make fast progress I planned to fill you in so you could check things out and report back to her. Now I've done it. Holly Sharma. Dancer. Tart. Lives in Orpington. Go and talk to her. You might catch Ray there if you're lucky. If you don't, I'm sure you can squeeze enough from Holly to take back to Lisa. You can bill her for the day and call it quits and the bad news won't have come from me. It won't be me wrecking her marriage.'

The street door opened again. Blew in another gale along with a trio of old guys who began yelling round the room about plans for everyone's Christmas, as if everyone was on starting blocks. On Christmas day most of them would be right here, the same as every other day. The trio commandeered the bar alongside us and redirected their shouting at the landlord, something they'd also be doing on the day. The noise was good for privacy. I turned back to Bonney.

'It's not as simple as that,' I said. 'Ray's staying away from home the extra days without giving Lisa a good excuse is odd. I'm struggling to see why he'd do that.'

'Puzzles me too,' Bonney admitted. 'But I've no doubt: Ray's just giving himself a Christmas bonus with his tart. He's usually smart enough to smooth things with Lisa, but maybe he doesn't feel the need any more. Maybe this time he's thinking of staying away.'

He looked at me. Toyed with his glass. Didn't re-order. I thought about burning bridges.

'I'll drive over,' I said. 'Talk to Holly. And Ray if he's there. It's going to be a little messy but Lisa's not hiding the fact that she's looking for him.'

Bonney nodded. Pursed his lips. 'Be good if you got back to her tonight.'

'If I've anything for her.'

'Let's close this thing off,' Bonney said. 'It's likely to be bad medicine for her whichever way things fall but it's better she knows now.'

He shifted on his stool. 'I'd appreciate it if you could give me a ring after,' he said. 'So we know what you've given her. We're going to have some smoothing over to do before Christmas, however it works out.'

He handed me a business card. I glanced at it and promised nothing. Lisa was paying the tab and Bonney wasn't privileged to hear what we took back to her, concerned father or not.

'The villains you mention,' I said. 'Are they connected to Ray's job at Odds-On?'

'Fully connected. But Ray's peripheral. This is not to do with work.'

'Who exactly does he work for?'

'The bookies are owned by Frank McLeod.'

He looked for a reaction. Got it. I raised my eyebrows. Bonney wasn't exaggerating when he said that Ray was dabbling with some bad types. Frank McLeod was one of the main operators south of the Thames. He ran a firm with fingers in all kinds of shady ventures. And as with Bonney and me, my path had crossed McLeod's just a single time back in the job. It was only a passing contact but the affair had been a firecracker. I'd become snarled by chance in a scheme to spring a villain called Nobby Snape from Whitemoor Prison, and had thrown a spanner that had stopped the caper. My chance involvement came about because I happened to be following two guys on unrelated business who turned out to be key players in the escape attempt. My involvement had remained low profile and

I'd never met either Snape or the lieutenant of his called Frank McLeod who'd organised the operation. McLeod himself had escaped the net that put four of Snape's people inside over the affair, and he'd later jumped ship to start up his own firm. By then I'd jumped ship myself, so McLeod's later career had passed me by. I'd spotted the dingy Odds-On bookies all over South London, passed them a million times without ever wondering who owned them. Now I knew: Frank McLeod. And that made Ray Elland one of his people, peripheral or not.

'What's a communications executive,' I said.

Bonney shrugged. Flicked his glass with a fingernail.

'Who knows?' he said. 'Ray's got some kind of job running round the places, keeping them in order, making sure the local managers are not skimming is my guess. But Ray's not part of McLeod's firm. Never will be. They've fed him the "executive" tag because that's the kind of person he is. Strokes his ego. But what Ray is is a glorified errand-boy. He puts in his hours like the rest. Just takes home a fatter pay packet than most unskilled workers. But the real action, the real operations, pass him by.'

'His disappearance could still be related to the job,' I said. 'If he's in with McLeod's people then things could turn against him for all kinds of reasons. There's always a risk when you work with the bad guys.'

'Yeah. Exactly what I've always feared. But I don't see it here. Ray's strictly small-time, nine-to-five. I talked to him only this last weekend and the guy was relaxed. Didn't give me any sense that he was playing games. The firm gives him a good job and a wage far higher than he's any right to expect, and if he didn't piss it all away, didn't spend his time running round chasing the good life and subsidising his tarts then he and Lisa would be comfortable. He could put money into the boutique and shift it upmarket like he's always promising her.'

A chorus of "White Christmas" got started across the bar like it was ten in the evening. I checked my watch. It was four p.m.

'Ray is just playing around on Lisa,' Bonney said. 'That's it. That's what this is about. He and I are going to have it out when this is over, but Lisa needs to know about Holly Sharma and it can't be from me. I don't want to be the one wrecking her Christmas.'

So he'd leave that to me. I smiled and finished my juice. Slipped

Bonney's card into my coat and went out.

CHAPTER EIGHT
Maybe it wasn't planned

I drove east and skirted the Bedlam hospital under the sodium glimmer of low cloud. LBC were still pushing rumours of snow. Latest estimate was thirty percent. When we control the weather we'll switch the stuff on to order so we can recapture the way it used to be. Maybe tie the snow in to the start of the Christmas retail season, mid-September. I don't go for tradition. To a private investigator, snow is the mess that soaks your feet as you stand a six-hour shift with a frost-bitten nose, watching the shadows in lighted windows where someone's having fun. The fun pays your wages but it's still damn cold and wet down on the pavement. Show me a P.I. and I'll show you a tropical beach guy.

Whatever Peter Bonney's motivation for getting involved, and whatever doubts I had about the reason for Ray's disappearance, his tip on Holly Sharma was my only lead. The first of the two days I had to wrap this thing up was almost gone and the afternoon's chasing around hadn't thrown up any other pointer. Ray had dropped way out of sight, and maybe the place he'd dropped into was Holly Sharma's Orpington apartment. And if he wasn't there, maybe she'd have an idea where he was, though if she was willing to tell me that much then I'd not need to find him. Lisa would have all the evidence she needed without the money shots.

A hands-free came in from Lucy. I told her we'd got confirmation of her earlier result. Holly was indeed the one. I gave her the address and said I'd meet her there. The way she agreed suggested that the afternoon's slog hadn't dampened her enthusiasm for the detective life. She hadn't stood around in snow yet.

Holly's address was a sixties apartment block constructed in buff-coloured brick sitting up on stilts behind a retail development at the bottom end of the high street. The place had somehow escaped the nineties' wrecking ball and was beached uneasily beside the upmarket four-storey developments that had gone up next door. Holly's flat was 1a which put her in one of the lower units over the parking and utilities level. The way in was up a driveway that climbed from the street to a row of garages and a rear entrance door. I backed the Frogeye into a pay by phone bay on the street and walked up the driveway. Found the building's entrance centrally located at the back, feeding a stairwell servicing a single flat to each side. The bell arrangement suggested that Holly's flat was the one on the driveway side which was all dark windows. No-one home. I took a gander round the parking area. There were only three cars there, none of them Ray's gold Capri. Ray wasn't here unless his car was hiding in one of the garages. I walked back down the drive and out to the Frogeye. Slid in and checked the time. Four fifteen. I keyed the Jarrett album back up and settled to watch. Five minutes later Lucy patted the vinyl top and I leaned across to let her in. Gave her an update.

'Her *father's* following you?' She shook her head. 'That's weird. Dodgy spouse and over-protective parents. You've got to feel for Lisa.'

'She's not in for a happy Christmas,' I agreed.

'But knowing the truth is better than having suspicion eat away at her,' Lucy said. 'What's she going to do if you confirm that Ray *is* playing around?'

'The same as most jilted spouses. Take the opportunity to re-consider her life. It's up to her. We just collect the evidence.'

'You think Ray will show up here?'

'Fifty-fifty,' I said. 'At best. There's a chance that the two of them are out of town. There's a chance Ray's absence is nothing to do with this woman.'

'Yeah,' Lucy said. 'A fling seems odd. How would he hope to get away with it? Maybe if he'd stayed away one extra night Lisa would have swallowed it. But if he was planning on sneaking a few nights away he should have given Lisa a credible story.'

'Could be it wasn't planned. A compulsive thing. Maybe Ray decided he could handle the storytelling later. Or maybe,' I repeated, 'it's nothing to do with Holly Sharma.'

We watched the building. The street was quiet and the driveway up to the parking area was even quieter. In an hour just two vehicles drove up the ramp but neither was Ray's Capri. And Holly Sharma's windows remained dark. Up at the junction traffic flowed steadily, homeward-bound, and Jarrett's keyboard slowed and drifted into

Funny Valentine as we watched the world from an island of tranquillity. I've had albums get me through eight hours straight, sardined in the Frogeye waiting for something that never happens. Jazz is a great time-killer because it takes you outside time. Pins you in the moment. Watching a building or a car or a doorway becomes one long moment. Lucy was more of a fast mover. The times she'd spent with me in the old Frogeye were nothing to do with sleuthing and didn't involve much staying still.

'I forgot how cosy this car is,' she said.

I grinned. Kept watching the building.

'As long as you don't move,' I said. 'It's like sitting in your favourite armchair listening to your favourite music. It's just the getting out that's a problem. Eight hours is a long shift.'

'You think she'll turn up?'

I shook my head. 'Our girl is a West End dancer. If she's working tonight then she'll not be back until midnight. We may have missed her.'

'Maybe Ray?'

'Not without her.'

Lucy concurred. The street lights and shadows touched her face and toned down her hair so you'd think she was just a natural redhead. Time was, I'd seen a lot of different colours in my old car though Lucy's smile had always stayed the same. Wide mouth. Smart, crescent eyes.

Then my gaze was drawn towards the end of the street. I grabbed my Leica and zoomed the telephoto to focus on a tall, blonde woman walking towards us. Young, late twenties or early thirties, long blonde hair, Burberry coat over jeans. Long legs. And sunglasses. The pavement was pitch black under the trees and she was wearing shades. I popped off a few shots, ready to bin them if she passed the apartment block but she didn't pass it. She turned and walked up the driveway ramp to the back of the building. Sixty seconds later the lights came on in the lower apartment and I pulled up the snaps I'd just taken. Lucy and I checked out the zoomed images. The woman was nothing out of the ordinary, just young and fit-looking, might or might not be a dancer and might or might not be able to see where the hell she was going with those shades. If the glasses were a disguise then she needed to sharpen her stealth skills.

And if this *was* Ray's illicit friend she was absent from her work. West End night off is Sunday. What would she be doing home tonight?

'She fits the description,' Lucy said. 'The parts we can see.'

We settled down to wait. If she came out again we'd see where she went. If she didn't come out we'd wait longer.

We waited longer.

CHAPTER NINE
What's the problem, ma'am?

Waiting can be a positive or a negative. Time to think about something you've seen or are waiting to see, a breathing space to push and prod at the jigsaw, or a null, when you're out of ideas in the low hours of a cold, wet night in a place where you can't imagine a single thing ever happening to take you forward. I've learned to focus on the positive. Play music and push jigsaw pieces, look for unexpected connections that show me something that I hadn't seen before. Then someone steps from a doorway or I spot a face out of place and it all comes together. Waiting is something I've learned, something I'm easy with. But tonight the clock was ticking. We'd a connection between Ray and the woman in the flat across the street but since Ray had dropped out of everyone's sight there was no reason to imagine that his resurgence would be here, tonight. He could be anywhere or nowhere. We were waiting because there was nothing else.

We sat for two hours watching the backlit blinds in Holly Sharma's flat and didn't see even a shadow move. No-one came out of the building. No gold Capri rolled up the driveway. No-one matching Ray's description tried to sneak in or out. I slotted in a Charlie Parker album and we listened and watched and I tried to ignore the ticking clock. Pushed away the thought that this was a dead end. Lucy was new to this. She mostly handled the coffee and invoicing side of the business. Was probably expecting fireworks or a body to come out of a window. But we got neither. We sat for two hours and saw nothing.

'Is it always so slow, Eddie?' Lucy said.

'Wait till we pull an all-nighter,' I said. 'Ask me then.'

She shivered. Slow *and* cold. It was December and we were waiting in a car with a soft-top. At least the cold keeps you awake. In the old days Lucy and I would have thought of a few ways to stave off the chills but this wasn't the old days. Lucy and I had gone our separate ways and there was no going back. And I wasn't even sure if Lucy was footloose. My memory seemed to have snagged hints of a name from her conversations in the last month or so. Stephan or Steve or something. Should have paid more attention. Probably not footloose. Women as good-looking as Lucy didn't stay alone for long in this town. Women as smart and trustworthy didn't deserve to stay alone. I grinned through the screen. That was the difference between Lucy and our blonde dancer: whoever Lucy was seeing he wouldn't be married. It kind of reflected my own views. But I didn't chase errant husbands to judge them. I chased them to put money in the bank. Without spouses fooling around the agency would be with the receivers.

This was Lucy's first stakeout. I could probably have managed alone but she was desperate to see what went down. She'd been trailing round all afternoon looking for Ray Elland and wanted to catch a sight of the guy in the act. Maybe she was keen to know how the elements came together to build one of the invoices she was always posting out.

Not that this invoice would amount to much. By tomorrow we'd have bled as much of Lisa's money as we were going to and the case would be closed. And that was starting to worry me. I couldn't escape the feeling that Ray wasn't going to show by tomorrow. With a normal infidelity case there's a fifty-fifty chance that a guy absent from home will show up at his girlfriend's door. But this wasn't a normal case. Ray had been missing completely and without explanation for three days. He'd jumped ship on his whole life in a way that was going to need more than lame excuses when he reappeared. If this was a spur of the moment fling at a five-star love-nest up in town or out in the country it might explain the three days but not the bridge-burning. And Holly Sharma wasn't up in town or out in the country. She was in her apartment behind those blinds. I watched her windows and wondered what had been going on up there the last three days.

Waiting. It's something I've learned. Something I'm good at. I've stood in the shadows for thirty-six hours waiting for a target to show up or sneak out, but time wasn't on our side on this one and the last two hours didn't have the feel of an investment, the prelude to a revelation. They had the feel of a dead end. And the answers weren't out on this street.

'Time for a house call,' I said.

We unfolded ourselves. Stepped out into the cold and walked the driveway up and round to the entrance and stood in front of a communal bell plate. I pressed 1a. Got no answer. I pressed harder. For longer. Got a result. The entry-phone crackled.

'Who is it?'

A woman's voice. Holly Sharma.

'Jehovah's Witnesses,' I said. 'We come with seasonal tidings.'

'Go away. I'm not interested in that kind of thing.'

'You should be ma'am. We're talking salvation. A one-time offer.'

'I'm not interested. Try next door.'

'They're not in. Only the Devil shall catch the straying.'

'I thought you people didn't believe in Christmas.'

'Normally we don't. But we thought, what the hell? Everyone else is getting a piece...'

'Well I'm not interested. Please go and bother someone else.'

The phone clicked off. I pressed the bell again. A good Witness knoweth perseverance. The crackle returned.

'Are you still there?'

'Yes, ma'am.'

'Please go away.'

'What's the problem, ma'am?'

'The problem is that you're disturbing me. I don't want to talk to you.'

You get this reaction. What is it about Witnesses?

'If we weren't Witnesses,' I said, 'would you talk to us?'

'It's more damn likely!'

'That's good,' I said. 'Because we're not. We're private detectives, here to interview Ms Holly Sharma.'

'You're *what?* Go away. I'll call the police.'

'Let's just think about that,' I said. 'The police are going to take at least half an hour to get here. Say forty-five minutes. And we'll be here the whole time. That's an awful lot of bell-ringing and door banging and general disturbance for your neighbours. On the other hand, if you give us five minutes we'll be through. That's better than any Witness ever offers.'

'What do you want?'

'Better in private, Holly.'

She gave it a moment. Saw sense and hit the door release. We went in.

Lucy looked at me. Made eyes.

'When you're a fully trained detective,' I said, 'you'll need to talk your own way in. I'll write you some notes.'

'Claiming to be Jehovah's Witnesses gets you through front doors?'

'Never,' I said. 'But when you start from the worst case scenario then the truth sounds a lot more palatable.'

A door half way down the hallway opened and the blonde with the tinted glasses poked her head out. She was still wearing the tinted glasses. She checked Lucy's hair. Decided that we really weren't Witnesses. Witnesses have a dress code. When she'd also decided that we were harmless she stood back and invited us into her hallway. She closed the door behind us but made no move to go further in. We stood in a cosy group whilst she waited for an explanation.

We were interested in an explanation too. Wearing sunglasses indoors on a December evening might be considered weird unless you were hiding bruising, which Holly was. Up close even the tinted glass couldn't hide the swelling behind them nor the grey-yellow bruise across her left cheek. Lucy glanced at me. Everyone had been painting Ray Elland as a loveable rogue. No whisper of a darker side. But Holly Sharma's bruised face made us wonder if there were things he kept hidden, whether Holly and Ray had fallen out. The bruises were new. Maybe twenty-four hours old.

'Can I see some ID?' Holly said.

I handed her my driving licence and agency card. The card had my name printed on it alongside my partner Sean Shaughnessy's. Most jobs involving straying husbands don't involve hand-outs. On most jobs the husband never knows we're around until the wife throws our report in his face. Tonight was a different approach. I'd need to explain to Lucy later, so she didn't get the wrong idea.

Holly handed back the ID and looked at me.

'What do you want?' she said.

'We're looking for Ray Elland,' I said. 'Heard rumours that he was here. His wife wants to know if he'll be home for tea.'

Showing our hand was not part of a normal investigation either, but we had twenty-four hours to close this job and we still hadn't caught the faintest whiff of the guy. Time for subtle to take a back seat. When she heard Ray's name Holly glared at me but didn't bother with denial.

'You're looking for Ray,' she clarified.

'We need to catch up with him. Urgently.'

'Well you've come to the wrong place. I don't know where he is and I don't care. If that's all you've come for you can leave.'

She re-opened the door and gestured. Lucy and I ignored the hint. We follow the Witnesses code in that respect.

'It's a little surprising,' I said, 'that you don't know where Ray is. Since you and he spend so much time together.'

But Holly wasn't biting. It's like we'd triggered something. The blood was flowing back into her face around the shades. Her bruises looked angrier than ever.

'Get out,' she said. 'I'm not talking about that bastard.'

We remained standing where we were. Holly's grip threatened to splinter the door.

'Have the two of you had some kind of tiff?' I said. But she was glaring into the hallway. Waiting for us to walk out. The glare was directed at something or someone distant. We weren't part of it. We weren't there. That's how angry she was.

But we were there. We stayed there. Holly glared at us.

'Get out! she repeated. 'And don't come back. Don't ever come here looking for Ray.'

So: a tiff. You sense these things. I wondered what the tiff had been about. I wondered whether Ray had been two-timing his dancer friend and been caught out. More burnt bridges.

She waited for us to move but we still stood our ground. I gave her a sympathetic smile and a knowing shrug.

'I'm sorry if the two of you have had a falling out,' I said. 'But we really need to talk to Ray. You must have some idea where he is.'

But she wasn't listening. The anger was a boiling cauldron. When she spoke her voice was a dangerous hiss.

'Get out,' she said, 'or I'll call the police. And if you see Ray, tell him to keep the hell away from me. The piece of–'

Then the anger burst. She turned and pulled herself inwards and tears streamed out from behind her shades. She cursed. Lucy reached out a hand but Holly shrugged it off and told us again to get the *hell* out, so we got the hell out. She wasn't going to give us any more. The door slammed the moment we were over the threshold and we walked back down the hallway in silence and let ourselves out. The electric lock clicked behind us and we were back in the dark and cold. Lucy looked at me, wide-eyed.

'Wow, Eddie. It looks like Ray's broken up with his lady friend.'

'The relationship shows signs of wear,' I agreed.

We walked round the building, back down to the road.

'Is Ray with someone else?' Lucy asked.

'Hard to say. But if he's just had a messy bust-up I don't see him leaving Lisa in suspense while he cavorts with the next name in his diary. If the fight was last night maybe Ray's about to show up at home. He might be in a bar right now working up the courage. I'll check with Lisa later.'

'End of case,' Lucy said.

'If he's shown up.'

'What if he's not?'

'Then we're gridlocked at square one. Still no idea what Ray's up to. If he's still missing tonight then his absence is nothing to do with Holly.'

We stopped by the Frogeye. Lucy looked up. Her face was in shade.

'Maybe Ray's not such a nice guy,' she said. 'Do you think that bruising was him?'

'We can't rule it out,' I said. 'There could be a side of him no-one's talking about. Maybe his friends just prefer the loveable rogue myth.'

Lucy jabbed her hands into her pockets. Bobbed up and down against the cold. 'We don't know where Ray is,' she said, 'and we don't know *who* he is. That sure *is* square one.'

I threw her a grin. 'Your map-reading's spot on, Luce. We're nowhere. If we look hard we'll figure it out, but not by tomorrow evening. It's just as I warned Lisa: we may bring her just enough to keep her worrying. She'll be in the same boat as before but with a lighter bank account.'

'So where next?'

'For you,' I said, 'nowhere. End of shift. I've a place I'm going to check out on the way home then we'll talk tomorrow. With any luck Ray will have shown up and we can leave him and Lisa to thrash it out. As long as it doesn't go the same way as with Holly.'

'Wow,' Lucy said. 'Some Christmas for Lisa.'

'Some Christmas,' I agreed.

Lucy said she'd see me tomorrow and headed off to her car.

CHAPTER TEN
I've never seen that before

I drove home. Took a shower then checked my fridge for something that might be converted into a meal. Found nothing. I'd run the fridge down to a duty watch of salad dressings and chilled beers for the season. In two days I'd be out of town, lording it at a country estate in Norfolk. Not my own country estate. I had a sister called Amber who was married to a tycoon called Bill Temple and the two of them lived in a house with twenty-three spare bedrooms. Or was it thirty-two? I could never remember and it seemed impolite to ask. More than enough spare rooms, anyway, to put me up. For Amber it had been a step up ten years ago when she'd moved out of her South Acton basement to start a new life involving decisions such as which twenty-three rooms you did *not* want to sleep in. I'd suggested a couple of weeks in each, which would get her round them all once a year. The step from surviving on a London Symphony Orchestra salary to being able to buy the orchestra if she'd wanted might damage a lesser person but my sister was a survivor. We'd toughed a few things out up in Yorkshire after our mother died. I'd been kind of looking after her in London until Bill Temple turned up to take over the job. I might have begrudged a fat-cat tycoon stealing my sister away except that Bill was a cat who'd earned his cash and knew its value and worried only about how not to waste it. And he'd have looked after Amber just the same if he'd not had a penny to his name and I'd have approved her choice just the same. The two of them were a matching set. So Amber needed less watching nowadays, but a tradition had grown up that I show my face at Christmas to try out one of the twenty-three rooms. It was a tradition that was hard to break in the face of a bedroom with a real fire and Christmas dinner and a thousand acres of parkland thrown in. The only excuse I needed to polish this year was an explanation for why I'd be showing up alone. Amber and my recent girlfriend Arabel had become attached to the point where it was clear that both of them were picturing longer-term arrangements. All arrangements had fallen through this last autumn when an investigation that was off the books jumped the rails and cost the life of Arabel's best friend, something even the most forgiving of girlfriends would find hard to overlook. I didn't know if Amber had read the papers but she knew I'd be alone this year and I knew she was disappointed. She wouldn't say it in so many words but she'd let me know before the year was out that it was about time I kept a closer watch on people close to me. If you cared for them you protected them. She should know. She'd protected me all those years up in Yorkshire.

But c'est la vie.

Protect those you care for.

The smart detective. Sees everything but the disaster racing towards him.

I closed the fridge door. Made a decision and headed out into the night to pursue the tip that Ray Elland was to be found at a place called the Carousel on Thursday nights. The chance of him being there tonight when he was nowhere else didn't seem high but I'd nothing to point me anywhere else and maybe I'd catch someone who knew something. That was after I'd eaten. I'd an invitation still outstanding to call in at an Italian restaurant called Quarto di Bue in Bayswater. The invitation was delivered on the back of a case we'd closed back in the spring. If the guy remembered me I'd be good for the chef's best attention. If not, they'd throw me out since they were probably booked solid. I fought stop-start mid-evening traffic through Chelsea streets that were still rush hour busy. Listened to LBC's warnings of frost overnight, snow still holding at thirty percent for Christmas Eve.

Westbourne Grove was bright as day, illuminated by late-evening store fronts and suspended Christmas lights. The pavements were busy with shoppers looking for inspiration. The bustle almost caused me to miss something on the far side. An alley cut back from the street under the harsh fluorescents of a stepped-up area fronting a building society and travel shop. Further in, where the shadows ruled, there seemed to be a couple of kids messing about. Some kind of scuffle. But I'd spotted a flash of brindle and white darting and dodging at their feet. I was already past the alley but I had a sudden bad feeling. I flashed an oncoming car and pulled across it onto the pavement. Left the Frogeye at an angle and hopped out and jogged back to the alley where two young toughs had the homeless guy

William backed up against the wall. The kids were late teen or early twenties with razored heads and bad attitude. One of them was holding William's coat open whilst the other was tapping him gently on the cheek and calling him "grandpa". Herbie had grabbed one of the boy's feet in a jaw like a vice but he was biting on Doc Marten and the kid couldn't feel it. Homeless guy's aren't the obvious targets for muggings but a day selling The Big Issue would have put seventy or eighty quid in William's pocket.

I walked in and grabbed the nearer youth – the one not anchored by Herbie – and pulled him clear. He cursed and swung a fist but I pushed it away and grabbed the wrist, hefted and twisted and the shoulder joint came out with a pop. The kid switched from profanities to blue murder. He pulled free, swinging his other arm, then came back at me despite the dislocation. He advanced the way he did at football rucks, using his weight in lieu of skill. I stepped aside and drove a punch hard into his abdomen, and he folded, bad arm hanging, and I dove under him and got him up in a fireman's lift and walked out to the pavement where Westminster Council had placed one of their bins. The bins restrict waste to the kind you can push through a nine-inch slot but this tub was missing its top, which made room for something wider. I heaved. Dropped the kid in head first. The bin was barely a quarter full but what was in there smelled unpleasant, and the kid went way down, into an impossible situation for a dislocated shoulder. I went back up the alley. Herbie had released the second guy's foot to watch the show but when I walked back in he resumed his assault and clamped his jaw back on the Doc Martens before I could claim it. The second yob had quit slapping William around and tried to shake Herbie off by kicking his foot out, but thirty kilograms is a lot to lift. When I came up the kid swung at me and I hit him hard and his eyes went up. I grabbed his lapel to try the fireman thing again, but his weight caught me out and when I looked down I saw I was lifting Herbie as well. The Staffie had only his left rear paw still on the ground. He wasn't giving up so easily. I yelled down to get the hell off unless he wanted to end up in the trash but then the shoe came off and Herbie fell clear and sat down next to William to give it a seeing to.

There were no more open bins so I put the boy down. His eyes had come back but they were unfocused. I walked him out and told him to help his pal. Getting him out was going to take effort, judging by the curses and screams coming from inside the bin and the way the kid's feet were flailing. I left them to work it out and went back to William. He was still up against the wall but there was a toothless grin patched across his face.

'Bin robbed marry a time,' he said. 'Never sin that before. You sin a guy in a bin, Herbie?'

Herbie was busy with the boot. He couldn't care less about bins.

'You okay?' I said.

'Naver bin finer,' William said. 'We showed the hooligans a thing or two, don't you think?'

We looked out at the street. The two kids were fighting the bin. The second was pulling on the first one's jacket, trying to get him out, but the dislocated shoulder was proving a problem. I heard a scream and grinned at William.

'We showed them,' I agreed. I looked down at the tattered rucksack at William's feet. Used for transporting his bundles of Big Issues. But I saw a rolled blanket sprouting from the top too.

'You're not on the street are you William?' I said.

'We're fine, my fren'. Lodgin' with me pal till we find somewhere else.'

'I thought you had digs.' The old guy had described a basement flat, a temporary let covered by his social. The place sounded like a dive and William's "comfitible" description brought images. But at least the digs had kept him off the streets.

'We got the boot, my fren',' he said. 'Me an' Herbie din' mix with the lanlor'. The lanlor' say no dogs. No exceptions. He say don't come back.'

'So where are you going?'

He told me about his pal, an ex-services guy living in a tower just across the Westway. He'd dossed with him before. A good man. A vary good man. Didn't mind Herbie at all. They'd be putting their feet up there tonight. William had a mile and a half to trek, though, lugging his rucksack.

'Want a lift?' I said. I wasn't sure how we'd all get in the car. It's not a people-mover. But William declined, declared that he was needing a walk and that they'd be on their way shortly and it was barely a dozen steps up to Wezzb'n. And Marry Christmas to me and all.

I looked at the street again. The Bin Twins had got themselves sorted. I walked out for a word to make sure they were clear about giving William a wide berth but they didn't wait for the message. They backed off towards Notting Hill, one of them hobbling on one boot, throwing obscenities and gestures. The kid with the popped shoulder was cursing like a good 'un. Give it a few minutes till the endorphins wore off and he'd find his full voice and his priorities would become clear. It didn't take a crystal ball to see a four hour wait in A&E somewhere in his future. William was safe for the evening.

I reported back to the old guy and he wished me Marry Christmas again. Herbie grinned up at me then turned circles and worried the boot. I headed back to the Frogeye.

The Quarto di Bue proprietor Giuseppe's memory of me was still fresh and still favourable and I got a seat in the window despite the place being packed. I also got a free meal and all the drinks I desired to wash it down. Since I was driving my desires were limited to fizzy water but the food was excellent, kicking off with a six course anti-pasti I hadn't ordered, also on the house. A waiter planted a plate of gnocchi and my mouth watered. The restaurant was packed and loud but for a while I was in my own world.

In a moment's break I called Lisa.

'Did you find him?' she asked.

I grinned. 'Jesus Christ,' I said. 'We're good, but we're not that good.'

The next plate was just touching down. I reached with a fork.

'Of course,' Lisa said. 'You said it would take time. I was just hoping you might have got lucky.'

'So was I. But it's not worked out. We've not had even a hint. We've talked to people all over town, most of the names you gave us. No-one has seen Ray all week. He's not turned up at any of his usual haunts. Ray's gone to ground, Lisa. It's a puzzle.'

'Is it another woman?'

I hesitated.

'Could be,' I said. 'There's some indications pointing that way. You may need to brace yourself for bad news.'

I heard a breath on the other end of the line. Sensed Lisa's powerlessness. She'd feared pushing this thing over the edge and now she was sensing the first rush of free-fall. No going back. But I held back on detail. Holly Sharma was more than just an indication that Lisa's fears were on target but Lisa didn't need detail at the moment. Just the warning that bad news was probably on its way. She be ready for the full dose tomorrow. And when I picked up more detail – or picked up Ray – maybe it wouldn't be Holly Sharma's name in my report. If the two of them had had a thing it was over. And if there was someone new then Lisa didn't need Holly's name.

But I couldn't hold back on the possibility that Ray's fooling about wasn't the reason he'd disappeared. Lisa needed to know that at least.

'You mean he's in trouble?' she said.

I finished the plate and a waiter swept it up to make room for the pasta and a salad main course. He brought a refill for my fizzy water.

'It's hard to be sure,' I told her. 'But something's not right. If Ray was fooling around that would be no reason to drop off the radar so completely. He'd be phoning you with excuses. Stuff about his business trip being extended. He'd need to staunch your suspicions. He wouldn't be burning bridges like this.'

'Unless he wasn't planning to come back.'

'In that case why not tell you, even from a distance? And why leave all his stuff behind?'

'So what's happened?'

'That's what I'm looking at. You say you didn't have a hint of anything brewing?'

'Nothing. Even when Ray phoned to say he'd be away an extra night nothing seemed wrong.'

'Did Ray ever mention a place called the Carousel?'

'Is that a club?'

'That's my guess. I'll be looking in there tonight. Then I'll continue tomorrow morning. We'll give it the whole day if needed. Ray has to be somewhere.'

'I can't believe we're having to look for him at all. This is scaring me to death.'

'Try not to worry,' I said. 'I'll catch up with Ray tomorrow and everything will become clear. If he shows up in the meantime let me know.'

'Of course.'

'Talk tomorrow.'

I killed the line. Was about to get back to my dinner when another call came in. Peter Bonney. He asked how things had gone and I gave him the news that Ray's dancer friend Holly had been a dud. I didn't mention the slapping she'd taken or her antipathy towards her presumed lover. Just reported that Ray wasn't with her and that she wasn't talking.

Bonney offered again to help. 'It's going to hurt Lisa whichever way this comes out,' he said. 'And I don't feel any better for having warned her.'

I forked linguine, rolled and dragged it through sauce. The sauce was astounding. The antipasti had been astounding. Even the fizzy water was astounding. Giuseppe had told his chef to be nice to me and he was being nice. Seemed Giuseppe was still happy with the job we'd done. Also, I hadn't eaten all day. I guess that helped.

'I'll hand Lisa whatever we dig out tomorrow,' I said. 'She'll have to deal with that. But it would be good to have some hard evidence to give her. If her marriage is about to be flattened then the bad news should at least be specific.'

'It's going to hurt her,' Bonney agreed, 'whatever comes out. I don't see a good Christmas coming.'

'Me neither. Best we can hope for is that it *is* just Ray having a fling, that they can somehow patch things over. But I'm wondering if we're looking at the wrong thing. Ray's disappearance doesn't have the feel of a simple extra-marital.'

'I hear you,' Bonney said. 'And I hope you're wrong. If Ray's crossed some of his criminal friends then things could turn nasty. But I know Ray. This is about him fooling around.'

I forked more linguine. Said nothing.

'No disrespect,' Bonney said, 'but I wish Lisa wasn't spending money on this.'

'None taken,' I said. 'And her spending ends tomorrow. After that she'll know all that she's going to without a major commission. She'll probably need to get the full story from Ray when he shows, if he does.'

'He'll show,' Bonney said. 'Like a bad penny. I never thought I'd see the day when I wanted to see him around but this uncertainty is killing Lisa. But once Ray's faced Lisa he's going to face me. If I get any sense he's not made things right with her, or has cut the knot completely, then things won't be pleasant. We're going to have a long discussion whichever way things fall. You've no kids Flynn?'

'None I know of.'

'You're lucky. They're a worry when they're helpless and tiny then a worry when they go wild and rebellious and a worry when they go out to make their own lives.'

He sighed. Close to the phone. I heard the sound even above Quarto's buzz. 'Lisa's a good girl,' he said. 'The best. And she loves this guy. And okay, he's been good to her in some ways. But I just wish she'd found someone else. Someone who didn't fool around or live on the margins of what's legal. So we're going to have a talk. After Christmas, if they patch things up. The man's going to start shaping up or get out.'

I guess I'd worry if I had kids. Maybe even feel that I could interfere in their lives. But from an objective point of view Bonney would be crossing a line if he pushed Ray Elland out. Ray was Lisa's affair. I chewed on linguine and attacked the insalata. Stabbed two cherry tomatoes. They burst in my mouth, fresh as if they'd just been pulled from the vine.

'Is there anything I can do?' Bonney said. 'An extra pair of eyes?'

I was inclined to say no. I didn't want Peter Bonney involved in this. I didn't want to be a collaborator in his interference. But Bonney was already involved. He'd been watching Ray long before Lisa called our office. His motives might be suspect but he'd uncovered Holly Sharma and he was a trained ex-cop and I had one day to find something positive that I could take back to Lisa. Maybe another pair of eyes would help.

'You could keep asking around,' I said. 'Double the chance of one of us catching a word. If I spot Ray with a woman he shouldn't be with then I'll have explanation enough to take back to Lisa. And if something else pops out of the woodwork we can think which way to go.'

'Nothing else will pop out,' Bonney said. 'This is Ray fooling around, pure and simple. And the woman he's fooling with is Holly Sharma.'

I thought about it. Decided that Bonney needed steering away from that dead end. So I changed my mind. Detailed the chat at

Holly's flat. Described her bruises.

'Damn!' Bonney said. 'I've heard Ray can be a little rough but there's never been any hint of it between him and Lisa. If this bastard's got a habit of smacking his women around that's going to be bad.'

'It's not good,' I said. 'But I think it rules Holly out as the reason Ray's dropped out of sight.'

Bonney cursed. 'There goes the quick and easy solution. Could be that the bastard's playing around with someone new though. There's still a few more places Ray might have shown his face. A few more people to talk to. I'll go and take a look. Any ideas yourself?'

'Just a couple of names and places from Lisa's list then I've a blank sheet.'

Bonney sighed. 'Okay. We'll talk tomorrow. If we get nothing new then I guess you'll have to take Holly's name back to Lisa whether they've broken-up or not. At least Lisa will know how things stand.'

I didn't commit myself. Tomorrow I'd decide what to take back to Lisa and whatever it was it would be between me and her. If she wanted to talk to her father about it that was her affair.

'Jesus,' Bonney said, 'this is a mess.'

I didn't disagree. The waiters were eyeing me as they passed by, ready to pounce with the next course. They had instructions that I shouldn't sit a second without a full plate in front of me. But my linguine and salad plates were still pretty full as far as I could make out. I grinned and gestured then killed the phone and went back on the attack.

CHAPTER ELEVEN
Deathhawk

It took me thirty minutes to locate the Carousel in an alley off a street called Kings Acre. A discreetly marked side entrance gave onto a cloakroom and cashier's window where a seventeen quid entry fee raised premonitions about the price levels inside. The premonitions were spot on. It seemed Ray was a big spender, Thursday nights.

The place was a piano and cocktail bar spread over four or five rooms all on different levels with steps up and down in every direction. The rooms were decked out in a fairground carousel theme, gaudy multicoloured panels and mouldings, rich woodwork, railings that guided you like the inside of a pinball machine. A blaze of white and coloured bulbs illuminated the rooms and the crowd that wanted to be seen for their seventeen quid.

I worked my way through the bodies, watching my feet and trying to look casual. Gabardine coats as the new cool. But the coat wasn't an issue. Everyone was decked out a range of gear – smart, casual, formal, punk and Goth, tight hairstyles, leather and little black dresses, tattoos and bling – that you couldn't say what was cool. So maybe different was cool and I was different.

I did the rounds and said hi and howsitgoing to people who weren't sure whether they should know me but mostly closed ranks with polite brush-offs to be on the safe side, trying to figure whether they'd seen the gabardine before. A few women flashed bright smiles. I moved steadily, throwing queries about Ray, and one in three who answered knew who I was talking about and said they hadn't seen him yet. Maybe later.

I worked my way up and down the steps, kept clear of the bars where waistcoated models were waiting to mix you a Daiquiri at tonight's special price of fourteen quid. Or something called a Last Laugh whose thirty-five quid tag told you exactly who was laughing. Then after ten minutes a guy in a suit wearing black Police semi-rims told me the same story as everyone that Ray wasn't around then asked me what was going on? I asked what he meant and he pinned me through his specs and told me that I was the second guy asking. I wasn't the only one doing the rounds.

I stopped.

'Someone else is looking?'

'Yeah. Same fashion sense.'

I grinned. Rolled my eyes. 'That must be Jim,' I said. 'Didn't realise he'd been in.'

'Two minutes ago. You need to get your act together. Why are you after Ray?'

If Ray was the popular guy I was hearing about then people asking after him wouldn't be unusual. No-one would notice. The only reason Police Spec had taken note of me was because I was in here in a gabardine coat. Seemed the other enquirer had stood out too. I asked where Jim was and Police Spec turned a lip at his pals.

'Just look for the coat,' he told them.

The pals chuckled. Lifted their own lips.

I held the grin. Told them to take it easy. Pushed on through the crowd towards where honky tonk piano music was coming from the end room which was four steps down beyond the end of the bar. I went down, looking for a man in a coat, but the only one I saw was me, reflected in a full height wall mirror framed by gold pillars and blue and red lights. In the lower room the piano was full blast and the player was pretty decent and the drinks were flowing very decently at fourteen quid a shot. The pianist was earning his keep. He was a gangly white youth in cords and waistcoat with a ring in his nose and a post-Goth deathhawk hairdo swept back into a bun. The bun was bobbing and weaving as the guy hammered the keys of a gaudy upright in a wood-panelled alcove framed by spots that highlighted the golds and browns in his hair. The hairdo suggested that this was Ray's pal Kevin Kobert, working the night shift.

I circulated and continued to ask about Ray and throw comments about how Kevin was pretty cool on the keyboard, and got just enough agreement to confirm that the pianist was Kobert.

Then I spotted the other guy. He stood out even better than me in a houndstooth wool overcoat that might have been a Lanvin, and black slacks and spit-shiny shoes. His clothes shouted money. Out-of-place like me but upmarket. The guy was mid-forties with a tough face and he was standing at the back of a booth with a drink in his hand watching the punters.

He saw me and turned casually away. Maybe clocked me as someone of interest or maybe not.

I went back up the stairs to cover the last couple of rooms whilst I waited for Kevin Kobert to take his break. The two rooms were more secluded but had the same decor, same drinks, same crowd, just a slower pace. A skirling electric guitar and B. B. King's throaty lyrics were piped in. And my queries drew the same answer. Ray hadn't been seen. Was usually in by now. Must be running late. You never knew with Ray. Could be midnight.

I wandered back and heard only piped music from the piano room. Kevin Kobert was on his break. I looked for him at the bar, though that was an unlikely place. One drink and his night's wages would be dust. The club probably topped up a complementary glass before each set to keep him lubricated. I checked the room but didn't spot him. I walked across and asked a bartender and she told me that Kobert had headed for the bathroom.

I followed the signs and found the men's bathroom and when I went in the houndstooth guy was in there with one hand on Kobert's chest, pinning him against the wall whilst the other cracked him hard on the face. Blood was running from Kobert's nose where the ring had pulled free. When I walked in Houndstooth looked up and clocked me in the mirror. He released Kobert and turned.

'What's up?' he said. 'Looking for somebody?'

'Everybody's looking for somebody,' I said. 'Let him go.'

'Let who go?'

'The kid,' I said. 'The one you're smacking about against that wall. See?'

Houndstooth turned to see. Looked surprised.

'This guy? We're just having a chat. Private. So get out.'

'Let him go,' I said. 'The chat's over.'

'You heard me?' he said. 'The bathroom's closed. Go piss somewhere else. Whilst you can still stand.'

I took my hands from my pockets. 'Final warning,' I said.

Houndstooth abandoned the kid and walked across. The kid was eyeing the route to the door but it was too tight. He wouldn't get past. So he stayed against the wall, dripping blood. Houndstooth came and stood two feet from me. Any nearer and I'd have had to poleaxe him on the basis that getting in the first strike gives the best chance of finishing things quickly. I could handle the guy but there was a risk I'd take damage and I had a busy day tomorrow. Didn't want to spend it nursing injuries. If Houndstooth and I were going to have an argument it needed to be one-sided and short, over before he knew it had started. I waited, hands at my side, while Houndstooth came to the realisation that I was another coat in a place where coats didn't belong. That I was like him. He stared a little longer, wondering who the hell I was, but he could see how things would go. He didn't want injuries either. He softened his stare, worked up a half smile and shrugged then stepped round me towards the door. I turned, ready for tricks, but he walked out. I went across to Kobert.

'You okay?' I said.

Kobert was dabbing his nose. Blood had run down his shirt and waistcoat and he didn't look like such a shit hot honky tonk player any more. He looked more like a scared kid.

'What did he want?' I said.

Kobert stepped across to a paper towel dispenser. Pulled sheets free and held them to his face and said he didn't know what the hell the guy wanted. Hadn't a clue. But he did.

'About Ray?' I said.

Kobert tensed defensively, maybe scared that I was about to continue the interrogation. Maybe I was a pal of the other guy. Like a good-guy, bad-guy act. I put him right. Told him that Lisa had asked me to find Ray and had given me Kobert's name.

'Assuming you're Kevin Kobert,' I said.

He didn't reply. His eyes darted and his hand pressed the towel and he bent to search the floor for the nose ring. A distraction. I repeated that I was here because Lisa was worried about Ray.

'Do you know where he is?' I said.

He quit looking for the ring. Stood upright. 'No,' he said. 'I've not seen him. What the hell's going on. That shithead wrecked my nose.' His words came out muffled from behind the mess.

'Any idea who he is?'

'No. He just barged in here and grabbed me. And who the hell are you?'

'I'm a private detective,' I said, 'working for Lisa.'

'A private what? That's crazy, man.'

'Was the other guy asking about Ray?'

'Yes. He thought I knew where he was. Why the hell's he after Ray?'

'I don't know,' I said. 'I just heard that he was asking questions out there. Any reason he took a particular interest in you?'

'I'm a friend of Ray's.'

'That's probably it,' I said. 'And you're sure you don't know where Ray is?'

'No. I've not seen him all week.'

Same old story.

'Did he mention anything about going away? Or about people coming after him?'

'Nothing. This is the first I've heard. Man, he's bust my nose!'

Yeah,' I said, 'Do you know Lisa?'

'Of course.' He examined the paper towels. Saturated. He bundled them and threw them into the waste bin. Pulled out more. 'Sure I know Lisa.'

'Then you'll appreciate how worried she is at Ray's disappearance. He's gone without warning and she's no way of contacting him. She's alone with the baby and scared to death. So think about it, Kevin: have you heard *anything* from Ray. Have you any idea what he's up to?'

'No. Really! We're just friends. He doesn't tell me everything. I thought he'd be in here tonight.'

'That's what you told the man?'

'Yeah. The bastard didn't believe me. Shit! My goddamn nose!'

It came out "By godda no."

'Best get it reset and stitched,' I said. 'It won't look too bad. No harm done.'

Kobert gave me a wild stare that disagreed. Hard to blame him. He'd come in tonight to earn a few quid and bumped into someone who'd almost certainly emerged from Ray's dodgy world to hit him like a bus. His nose would be fine but his nerves would be shot for a long time. I wondered how far Houndstooth would have gone if I hadn't walked in. He probably had no specific reason to believe that Kobert knew where Ray was but his tactics were clear: go in hard and inflict damage. And if there's no information to be had there's no loss.

I left Kobert and went back out and checked the rooms to see if Houndstooth was still around. He wasn't. When I reached the street an Audi was pulling away from the kerb twenty yards up. I watched it come by and saw two faces behind the screen. The driver's was obscured by the reflections but the passenger was Houndstooth. He fixed me with the same look he'd given me in the club. Filed my face in his memory.

I filed his too, knowing that I was looking at the explanation for Ray's disappearance.

Ray's absence had nothing to do with his extra-marital fling.

It was all to do with hiding.

And the people in the Audi were the ones he was hiding from.

The car reached the main road and its brake lights flared and it disappeared into the traffic.

CHAPTER TWELVE
A different class of people

I went out in the black dawn to run my circuits of Battersea Park. My last exercise before I left town. The temperature had touched minus two overnight and ice glistened on the path, threatened to land me on my backside, and the black sky seemed like it would never lighten. My feet lost traction. For a moment things hung in the balance but the moment passed. I upped the pace. Challenged fate. If it happened it happened.

A new day. New optimism. How hard it could be to catch up with a guy as popular as Ray Elland, driving a car as conspicuous as a vintage Capri? Damn hard, perhaps, if he was hiding. The agency had found plenty of people who didn't want to be found but not in thirty-six hours, of which I now had twelve left. Right now all I'd be handing to Lisa was the news that her husband was indeed playing around on her but that the playing around wasn't the reason for his absence. That it looked like he was caught up in something. Which would leave her where she'd started, waiting for Ray to show up. And if he didn't, she'd be left with the new fear that something had happened to him, that he might not be coming back. She'd need to decide whether to talk to the police or us after Christmas.

If Ray *was* in some kind of trouble would that tie in with Holly Sharma's hostility? What if the dancer's bruises weren't Ray's doing? What if she'd had a visit from Houndstooth?

I turned away from the river and passed a lone jogger coming the other way. No acknowledgements. Too dark. Too cold. My energy was focused internally, sculpting a challenge: find Ray Elland by the end of the day. Save Lisa's Christmas. Or destroy it.

I ran a final lap, city lights flaring and flowing across the river, the sound of horns on the breeze, the hiss of the city coming awake. A hint of grey had come into the east. I ran towards the growing light and decided that Ray was findable.

I jogged homewards. Showered and drank a coffee watching the street brighten. Cars crawled out towards the main road. The last working day before the break. I called Lucy to intercept her before she headed for the office. Gave her a fresh assignment: Ray's base, the Odds-On branch in Mitcham. She could watch the place, see who turned up. Pointless me chasing round Greater London if Ray showed up at work. Then I called Lisa to make sure that Ray hadn't already turned up but her phone went to voicemail. I left a message.

I donned my Burberry trench, pulled it tight and went down to warm the engine. Rolled out to the main road just before eight thirty and worked south against the incoming flow. Reached Tooting a little before nine.

Army Outlet was still closed. I grabbed a parking spot three streets away and walked back down. The shop's sign promised a nine thirty opening which wasn't good since kicking my heels for half an hour wasn't a productive way to spend my twelve hours. Not good, too, because the sign also said that they should have been open yesterday, which they weren't. But I decided to risk the half hour. Ray Elland's gun-collector crony would either show up by then or I'd scratch him from the list.

I walked to main drag to kill time. Passed closed-up pound-stores and kebab takeaways, big-name betting shops that represented the other end of the market from Odds-On, though it wasn't clear there was another end. Just flashier street windows, better screens inside. Your money would go as fast in any of them.

My conversations yesterday hadn't got me any nearer to understanding Ray's job. Maybe Odds-On dispensed with formalities such as job descriptions, just let their people oil the wheels as they saw fit. As long as the cash kept flowing they were doing it right. I wondered about Ray's weekly round of the Odds-On outlets. Was that part of the communications executive remit? Or had he invented the trip for Lisa's benefit? A reason to stay out every week. But Monday was the wrong night for his dancing girl. Holly Sharma's free evening would be Sunday. That's when the West End shows took a break. So maybe the trip was legit and Ray had to fit things in as best he could, meet Holly for a late drink after the show before retiring to her place or to his Travelodge. If I didn't pick up a scent this morning I'd take a drive out to Dartford and see whether the hotel staff had anything they could convert to cash. If Ray had a long standing weekly booking then they'd know him.

I walked back up the street and saw that the lights were on inside

Army Outlet. I rapped on the door and a big, untidy guy materialised and waved me away from behind the mesh. I stayed put and made urgent gestures and he threw the locks and came out. Filled the doorway. Scruffy jeans and stained tee-shirt hanging free over an impressive beer gut. The weak daylight illuminated a wide, florid face with dark-set eyes, a razored head.

'Open nine thirty, mate,' he said. He backed away and started to ease the door shut but it jammed on my foot.

'I'm not a customer,' I said.

He looked me up and down and the Burberry's formal air registered. He asked who I was. I told him I was here for Ray Elland's wife. Family business. Barr looked dubious, but curiosity put him off-balance. He eased the door back and came out again.

'What's up?'

I told him. Asked if he had any idea where Ray was.

'Who are you? Her old man?'

'Just a friend,' I said. 'We're kind of worried. He's dropped out of sight and Lisa needs to get hold of him. Any idea where he might be?'

'Haven't a clue.'

'I hear you and Ray are close.'

'Pals, yeah. Shared interest. Military antiques. We do the fairs and markets.'

'You didn't see him at the Bay Horse this week?'

He looked up and down the street. The temperature was zero. I was cold inside my Burberry but Barr had his own insulation.

'No,' he said. 'He didn't show.'

'You expected him?'

'Yeah. He said he'd be in. Owed me for some rail tickets.'

'Any idea why he didn't turn up?'

He looked at me.

'It's just that Lisa's worried,' I said. 'She's got me running all over town.'

Barr folded his arms across his chest and shook his head. The tee-shirt fluttered. His biceps flexed. His goosebumps mottled.

'I'd love to help, mister,' he said, 'but I've not talked to him.'

'He always shows up Wednesdays, right?'

He shrugged. 'Most weeks. Ray's a steady guy. Got his work. Got

71

his routines.'

'And he and Lisa are okay?' I said. 'Nothing between them?'

'We talk antiques. Firearms. Not marital affairs.'

'Appreciated. What about work? Lisa hasn't told me much about what he gets up to there, though I've heard the bookies are a dodgy outfit.'

'Wouldn't know, pal. Far as I know they're legit. There's some South London people running the shops, into all kinds of things, but Ray's not involved. Just works the shops. Are you digging for dirt?'

'I'm digging for whatever will get me to him. It's kind of hard on the wife and kid, Ray dropping out of sight just before Christmas. What do you know about the people who run the shops?'

'Nothin'. They're dodgy. That's it. And Ray's not into that stuff. Just does his job. Works hard.'

'Any idea what a communications executive is?' I said.

Barr watched the street.

'Communications stuff or something,' he said.

I turned to watch the street with him. Cold and noisy. Litter on the ground. Barely a Christmas light on display. Wong part of town.

'Does Ray have any problems?' I said. 'Anyone he doesn't like?'

Barr shrugged again. Bounced on the balls of his feet. Wagged his head side to side, deciding whether to give me any more. Concluded that it was more interesting gabbing on the street than tidying up inside the shop. Stayed to talk.

'There's a geezer in Merton,' he said.

'What geezer?'

'Ray had a set-to with him a couple of weeks back.'

'What happened?'

'Nothin'. You'd be wasting your time. Ray's not hiding from that bastard.'

I've wasted time before. Sometimes it's the wasted time that gets results.

'Who is he?'

'A dealer. Military gear. Antique firearms. Mike Malik.'

'What happened?'

'Ray got scammed. He's a collector but he's not an expert, and Mike took him for two grand on a pair of fake pistols. Sold as 1850s Harvey and Son travellers, original box and everything, only they didn't seem kosher to me. The bullet mould was a modern casting for a start. Ray checked with a guy who knows and it turned out that the set was made in China. They were a nice reproduction, okay for decoration for a tenth the price. So Ray went back to Malik and demanded his money back.'

'Malik wasn't keen on a refund?'

'Not a bit. He told Ray he'd bought the set as-seen. No provenance offered. Malik's a piece of work. Mixes everything: legit, fake and nicked. Flogs to customers he hopes he won't see again. And he's a tough geezer. Ex-Marines. Someone you don't mess with. Didn't stop Ray trying it on. He pushed Malik for the refund but when he got insistent Malik whistled up a couple of guys from the back and had him frog-marched out of the shop.'

Barr laughed and manoeuvred past me onto the pavement. Strutted and turned. Flexed. His story was good drama.

'Ray's a good 'un,' he said. 'He was going to get his money back. So he went away and came back with a couple of mates of his own, from the bookies business. Different class of people to Malik's boys. Malik and his friends ended up in hospital and Ray got his consumer rights.'

'Where does Malik live?'

Barr described a shop on Merton High Street.

I decided to go and talk to the guy.

CHAPTER THIRTEEN

Is this going to bring trouble?

I didn't see Ray going missing over a squabble about phoney antiques. And the squabble hadn't produced last night's assault on Kevin Kobert. But I needed to be sure. I needed Mike Malik to convince me that there was nothing going on between him and Ray. And maybe I'd get a bonus. Maybe Malik would spit out something Ray's pals weren't telling me.

I spotted a corner shop on Merton High Street with the name Militaria up on the fascia. The windows were obscured by a heavy mesh security grille but lights were showing behind them. Maybe the grille stayed down. I guess when you're selling fakes at two thousand quid a shot you feel the need for security. I went in.

The shop was jammed with cabinets displaying medals and badges, knives, daggers and swords. A firearms case ran the length of one wall, displaying guns ranging from deactivated World War Two sidearms and infantry weapons right through to a set of duelling pistols with gold inlaid engravings that would have Dick Turpin grabbing his wallet.

The shop itself was a gloomy contrast with the display cases. Dark wooden floors. Black ceiling tiles. Window grilles blocking the daylight. A chime sounded in the back and a moment later a guy came out and stood behind the counter. He was big, six-two, a little heavier than me, mid-fifties, mean-looking. The meanness was accentuated by a line of stitching across his bruised left cheek. You had to admire Ray Elland coming back for his refund. Mike Malik's face didn't have consumer rights written across it. But the bruising and the plaster cast on his left hand showed which way the argument had gone when Ray returned with the troops.

Malik looked at me like he was ready to roll the dice again and I wondered what weaponry would appear from behind the counter when the shoplifters came in. And thieves had to be a possibility. If you took the display prices at face value the shop was worth knocking over.

'Looking for anything?' Malik asked.

'Ray Elland,' I said.

Malik tensed and came alert. Didn't wait for me to explain further.

'Get out of here,' he said. The sound of Ray's name had moved him an inch or two closer to whatever was beneath the counter. Eighty-eight percent of people are right-handed. So it was an eighty-eight percent probability that Malik's uninjured hand was his favoured one, and that whatever was stashed behind the counter was waiting down on that side. Malik was ready to rumble, plaster cast and all. A tough guy. Ray Elland must have brought impressive backup to negotiate his refund.

Mike Malik wasn't the explanation for Ray's disappearance but the clock was ticking and the best information often comes from the enemy. Malik had been a regular at the Bay Horse. He'd known Ray. Maybe was even pally with him before their gun duel. So maybe he knew things about him.

If my hunch was wrong, if Ray's disappearance *was* connected to Malik, then he'd not talk to me at all. So first question: would he talk? I turned to admire the wall cabinet beside the counter and gave him time. The cabinet was stacked with nineteenth century rifles and carbines. Presumably deactivated or made in China.

'Do you know where Ray is?' I asked.

Malik coughed out a laugh. 'Why the hell would I know where Ray is? Is he looking for more trouble?'

'The opposite,' I said. 'He's trying to avoid it. I've a client Ray owes money to. Today is pay day. My client would like to talk to him.'

Malik's stitches realigned and pulled up a lopsided sneer.

'So the jerk's got himself into a hole,' he said. 'Well good luck finding him. Give him a smack from me.'

'That's my problem,' I said. 'Can't find him. Gone to ground. I heard he's a collector. Thought he might have been in.'

'You heard wrong,' Malik said. 'Elland's not one of my customers.'

'Okay,' I said. 'Bad info. Any other place you collector types go? He's not in work today. Not in his usual places.'

'Can't help you, pal. But I hope you find him. Just watch out for his babysitters. The punk acts tough when they're around.'

'Ray's got protection?'

'You kidding? The bookies he works for is one of Frank McLeod's businesses. You heard that name?'

I'd heard the name. Gave Malik impressed.

He sneered. 'Elland's a real tough guy when those guys are behind him.'

I switched from impressed to worried. Looked thoughtful, weighing pros and cons.

'I didn't hear Ray was one of McLeod's,' I said. 'Is this going to bring trouble for my client?'

Mike Malik relaxed. Eased away from the surprise hidden behind the counter and splayed his fingers on the top. His smile threatened to bust his stitches.

'You've just got to play it smart,' he said. 'Get Ray on his own and beat the living crap out of him and tell him you'll do the same again if he makes trouble. Elland doesn't walk round with his protection.'

'Just being cautious,' I said. 'My client wants his money back but he doesn't want to start a war. If Ray's working for McLeod then that could be a problem.'

'He's not one of McLeod's soldiers,' Malik said. His smile had switched to something way more intense. He'd seen a chance to do Ray Elland a bad turn and he didn't want me nervous and backing off. If my client or I caught flak later for going after Ray, Malik couldn't care less.

'Ray thinks he's a big shot,' Malik said, 'but he's a gofer. He works for the bookies. Keeps things tidy, running round the shops. But he's a nobody. Same as the cashier taking the tickets. Same as the toilet cleaners if they ever clean the toilets. '

'What's a communications executive?' I said.

'A communications *what?* The only communicating Ray does is running round the branches, distributing dirty cash. They gave him a fancy job title because he's the kind of guy titles matter to.'

'The bookies redistribute their takings?'

'Not the shops' takings. This is the stuff going *in*. McLeod's cash that he's washing through his businesses – the bookies and his other shops. Elland's a loud-mouthed drunk. Tells everyone he organises the money. Thinks we're impressed. All he actually does is carry the purse round the shops once a week. He's an errand boy.'

So that was Ray's regular Monday trip. I thought about it.

'Could that be where he is?' I said. 'Travelling?'

'Don't know, mate. You're going to have to burn shoe leather.'

'You say McLeod has other businesses? Does Ray visit those?'

'All of them. Once a week.'

'You know which businesses?'

Malik named a few. A body shop in Surbiton, a scrap metal merchant called Jack Lees with one place in Redhill and another in Dartford, a dodgy used-car sales in Sevenoaks and a high street instant cash shop called Lay-Z-Cash by Norbury Park. All McLeod's. All fronts for laundering, Malik said, the same as the bookies.

'Keep looking,' he said. 'You'll find him. Catch him on his own and he'll not have back-up. Easy.'

'Good to know,' I said. I walked out.

I went back round to the car. Ticked Malik off the list. He was too keen to urge me on, to chase up my client's money and hand out some bad medicine to Ray Elland. He was too keen to assure me that I could do that with impunity, which was a straight lie because his assurance that Ray was just a gofer in the bookies' business was a lie and the bruises on his face, the cast on his hand, told a different story. If Ray was moving a villain's money around then he wasn't a junior employee. He'd have protection whenever he needed it. And I'd find that out pretty quickly once I'd given him the grief that Malik was urging. The one consistency in Malik's story was that Ray wasn't part of the inner circle. That tied in with what everyone was saying. So maybe Ray was just a trusted courier, handling the inflow of cash to McLeod's laundering shells. But that cash wouldn't be peanuts. Was his disappearance to do with the money? Had he poked a finger into the pie? Possible. But did it make sense? Ray had a secure and well paid job. Why would he get involved in something that upset the apple cart? The picture I was getting was of a guy enjoying life. A guy who lived in the moment, liked to get around, liked socialising, liked dancers and nights away from home. Would Ray risk all that? Who was Houndstooth, the guy who'd assaulted Kevin Kobert last night?

I'd just pressed the starter when my phone rang. I killed the ignition and took the call.

It was Peter Bonney.

'Nothing,' he said. 'Not a damn person has seen Ray all week. What the hell's the guy's up to? I can't believe he's just upped and left town.'

'Ray's hiding,' I said.

'He's what? How do you know that?'

'I don't know for sure,' I said. 'Just a theory. Signs I'm seeing. They're pointing to some kind of trouble. Maybe with Frank McLeod's people, maybe with someone else.'

'What have you got?' Bonney asked.

'Nothing specific. I'm still talking to people,' I said. For the moment I was keeping my non-specifics to myself.

Bonney sighed. 'If the bastard's got himself into a mess I'm going to jump all over him.'

Firm words but I could hear something in Bonney's voice. Tension. Stress. Maybe fear for his daughter. I guess the prospect of a truly black Christmas was looming.

'We're going to have a face to face when he turns up,' Bonney said. 'But my first priority is Lisa. She needs to know the truth, good or bad, so she can move on. Preferably without Ray.'

'We've the rest of the day,' I said. 'Then I'll give her what I've got. Which may be nothing.'

'Let's keep looking,' Bonney said. 'We might get lucky. Is there anything I can help with? Places I can look?'

I detailed the businesses Mike Malik had identified. It was a million-to-one Ray would be at any of them doing communications stuff but if Bonney checked it would save me the footwork

I said we'd talk later and we ended the call and I sat in the Frogeye deciding on my next move. I'd covered Ray's social scene, and Bonney was heading out to prod a few nests on Ray Elland's work circuit, and over in Mitcham Lucy was sitting outside Ray's base, the centre of the spokes. I called her for an update and she told me that Ray hadn't shown up but that she'd seen some dodgy types going in.

'Serious guys,' she said. 'Two heavies and an older guy in a blazer. They've been in there thirty minutes. They didn't look like gamblers.'

I was two minutes away. I told her to hang tight.

CHAPTER FOURTEEN
He wasn't coming back until someone pressed the button

Lucy was across the street from the bookies, operating covertly from behind a newly-erected advertising totem whose cracked screen attested to a collision with the pavement traffic it was blocking. The working part of the screen said "For a better con..."

Lucy read me the detail on the shop's visitors from a Post-it block.

'Old guy,' she reported. 'Mean. Sunglasses. Blazer. Frizzy hair. Retired bank robber. Two other guys. Accompanying. Younger. Big. Mean.'

I filed the detail and asked if the three were still in there.

'Yes. They went in half an hour ago.'

'Anyone else?'

'Just a few customers in and out.' She flipped more Post-its. 'Hoodies. Trainers. Tracksuits. Nikes. Likely regulars. Most out within thirty minutes. Unhappy.'

The way the machines were rigged that made sense. You don't see fobty addicts popping the champagne. But the machines are the future. Their main advantage is that you can start early. No need to wait for the racecourses to open up.

The digi-sign beside us flickered. The ad. changed. The new one was some kind of political drum-beating. It said "Here illegally? Face a rest..."

The morning was evaporating fast. Time was moving and we needed ideas. I wondered what the big shots were doing at Ray's workplace. And the old guy in the blazer was a big-shot. I'd bet my hat on it.

Then a guy I recognised walked round from the main street and my bet said that he knew something too.

It was Spud. The potato and wire brush guy who'd visited Lisa's shop yesterday for his weekly protection money. He walked up the street and turned to jog up the Odds-On steps and my hunch that something funny was going on was confirmed.

What was a guy who was extorting Ray's boutique doing popping into his workplace? He wasn't here on extortion business, that's for sure. And the confident way he strode up and disappeared inside said that he *belonged*. Not an interloper and not a punter. The suede coat and dark slacks, shiny black shoes, told me that. The Odds-On shop was routine territory. But if the guy was connected to Ray's work then he wasn't extorting his boutique. Which meant that Lisa wasn't paying those guys off yesterday. So why had she lied? Why were Spud and Franco at TomCat? The obvious answer was that they were looking for Ray. And if Ray's dodgy work pals were looking for him then it meant he was off without a doctor's note. In some kind of trouble with these people. Was this what he was hiding from?

Another hunch: the people inside the bookies had the answers.

I told Lucy to hang tight and walked over. The ad. display flickered as I passed. The working pixels said "Every little hel...".

I went up the steps and into the shop. Found two customers in, working the fixed-odds machines with an intensity that said *this time* but which didn't change the odds in their favour by a millionth of a zillion. There was no sign of the old guy and his pals or of Spud. My guess was that they were behind the security door at the back of the shop.

The same red-jacketed cashier watched me from her security pen as I came in. I pulled a ticket and wandered over to the table. Stooped and got busy writing to kill time and see what happened. I didn't know much about horses and hadn't picked up any tips so I wrote out Coleridge's Kubla Khan which I'd had thrashed into me at school and had never shaken. I used to recite the poem complete – all fifty-four lines of it – at job parties which impressed the WPCs no end, even if they suspected I was making most of it up.

I wrote slowly. Odds-On provided short blunt pencils in lieu of biros, and writing was painful, stooped over the table and gripping the inch of pencil to keep it straight. The poem came out a little rough but it achieved the effect. Redcoat had switched her attention back to her smartphone. I was forgotten. I scribbled away, working on the question of whom Spud was talking to behind the security door.

I filled the front of the ticket. Flipped it over to continue and got as far as "Five miles meandering with a mazy motion" when the back door opened and a guy came out. I dropped the pencil and stepped over to slip through the door before it snicked shut and before the guy, who was Houndstooth, the one who'd smacked Kevin Kobert around in the Carousel last night, spotted my move. He turned and yelled something but it was muffled by the door which had snicked shut. The guy wasn't coming back in until someone pressed the button.

I was in a storage area cluttered with defunct slot machines and modular shelving units stacked with admin files and stationery supplies. The door to the cashier's kiosk was to my left. Two more doors faced me. One of them was open and dark and looked like a bathroom. The other was closed and looked like it might be hiding people.

The cashier's door opened and Redcoat's head popped out. She started to say something but I grabbed the handle and eased her back into her cage and told her to stay put. Then I stepped across and eased open the back door and went in.

Lucky guess. The door got me into the action. A back room, thirty by thirty with subdued lighting and a small bar. Five large game tables. A cluster of six men round the centre one. Busy gabbing. At least before I stepped in and the vibe got round and stopped them. Then six pairs of eyes turned to stare at me. Four of the men were seated at the table. The two others were standing nearby. One of the standing guys was Spud. Three of the four table guys tensed and pushed their chairs back but they didn't get up, and none of them spoke. The guy with the speaking pay grade was the fourth one, sitting on the far side of the table facing me. He was the older guy Lucy had seen come in. The retired bank robber.

Lucy's notes weren't far off. The guy wasn't retired but he'd robbed a few banks in his time.

His face was a decade older but I knew him. Early sixties. Clipper-cropped receding hair; navy blazer and open-neck checked shirt; aviator sunglasses floating over thin lips and denture folds. A face I knew from back in the job, though he didn't know mine. His name was Tommy Vance and he'd worked for Frank McLeod, the guy who owned this shop. I knew both McLeod and Vance from the Nobby Snape affair. Nobby had been their old boss back in '02 when I'd spannered his attempt to go over the wall at Whitemoor. With the big guy looking at another couple of decades inside some of his firm had decided that a future taking commands via scribbled notes and secret codes was less than attractive, and Snape's second in command, Frank McLeod, had jumped ship to set up his own enterprise, taking Tommy Vance with him.

Vance's face was a decade older but he'd still be recognisable at ninety. The face had a meanness that is resilient to age. But he didn't recognise me, which was good. He just watched me calmly, waiting for an explanation.

Calm. Puzzled. Surprised that a punter would come busting through from the shop to gate-crash his business meeting. The other guys looked puzzled too. Only Spud knew the score. He was surprised but he knew what was happening. When he twigged that he was the only one who did he stepped past me and closed the door, blocking my exit. Yesterday it was an open door. Today, closed. I turned and threw a knowing grin at him then returned my attention to the table.

The men with Vance had all come from the same factory. They all looked like boulders. They all had the same bored look of professionals between jobs.

Vance caught up. He knew I wasn't a punter come to complain about the sell-by date on their machines. He already knew that something was off. And when he finished decoding the message that Spud was transmitting he knew what it was. His aviators angled and caught the light.

'This is the guy?' he said.

His voice was quiet. It rasped like he had a bad throat.

'What the fuck's he doing here?' he said. He was talking to Spud. The voice was quiet but it had a dangerous edge. 'What's he doing coming through this door?'

Spud didn't know.

Vance's shades realigned, looking at me. His dentures worked and his cheek ticked. He watched me for a moment. Then his finger pointed at the table top.

'Sit down,' he said.

'I'm fine,' I said.

I sensed movement. Turned and side-stepped to prevent Spud's lump-hammer fist connecting with my kidney. He tore air with a grunt but the other standing guy had stepped forward along with one of the table guys and their hands clamped my shoulders. Good tactics said to go with the flow. Spud was ready to follow through but whilst these two had me he was blocked. His moment had gone. You never get a second chance to land a sucker punch. So Spud held back, breathing heavily, while his two pals eased me down into a seat.

Tommy Vance and I looked at each other across the table.

'You're the guy chasing round after Ray,' he said.

I guess Lisa had answered a few questions when Spud and his friend returned to the boutique yesterday.

'That's a private matter,' I said, 'between me and my client.'

Vance's face stayed expressionless but his low voice hardened.

'I'll ask you again.'

I was watching him and watching the two characters in my peripheral vision, waiting for the flicker on Vance's face that would give them the green light. But if his guys were tough they weren't smart. They'd left me sitting a foot too far from the table and they were standing a foot too close to me. They'd given me space and restricted their own and they'd not spot my intentions before I moved. There was nothing to choose between them, but a tenth of a second decision-making would be a tenth of a second wasted if Vance gave the nod so I'd already made the decision. The left hand guy would take first strike. He was lined up to favour my right hand and he'd take a hard hit before I rolled away from the second guy and lifted the chair as a shield. A good push would send the second guy backwards for the moment it would take to turn again and complete the job with the first. Then I'd be moving towards the door. The flaw in the plan – a significant one – was that Spud was between me and the door and that was going to cost me time. Two or three seconds. Which was sufficient for the guys sitting round the table to get their act together. I'd be lucky if I made the door.

But leaving seemed pointless. And keeping quiet seemed pointless. My work for Lisa Elland was confidential but it was getting nowhere. My two-day deadline favoured a more open investigative technique. And Tommy Vance had answers. So talking to him was the best option.

'Your information's right,' I said. 'I'm looking for Ray. Have you seen him?'

Vance said nothing.

'I was thinking he might be here,' I explained.

Vance stayed quiet. His shades stayed motionless, figuring me out. I was still pretty sure he didn't know me from the old days. My name had never got out over the jailbreak caper and so all I was to him was a private detective whom Ray's wife had hired, an inconvenience, someone getting under their feet.

But even that could be worked up into something more serious. Professional thugs have a habit of looking for grievances. Vance's mouth puckered and his voice rasped.

'A pissant little P.I.,' he said. 'You come barging in here like we're a post office.'

'If Ray worked at the post office I'd go there,' I said. 'But he works here. So it seemed a good place to start. We P.I.s have this logic.'

'And bookies and post offices both have security doors,' Vance said. 'They're there for a reason. They mean "Keep Out". Even a knucklehead private investigator knows that.'

'You don't get results by sticking to the rules,' I quipped.

'No. But you get to stay out of hospital.'

I thought about it. Vance's own quip wasn't rhetoric. His aviators flashed across the table as he let the thought register and he finished making his decision on whether I was going to walk out of here. I estimated his calculations to be at the sixty-forty against stage. People rarely crossed McLeod and his crew back in the old days. If they did then hospital was the least unpleasant of their futures. McLeod and Vance were gangsters from the mould. Swatting aside problems and maintaining reputations was part of their day-to-day operations. I watched Vance and stayed ready for his signal. His men would take collateral damage, but one nod from Tommy and I was going down.

But Vance held off on the nod.

'Why exactly do you want Ray?'

'Your monkey already asked Lisa that.'

Vance's head turned fractionally towards Spud. Cogs were still turning. Options were being sifted. Then he sat forward and rested his arms on the table.

'We heard it's a family matter,' he said. 'A little private investigation.'

I shrugged. 'There you are,' I said. 'That's it.'

'Why did she come to you?'

'Beats me,' I said. 'Probably our Yellow Pages ad. We took a box this year. A fancy border. It's pretty good. Stands out.'

'There's no other connection?' Vance said. 'You don't know her or Ray?'

'Never met them before.'

I didn't mention Peter Bonney. Vance already knew that Ray Elland's father-in-law was an ex-copper, and the knowledge would ensure that Ray Elland was never conscripted fully into the firm, but Vance didn't need to know about my own connection to Bonney. And he didn't need to know that I was an ex copper with a history that had crossed his own. An open exchange of information wasn't going to help the discussion at this point.

Vance's head moved, barely discernible, left and right, checking in with the goons at my side. Still no signal.

'Did you discover anything?' he said.

'Not a damn thing,' I said.

The corners of Vance's mouth twitched upwards.

'No sight of Ray's extra-maritals? No dirty pics?'

'It's hard to get a sight of anything until I know where he is.'

'Gotta be some whispers. Word going round...'

'Not a squeak,' I said. 'I was hoping someone here might give me a pointer.'

I sensed movement behind Vance's shades. His eyes opening a little. I kept watching for the signal. Kept my hands on the table top, ready.

The room was quiet a moment. Then Vance re-focused.

'If I thought you were lying,' he said, 'I'd have you carried out in bags. But I'm assuming you're not. You're a nobody, Flynn. A jumped-up Tesco security guard ripping off girls like Lisa who don't know any better. Girls who shouldn't marry guys if they're going to spy on them.'

He sat back slowly and gripped the table edge.

'I'd like to teach you a lesson about security doors,' he said, 'but we're busy and it's almost Christmas and we don't have time to mop up. So you get a break, Flynn. When you leave here you'll close your investigation and Lisa will sort things out with Ray herself. Is that clear?'

I grinned. 'Sure,' I said. 'Blindingly.'

Vance didn't grin back. He looked like he was reconsidering his offer. He waited a moment, watching me, then sat forward.

'Get out and stay out. If I see you again you'll be sorry.'

'One last thing,' I said.

Vance froze. The goons waited.

'What's a communications executive?' I said. 'What does Ray actually do?'

Vance stayed frozen. Kept control.

'I'm offering you the door, Flynn,' he said.

I shrugged. 'Just asking.'

'Ray's job is of no interest to you.'

But it was. Ray's job was suddenly of considerable interest. Lisa thought Ray was cheating on her and he was. But at its heart her fear came from concern about him. Misguided, perhaps, but he was her family. And now Tommy Vance and Spud and Houndstooth and the rest of the friendly faces round this table had confirmed that Ray was in something a little more serious than a marital fling. He was in trouble. And they'd confirmed that the trouble was with them. With Frank McLeod.

I liked Lisa. I might even like Ray if I met him. So if Ray had a serious problem I needed to let her know. And if she asked me to help then I'd help. If these people were after Ray then Lisa was in danger too.

I held the grin. Stood and turned. Walked out.

I went back into the store room and out into the shop where Houndstooth was waiting, looking a little stupid. He stood close as I passed but made no move to get involved. I turned at the street door and saw that Spud had come out to stand alongside Houndstooth. They were both watching me. Redcoat was watching me. The punters were still watching their terminals. Civil war could break out and they'd still be focused on their millions.

I went out and crossed the road.

Lucy stepped from behind the digi-sign and asked if I'd got anything. I told her I had. I'd got confirmation that Ray Elland was in trouble, that this wasn't about a fling, that Ray was on the run from the people he worked for. I just didn't know why he was running, though the money he couriered for them might be a good explanation.

'Wow,' Lucy said. 'That puts us back at square one.'

'Not even there,' I said. 'We're still at zero.'

The damaged digi-board flickered and changed. The message said "Life's a ...bit ch...".

CHAPTER FIFTEEN
That's not going to happen

Time for Lucy to stand down. Her afternoon job was waiting – the paying one. When she wasn't fighting the forces of disorder in our offices she ran her Uncle Umberto's music shop over in Bethnal Green, a job arguably better suited to a music degree and cherry-red hair than undercover surveillance. Tomorrow was Christmas Eve. The shop was entering its busiest trading period of the year, and chasing retail revenue was likely to be more productive than chasing wayward husbands. My own knocking-off time was less certain. My start of day resolution to catch up with Ray Elland was taking on a more realistic slant. A less than marginal one. I'd warned Lisa that we might draw a blank but the nearer I got to delivering her the bad news then clearing off the less I liked it.

'Are you going to let Amber down?' Lucy said. 'She expects you to show up.'

Same as every year. The same as when I used to take Lucy there.

'I'll be there,' I said. 'Tomorrow. I just want a better idea of what's happening to Ray so I've something more positive to scare Lisa with.'

'You sure I can't help?'

'I don't know what help I need,' I said. 'And if things turn hot with Ray's work cronies the fewer involved the better. Go look after your uncle. Say hello from me.'

Lucy still looked uncertain but until I got a scent of where the hell Ray Elland was there was no way she could help. If I needed extra footwork I had Peter Bonney to call on. He was an ex cop. If Ray had been pulled into something bad then Bonney would understand. He'd know what was needed. He'd know the risks attached.

Lucy looked across to the bookies.

'Don't get drawn in,' she said. 'Go to Norfolk, Eddie. And stay safe.' She tiptoed to peck a kiss then disappeared towards her car. I watched her. Said nothing. I was already drawn in.

I phoned Lisa but she didn't pick up, which was inconvenient. We needed to talk. If I didn't catch her this afternoon I'd be forced to drive up to Wandsworth. This wasn't a good time for her to be out of touch.

I made another call and set up a meeting with my old pal Zach Finch. Zach was the Met detective sergeant who'd been at my side for most of my time in the job. Zach had nearly jumped ship when my own career hit the rocks but I dissuaded him with dark warnings of life beyond and he reconsidered. Stayed with what he was good at and was still there, way past minimum retirement and looking set for another decade. From time to time I squeezed him for favours. Now was one of the times. I needed up to date info on the people Ray Elland was working for and I needed it fast and unredacted.

Zach picked up. I said Merry Christmas and told him what I wanted.

'We're just going out,' he said. 'Christmas bash. Come and say hello to the crew. They're still rolling in the aisles over September. Johnny Scrivens wants your damn autograph.'

I didn't roll about much myself after September. September was when we'd caught up with a bad guy and swung a collateral broom around inside the Metropolitan Police Service at the same time. Apparently, working coppers were still gabbing about the damage. But all the case meant to me was the death of an innocent woman whose only crime was to be close to my then-girlfriend. I'd not done much laughing when my girlfriend's father told me he'd kill me if I went near her again.

'Another time,' I said. 'I'm on a schedule today.'

'Half an hour,' Zach insisted. 'Just show your face. I don't know a thing about Frank McLeod but Andy Lamb does. He'll give you the whole story.'

I thought about it.

'Okay. Thirty minutes. In and out.'

Zach named the old place in Putney, a scruffy town pub called the Blue Monkey. 'They're gonna laugh,' he repeated. 'And they want to know what the hell happened in the Caymans.'

That was something they weren't going to hear. Nothing happened in the Caymans. How the hell the Metropolitan Police grapevine sniffed this stuff out I didn't know. And drinking buddies or not, the Met weren't going to hear different today. I'd tell Zach one day but not his pals.

I fired up the Frogeye and fought heavy traffic up through Merton and Wimbledon. Crossed the A3. The carriageway was stationary below me and the slip roads were backed up to the roundabout. The Christmas exodus had begun. Half the cars would still be on the road by the normal rush hour. And if they were heading far north or west they'd still be there at midnight, consoling themselves with the late bulletins reporting railway pandemonium, stranded masses and cancelled trains.

I parked by the bridge and walked down Putney High Street through a crush of mid-day shoppers and stalled traffic. Gusts slapped my face and sent the clouds scudding low overhead. Failing light emphasised time running out. I needed to get a wider picture. Understand what kind of operation Ray might be mixed up in with his bookies job. The last twenty-four hours had given me a good idea. The link to McLeod was not a good omen and Tommy Vance had strengthened my impression in the bookies' back room. An errand-boy, Bonney said, but I wondered whether he'd missed the picture. Why was Tommy Vance so tense about the kid? I needed to know exactly what Frank McLeod was up to nowadays. Needed to understand how Ray fit in.

A guy in a red coat and white beard stepped out to block me beneath the Exchange Centre lights. Clanged a bell in my face. I side-stepped to avoid being brained and he jabbed a fistful of tokens at me. People jostled my shoulders, steering clear.

'One-time bargains,' he yelled. 'Merry Christmas!'

I waved him off. 'Not shopping, pal.'

'Then eat!' he said. He jabbed more tokens. 'Eat!'

'Not eating.'

'Hey! Just take the damn things! I've a whole fucking bag here.'

'Kinda busy,' I said. I was already moving away.

'Suit yourself,' he yelled after me. 'So pay full price! Merry fucking Christmas, *asshole.*'

He shook his bell like a mad dog and went to ambush someone else. I turned into a side street and went into the Blue Monkey, which was just as packed as the street. I heard a racket coming from the back lounge. Clamour topping the clamour. I eased my way through and walked into a cops' coven. Thirty Met detectives heading home for the break by way of a skinful. I spotted Zach at a table and tried to push through but someone spotted me and heads started turning. People were jostling, yelling my name. I grinned and nodded at old faces, shook hands, waved off questions, kept moving. The room's racket had gone up as if a celebrity was visiting but I was no celebrity. Never had been, no matter the firm handshakes and back-thumping. And I was out, no longer part of the elite. Just a civilian intruder. The beer was making them forget. But the racket had gone up and faces I didn't know were asking how the hell was I? I told them I was fine and kept moving. But these guys were heading home for the holiday and I was stuck in a stalled job with a client whose husband was in trouble and no chance of knocking off any time soon. And whatever Zach's pal told me it wouldn't be enough to explain where Ray Elland was. At best I'd get an understanding of how Ray's bookies serviced Frank McLeod's underworld operations.

I reached Zach's table and sat down opposite my old buddy and a guy beside him whom he introduced as Andy Lamb, an inspector from SCD7. Lamb was a big man with a pale face in a dusty suit and red tie. He had a pint of mild up on the table. He raised it and toasted me.

'So you're the guy got Baker fired,' he smiled.

I gave him a noncommittal shrug. The toppling of a corrupt Deputy Assistant Commissioner as collateral from our case last September might have been a source of satisfaction if the guy's activities hadn't pushed things towards a bad outcome. Half the Metropolitan Police were glad to see the guy go but that was their business. I couldn't care less. It was nothing I'd be telling stories over.

'Eddie's not here to brag about how he's doing our job for us,' Zach said. 'I enticed him with the promise of info.'

Lamb dropped the smile. 'Sure,' he said. 'Frank McLeod. You want intel. That's interesting, Eddie.'

He was looking at me with the standard cop-P.I. suspicion. He took a sip at his beer and planted his glass. 'What are you up to with McLeod?' he asked.

'I'm looking for a guy who works in one of his legit businesses,' I said. 'Wondering if he's got mixed up with the bad stuff. I'm wondering what exactly the bad stuff is nowadays.'

Lamb held his suspicion. 'It's interesting you should ask,' he repeated. 'We're wondering the same thing. We fished a body out of the river yesterday over by Frog Island. Beaten and knifed. ID'd as one of Dixie Martin's crew. Martin's had a few set-to's with McLeod's firm recently and we got a whisper that the killer was McLeod's. So we're wondering if something's brewing between the gangs. Does that strike a chord with what you're looking at?'

It didn't. Ray Elland was peripheral to McLeod's organisation and its turf wars, though Mike Malik's story that he moved money around for them said he wasn't *that* peripheral. But Ray hadn't been painted as one of the soldiers. He wasn't the inner core. Wouldn't get involved in disputes. A tussle between McLeod's firm and a rival gang would be above Ray Elland's pay grade.

Though the timing was interesting.

The timing gave a tinkle on the bell attached to the First Rule of the investigation business, which says that there are no coincidences. McLeod's people knocking off a rival soldier and McLeod's people losing track of one of their own had all the potential for connection. I moved on.

'I'm told that McLeod's still running the old games,' I said.

'All the old games and more,' Lamb said. 'I don't know what I can give you though, Eddie. We need to be careful with our intel.'

'Broad brush,' I said. 'Scope. I want to know what a lower echelon guy moving money for the firm might get involved in.'

'Like I say,' Lamb said. 'We need to be careful here.'

Zach planted his drink and leaned in towards Lamb.

'Andy,' he said, 'take the pickle out of your arse and tell the man.' He fixed Lamb with his evil eye, the same one he used when he worked for me.

Lamb glared back. 'Tell the man, *sir*,' he said.

'Jesus,' Zach said. 'Tell the man fucking *sir*. Were you listening to me at all Andy? It's Christmas and Eddie's probably wrapping a present for us right now.'

Zach. The model subordinate. A real partner. Though he never called me *sir*. The racket was getting louder around us. People were pressing in. Someone planted a Pride in front of me and I grinned and lifted it. Good to see they remembered. I touched a few glasses and took a sip. Zach and Lamb were still glaring at each other. When they'd finished Lamb shook his head and sat forward to be heard.

'McLeod's running all the old games,' he said. 'Extortion, unlicensed gambling, loans, girls. Protection round half the boroughs. His bookies are legit Licences all in order, though we're going to put a stop to that since we know they're part of his shell operation and we know they're generating black revenue in their own right. The bastard's running too many side scams on the premises. Back-room gambling that never gets on the books. Loan sharking right out of the cashiers' tills. He draws people in for payday loans at ten percent interest for the week. The only problem: if they don't repay fully then the interest goes up to a hundred percent a week and the borrowers are locked in for life. Their debts rise to lottery levels but McLeod's fine with that. He doesn't shoot the ones who can't pay. He knows they'll never clear the tab. Just forces an "affordable" repayment plan on them and they know they'll get seriously hurt if they don't stick to *that*. So McLeod gets his instalments each week from hundreds of bad-debtors.'

'Straight extortion.'

'Straight extortion. And his people work the clubs and pubs and retailers. Standard stuff. "Insurance" instalments. And he runs girls and acts as middle man for some Albanians bringing people and drugs in.'

'All laundered through the bookies?'

'About half of it. McLeod runs twenty businesses around the area. Bookies and other shops. Out as far as Chatham. The businesses make money in their own right but the bulk of their takings comes in as washing. He's got a car auction place, a houseware retailer in Gravesend, a chicken takeaway, salvage car parts shop and a buy-sell instant cash place over in Streatham. All shells for cleaning his money.'

'The word about my man is that he delivers the cash,' I said. 'Maybe you've heard of him.'

I gave him Ray's name but Lamb shook his head. 'Don't know it,' he said. 'Not one of McLeod's main people. But McLeod's laundry operation is slick. He knows how to move money without making ripples. Keeps his people clear. My guess is that this Elland guy is the civilian part of the operation. We'll look into it.'

'What kind of turnover are we looking at?' I said.

'For the shells? McLeod launders the maximum the businesses will take without the ripples,' Lamb said. 'We estimate one to five thou' a week. Average two-five. Not a fortune but when you've got twenty feeds you're talking about nearly a quarter of a million a month. The operation costs McLeod in tax but gives him clean money. And we have him for another quarter to half mill. flowing out through other routes. Online financial services, virtual gaming sites, peer-to-peer transfers, cash salaries for his people. All untaxed.'

'Is Tommy Vance still his hands-on man?'

'Yeah. He's McLeod's enforcer, just like he was for McLeod's old boss.'

'Nobby Snape,' I said.

Lamb stopped. Smiled.

'You know your names, Eddie,' he said, 'for a guy who was never in Organised Crime.'

He looked at me and looked at Zach. Zach threw back a grin to tarnish mirrors. If Zach hadn't been my reliable sidekick back in the job and wasn't still a pal I'd describe him as the ugliest bastard I'd ever met. It was part of the reason he could stay a sergeant and still kick his superiors around. His looks put the shits up them. The looks did their job now and staunched Andy Lamb's appetite for being a smart alec. The look said just forget it – *sir* – there's things you don't know and won't ever know. Zach knew all about the Whitemoor jail break, knew I was the cop who'd stymied the caper. Maybe a few more people knew by now but Zach wasn't the one spreading the word. Lamb gave up and turned back to me.

'So you know these people,' he said. 'Then I don't need to tell you about them.'

'Yes you do,' I said. 'I've been out a while.'

Lamb looked at me. 'Well: that's the scene,' he said. 'Tommy Vance is Frank McLeod's fixer. Word has it he's also the hands-on guy for the bookies and retail operations. He's in and out of their places all the time. And if the body in the river yesterday *was* McLeod's doing then Tommy Vance was probably the guy with the bat and knife. If you've a photo of your man Elland we'll look him up, but if he's in a scrape with McLeod he'll likely be taking the next swim over to Frog Island.'

I pulled out Ray's photo. Lamb looked at it without recognition then pulled his phone out and angled it to get a copy to take back to the office. Next week. More likely, after the New Year. Whatever he did with the photo wasn't pertinent to my search so I didn't care. The main thing I'd just picked up was that Ray wasn't one of the upper echelon players. He'd not come up on the Met radar. But anyone shifting fifty K of McLeod's money each week wouldn't be too far from the firm's heart.

'You say the guy is missing?' Zach asked.

'Took a regular trip on Monday, doing the rounds with the cash. Dropped out of sight. McLeod's people are looking for him.'

'And where do you come into it?' Lamb said.

'Ray's got a wife and baby waiting at home. The wife suspects that Ray is playing around with another woman and she's brought us in. But marital problems are the least of her husband's concerns.'

'The guy's crossed the firm,' Zach said.

'It's looking that way. But if he's done a permanent runner it's kind of odd. He's upped and left without his latest love interest and without his belongings or documents or passport. And without letting his wife in on it.'

'So she says.'

'She hired me to check up on him,' I said. 'Her story's kosher. If she was in the thing she wouldn't waste money on a pretend-search. That kind of smoke wouldn't fool McLeod.'

'So the wife's legit?' Lamb said.

'She just wants to know what her husband's up to. Wants him back safe for Christmas.'

Lamb looked at Zach. They both looked at me. Lamb raised his glass. Smiled.

'Not going to happen,' he said. 'Cheers anyway. Happy Christmas, Eddie.'

I raised my own glass and took a swallow. The beer was good. I planted it back on the table and nodded to Zach and said I'd see him in the New Year. Then I pushed out through the mob, dodging another wave of calls and back-slaps.

Happy Christmas.

Not going to happen.

The question was how far to take this thing. It was one fifteen, Friday afternoon and everyone was heading home or in the shops. Tomorrow was Christmas Eve and the street was busy and cold and the clouds were lower and slower, threatening to drop the promised snow. I walked back up to where Bad Santa was still hassling people outside the Exchange, force-feeding flyers and vouchers. I skipped across the road to give the bastard a miss, jogged through gaps between busses. Would have made it if air horns hadn't thwarted my attempt at stealth. Santa head the din and spotted me. Pushed to the kerb to give me the bird. Yelled something I couldn't hear. He was still holding up a fistful of vouchers.

Not happening.

Merry Christmas.

CHAPTER SIXTEEN

His antics had the appearance of something unplanned

I crossed the river in stop-start traffic and worked my way back to Paddington. Traffic reports had the Orbital congealing, the M1 solid at Watford, and Euston and King's Cross declaring delays and cancellations. Everyone wanted to get home. Everyone had left it a day late.

I parked behind the building and walked round. The front door was blocked by a noisy rabble. I wondered if we had a fire. But I didn't hear any alarms, just the racket of the group chin-wagging out in the cold. I saw that most of them had drinks and fags. The drinks explained things. Christmas party. I waited for the sea to part but saw that manners weren't going to work. Opted for the shoulder technique. Pushed through, trailing shouts and slopped drinks. Luckily the glasses were mostly empty. I got clear and went up the steps towards the blast of music from Rook and Lye's door. Smelled warm punch. I guess even ambulance chasers turn off the sirens once a year. As I pushed through the vestibule Bob Rook was just heaving himself out of their clinic door to join the smoking brigade and foul the street with one of his monster Havanas. He illuminated me in a tipple-assisted smile for the fraction of a second it took to recall who I was. Then the smile was whipped away like a cloak in a bullring and I skipped sideways to avoid what was coming after. Yelled Merry Christmas and grabbed for the stair rail. The bull snorted.

Upstairs I unlocked and went in. Flicked on the reception lights but left the tree dark. I stood a moment in the empty room. The Christmas decorations already had that cheerless, post-New Year wilt. The thump of Rook's music came up the stairs. An oldie. Pre-Slade. An amplified chink of cash registers. Electric guitar. Bass thump. *Money,* booming loud.

I pictured Gerry Lye hunched in his office finishing up the year-end accounts while Bob Rook got down and dirty and talked profit trends with the crew. I pictured tonnage hurtling, wine flowing, paralegals scattering. I sighed. Turned and closed the door and went through to my room and swivelled the chair to get my feet onto the sill and gaze out beyond the phoney snow at the grey tower blocks sailing below grey clouds. My phone rang. I reached backwards onto the desk and picked it up. Peter Bonney.

'Not a damn sight of him,' he reported. 'I guess he's hiding, like you say.'

'No doubt about it,' I said. 'If we've nothing by the end of the day Lisa will need to decide whether she wants me to keep looking.'

If we'd nothing by the end of the day then Ray was either *deep* in hiding or already caught.

'Damn,' Bonney said. 'You've not heard even a whisper?'

I'd had whispers but I wasn't ready to share them.

'Let's give it the afternoon,' I said. 'We'll talk this evening.'

'I've had a thought,' Bonney said. 'Ray's got a cousin down in Exeter. Pressed from the same mould. The two have got themselves into a few scrapes over the years. If Ray's hiding from someone then that's a likely place. You fancy taking a run at it? I'm heading across to Brentwood to check one of Ray's old flames. A tart he still sees now and then. I'm thinking that her place would be a good place to hide out too. I'll catch her this afternoon but I'm not going to get to the cousin.'

Bonny sounded weary. Scared, almost. The guy had no time for his son in law but I guess the picture of his daughter's family cracking open, leaving her high and dry, was now too real. The time for innocent explanations had run out. I took details of the Exeter cousin and said I'd think about it. But Devon was a long way. The drive would eat up the rest of the day and I'd other ideas, closer to home.

'I've a feeling about Devon,' Bonney said. 'Ray's with someone he knows. If it's not the Brentford girlfriend then it might be the cousin.'

I repeated that I'd think about it and ended the call. Planted the phone back on the desk and continued watching the Westway. Thought it through. The floorboards shook beneath me and the window glass vibrated. *Money* again. Lyrics pounding through the floor.

Ray moved money around for Frank McLeod. Shuttled fifty K between the villain's businesses each week, feeding packages over the counters. He probably worked from his Mitcham base, from that heavily staffed back room. The money would come in from McLeod's off-the-books operations and they'd count it and package it and make entries in some unofficial ledger then Ray would walk out with a bag and hit the circuit. Was his disappearance related to the cash? Had he decided to rip McLeod off? But even if fifty K was a tidy sum it wasn't a fortune and if you scammed professionals you were going to bring down a whole truckload of grief on yourself. If you scammed the gangsters you'd need to disappear completely. Abandon your wife and kid and abandon them for good. Maybe a new love interest would drive a man to that kind of risk, but the love interest wasn't Holly Sharma, the woman Ray had been seeing for the last four months. Whatever the reason for the bust-up, that affair was dead in the water. And would Ray disappear without his prized possessions or passport? I couldn't see it. Ray's vanishing act had all the appearance of something unplanned. So if he'd nicked the gangsters' money had he done so on a whim? An opportunity that came up?

I watched the drift of cloud above the Westway and tried to make sense of things. A guy with fixed roots, a steady job, family, social circle, woman on the side. Ray wouldn't give all that up lightly. But Tommy Vance was looking for Ray about *something*.

And no matter how I looked at it the only *something* I could see that made sense was the money.

If Ray had done a runner with McLeod's cash how would it go down?

I swivelled the chair back to my desk and grabbed a felt-tip, pulled my Kent A-Z across and opened it at the key map, London to the south east coast. Dotted on the locations of McLeod's twenty operations. The Odds-On shops and the businesses Mike Malik and Andy Lamb had given me. Frank McLeod's laundering ring. I added the Dartford Travelodge where Ray overnighted on his circuit. Then I joined the dots. Started at the Mitcham Odds-On bookies and worked anti-clockwise. Got an oval stretching from Surbiton and Leatherhead in the west to Gravesend and Chatham in the east. A hundred mile circuit, maybe one-fifty road miles. McLeod's bookies and fast-cash shops, dodgy car sales, scrap metal merchants and bargain retailers.

I pictured Ray walking out of the Mitcham bookies each Monday morning with a bagful of cash. Circling the route. Which way? Clockwise or anticlockwise? Anti- made sense: it put two thirds of the deliveries behind him when he hit the Travelodge on Monday night. Left him an easy run back into town to finish up Tuesday lunchtime. Left a lighter load in his overnight bag when he put his feet up for the night.

Would Ray do the circuit alone? Fifty thousand pounds was a lot of cash to entrust to a single guy. Then again, if the guy was a long-term employee, if he had a steady job and very nice pay, and if he had a family he wanted to keep safe he'd not be inclined to play high-stake games. Still, all that money... week after week, year after year. The temptation had to be there.

Ray had started his run as normal on Monday according to Lisa, with or without an escort. Lisa hadn't mentioned anything about a travel partner, so maybe without. Did he finish the trip? Or did he jump ship part way round?

I'd no other leads. No other place to go. And somewhere along that circuit would be the place Ray was last seen, and maybe a clue as to where he'd gone, and why. If he'd finished his run on Tuesday then I was looking at the wrong thing. But maybe he hadn't finished.

I grabbed the A-Z and shut up shop. The party was still going strong down below. I went down. The mob was still blocking the doorway. I steeled my shoulder, sucked smoke and pushed through. Hit the street.

CHAPTER SEVENTEEN
Ponced-up Cortinas

I crossed the river at Fulham and drove towards Wandsworth. My anti-clockwise theory made Ray's first stop a branch of the Odd-On chain in Wandsworth, just a quarter of a mile from their fashion boutique. Maybe someone had seen Ray there on Monday and could confirm my guess about his route. I threw in another guess: that no-one in McLeod's shops would enlighten me. If something was up, if there was a problem with the money, then they'd already be in lock-down. I needed outside witnesses, people who'd spotted Ray going in and out of the place. The drop-off would be brief but if Ray parked his gold Capri outside the shop at the same time each week someone would know it.

The afternoon was grey under steel wool clouds. Lights already on. Stalled traffic. The LBC weather broke in and they were still talking up the prospect of snow, boosting the odds with reports of overnight falls in the Scottish mountains, which had as much relevance as a report of sun on the Côte d'Azur. I struggled free of a traffic light failure at the bottom end of Upper Richmond and headed east. Glanced at TomCat as I passed on my way into Wandsworth. The boutique's windows were dark. Seemed Lisa had given up pretending that things were normal. Called time and closed up at the busiest time of the year. Lisa's Christmas bonus would materialise if Ray showed up and the two of them were still together by Boxing Day. But why was her phone off?

The Wandsworth Odds-On was located up in the one-way system. I parked and walked the street, poking my nose into the neighbouring shops, showing a picture of a gold Ford Capri I'd ink-jetted back at the office. Lisa hadn't given me a snap of Ray's vehicle but the generic inkjet print would do the trick. Jog memories if anyone had spotted the car.

The one-way system was protected by double-red lines. Stop for any reason and you're tow fodder. But Ray had a hundred and fifty miles to cover and I didn't see him slotting in coins at the nearest NCP. He'd park outside the shop. Run in and be back within sixty seconds. As long as there was no warden within sprinting distance there was no risk.

And if his gold Capri was parked here each Monday morning then someone had noticed.

So went my theory.

The first three shops threw cold water on the theory. The people inside gave me idiot looks at the idea that anyone would notice anything going on outside their windows.

No luck.

The investigation business is all about simple ideas that don't work and three negatives in a row threw up the possibility that I was whistling in a gale. I came out of the third shop and looked round through the ear-busting roar of busses and vans. The pavement was mob-rule and the idiot looks suddenly seemed apt. Maybe no-one noticed anything around here.

Except at the business next door to the Odds-On shop. They'd notice all right. The place was a tyre and exhaust drive-in, and you don't park a vintage Ford outside the open doors of a shop full of mechanics without it being spotted. I went in and got lucky. The first blue-overalled guy I spoke to said yeah, there was a Capri that showed up every week. And he also told me that it had been parked there this last Monday, mid-morning. It had rolled up and planted its wheels on the kerb and the same guy as always had jumped out and gone into the bookies. He was in there maybe a minute then came back out and drove off. The same as always.

Theory comes good: people do notice. People *had* noticed this week and confirmed that Ray Elland had started his regular run here on Monday morning with a bagful of cash and a schedule.

I asked the guy whether Ray had been alone. Got a negative: the mechanic had never *noticed* a second person in the car, this week or any other. But only one guy had got out of the car. I asked another question but he'd never noticed the guy carrying anything. If Ray had had a bag the mechanic would probably have spotted it. So maybe Ray took individual packages into each shop. Nothing conspicuous. Just fat envelopes. Ray probably pulled the packages from a bag in the boot. I squeezed the service guy and he recalled that he *had* seen the Capri's boot open from time to time.

I thanked him and went back to the car.

So Ray had started his round on Monday morning. He hadn't simply done a runner with the firm's money. Not from the start, anyway. Maybe he had a place further on that was better to scarper from, worth losing some of the packages. Or maybe I was guessing wrong. Maybe he'd finished the round. Maybe this wasn't about the cash.

I sat in the Frogeye and thought about the circuit. A hundred and fifty miles. A long trail to follow. Too long for the time I had, too much time wasted if all I proved was that Ray completed his rounds, dropped off his last package. I needed to cut things short. Needed to look at the other end of the job.

My guess said the last delivery would be at a shop called Lay-Z-Cash over by Norbury Park, a mile or so from Ray's base. It was the logical place to end his circuit as he came back in, Tuesday lunchtime or early afternoon. If he'd been spotted there then he'd finished his round and this wasn't about the money. I could give up the theory and head to Exeter to chase up Bonney's lead.

I headed for Norbury Park and located the Lay-Z-Cash on the main road west of the park. A shabby retail window in a two storey block of fast-food takeaways, bargain basement off-licences and charity shops. I hopped out and worked the street either side of the shop. Poked my head into doors fifty yards up and down. Got nothing. Crossed the road and continued on that side. Found no-one who'd seen a gold Capri, this week or any other. A true negative: the result told me nothing.

I continued back-tracking. Drove into Streatham and located another Odds-On bookie. The second-last call on Ray's round. Another dud. No gold Capri seen this week. No gold Capri seen last week or any week.

Another negative. Not the definite kind that said Ray hadn't been here on Tuesday. Just the blank of no-one noticing anything. Ray might or might not have got this far with his deliveries.

The two duds balanced my earlier hit in Wandsworth. Gave that one the feel of beginner's luck. I continued reversing Ray's route. My next stop was another Odds-On branch in Lewisham. A third dud. Ray's gold Capri had never been sighted, this week or any other.

The light was fading. Traffic was hell. This was going to take a week. I turned south down the Bromley Road stifling negative thoughts. The next place – the fourth last on Ray's round – was a car parts salvage business called Water Street Auto. The shop sat at the corner of a dead-end street three hundred yards from the centre of Bromley and was closed. The adjacent yard was protected by an eight foot wall and razor wire. The yard gate had gaps in the rotting wood which gave me a view of a space thirty feet across jammed with scrapped vehicles. A faded board beside the office window promised premium auto parts. All rust scraped clean. The place was locked up. Dead. Maybe it had been open earlier today or maybe not. But if it was a front for money laundering then day-to-day custom wouldn't be a factor. As long as the shutters went up once a week, around midday on a Tuesday, the books would look good. I walked the far side of the main road and poked my head into a dry-cleaners and an electrical hardware shop, an estate agents and cheap furniture store. Got nothing. The traffic roared past in unbroken convoys and cost me minutes getting back across to a tiny shop opposite the salvage yard, just back from the corner. The place had whited out windows and a simple name over the door. No hint of what its business might be. I went in through the narrow doorway and found a dark interior, a long, narrow room stacked with carpet rolls and sample stands. Deep in the back was a counter. I walked across and palmed a bell.

Got a hit.

A positive negative.

The guy who came out was mid-sixties and wore a brown shop coat and a disinterested look on his stubbled face that didn't promise much conversation. Once I'd confirmed that I wasn't looking for a carpet it promised even less. I asked anyway, and it turned out that the guy did know about the gold Capri. He knew about it because it was out there all the damn time, which turned out on closer interrogation to mean every Tuesday morning. For ten minutes. Ten minutes was a long time. Maybe Ray was taking advantage of the easy parking and his light load to stop for a cuppa. With only three more deliveries he could relax a little. The reason the carpet guy remembered so well was that nine times out of ten the Capri turned up at eleven thirty, just when his van was coming in to load rolls, and parked right opposite his door so that his own guy was forced to park ten yards further up. Ten yards wasn't a hike even for loading carpet but the Capri was a sufficient irritant to have lodged in the guy's memory.

And his memory said that this Tuesday the Capri didn't come.

I asked the carpet guy how he could be sure and he told me that his van had been late and he'd been standing in his doorway for forty-five minutes and the Capri hadn't shown up the whole time. The first time his van didn't needed the spot and the Capri didn't show.

I asked whether the Capri might have called earlier or later and he asked me how the hell would he know that? It wasn't there at eleven thirty. That's all he knew.

'How come the scrap place is closed?' I said. I nodded towards the distant doorway.

'It's always closed,' he said. 'A couple of half days is all they ever do.'

'Was it open Tuesday morning? When the Capri didn't come?'

He thought about it.

'Come to think of it,' he said, 'they weren't.'

'So they weren't waiting for the Capri.'

'Looks like it. The Capri didn't come and they weren't open. Bloody rubbish cars, those. Even in their day. Ponced-up Cortinas!'

'I heard they were popular.'

The old guy laughed. 'There's no accounting for taste, mate. It was Bodie and Doyle done that. The only reason Capris were popular. And that's this guy all over. Bloody Doyle in his gold Capri. Crap car. Crap show.'

I took his word on the TV history.

'What were your own wheels?' I said.

'Nothing flashy like that,' he said. 'I had a Reliant Robin. Fifteen years. Never broke down once.'

I grinned. Threw him a salute and walked out. His view of Capris made sense.

So Ray Elland hadn't made it to the end of his round on Tuesday. It could be that he skipped this stop but I wasn't betting on it. The shop had been told that Ray wasn't coming and kept its doors closed. Ray's round had hit the rocks before he got here.

So how far had he got? If he'd eloped with the firm's money it had to be near the start of the round. No point handing most of the cash away.

Somewhere after his first stop in Wandsworth something had happened.

And that something was the reason he was missing.

CHAPTER EIGHTEEN
Positive negative

My A-Z suggested that Ray's first stop after Wandsworth would be a car body shop called London Auto over in Surbiton. I headed that way.

It was four fifteen and already dark. I fought forty minutes of South London rush hour. The slower I crawled the faster the clock seemed to tick. Logic said that traffic should be lighter since everyone had got a lunchtime start. Logic was wrong. Way wrong. The traffic was worse than normal. Or more obstructed. I hit a fast-building jam at the London Road junction coming into Kingston. A white van had rear-ended a bus and stalled the traffic. Solid oncoming traffic precluded queue-jumping. I swung the wheel the other way and pulled onto the pavement, squeezed between lamp posts and street signs. The advantage to driving a car that's only fifty-two inches wide. I got clear of the blockage and out through Kingston and put my foot down.

London Auto was a small garage with its street door slid open to give a view of a regular repair shop. I guess McLeod had to keep up appearances. I parked nearby and spent ten minutes canvassing neighbouring businesses for anyone who might have noticed Ray's gold Capri on Monday. Got nothing. Another dud. No-one had noticed, this week or any other. Maybe Ray had called at the repair shop, maybe he hadn't.

My next stop was another Odds-On branch on the main drag up in Rose Hill.

That's where my luck returned.

Right next door to the bookies was a funeral directors. A dark place with memorials and token plastic flowers on display in the windows. No Christmas lights. I went in and found an old guy in a dusty three piece suit and liver spots the size of saucers tidying up in the front shop. He hid his disappointment that I'd no deceased in tow and opened up in his dour, disapproving way to confirm that a gold Capri had indeed parked outside their window on Monday morning just as he was closing up to head out to a funeral. The car was a regular. He saw it at the same time most weeks. Was confident that it had been there at eleven a.m. this Monday when he went out. I thanked him and he watched me go back out with sad eyes.

The bookies was the third of Ray's drop-offs. I wondered how many packets he'd delivered before his schedule was interrupted. How far before the trail fizzled. If this was about him heisting the firm's cash it had to be soon. No point handing all the dosh over before running.

Same thing if someone intercepted him. No point waiting until the swag bag was empty.

All still speculation. Sure, the money would set Ray up nicely, and sure, people would know Ray's routine, knew that he carried cash every Monday. But anyone who knew about the cash also knew whose money it was. Knew that if they took it McLeod would come after it and that he wouldn't be constrained by police procedures or the reading of rights. McLeod would operate fast on the basis of rumour and suspicion, and collateral damage would be no object until they homed in on the thief. Anyone snatching McLeod's money would know they'd be on the run from a firm who wouldn't stop until they'd got it back. If a rival gang had ambushed Ray they'd know they were starting a war. I thought about Andy Lamb's info, the body pulled from the Thames. One of Dixie Martin's crew. Andy had wondered whether something was kicking off between the gangs. But if a rival gang had trodden on Frank McLeod's toes there'd be more than one body by now.

All I had were theories, what-ifs and maybes, a notion that Ray's disappearance was connected to the cash.

And if I was right then somewhere up ahead was Ray's last stop. Up ahead was a crime scene. And crime scenes talk. Open your eyes and you'll pick up more than any forensics team. Whilst they're scraping for traces they don't yet see you'll pick up the key element: a sense of direction. And that's what I needed this afternoon. Problem was, if I found the crime scene it would be more ethereal than any I'd ever walked.

But it would be all I had to give me that direction.

I had the rest of the afternoon and evening before I reported back to Lisa and packed my bags for Norfolk.

Not long enough, whatever I found.

~~~~~

I covered Ray's next three drop-offs in an hour and ten. A cash-for-goods shop in Cheam and a car auction showroom up in Sutton centre, another Odds-On branch out in Leatherhead. The three were negatives but not the useful kind. I didn't find anyone who'd noticed a gold Capri near the businesses, this week or any other. And my supply of potential witnesses was drying up. Shops and businesses were closing. The few people I collared were not inclined to hang around to discuss things. They just wanted me out of their faces so they could get home. So I had negatives that didn't mean anything. Ray might have got as far as Leatherhead on Monday but no-one could tell me one way or the other.

Six p.m. Dank black streets. Racing headlights. Screaming busses. Bicycles up your backside every time you tried to hop across a road. Businesses shutting up fast. Street trade shrinking to coffee bars and restaurants, a few clothing and gift stores open late for the Christmas shoppers.

I'd crossed the Orbital thirty minutes back and the traffic below me had been solid streams of white and red out to the horizon, but the southbound tail lights had been moving. I took a chance. Drove down and merged in. Drifted with the flow as far as Reigate and worked through the town towards the scrap metal merchants Mike Malik had given me. I found the place, a tiny brick office adjoining an eight-foot wire mesh yard at the end of an industrial cul-de-sac between converging railway tracks. The name Jack Lees up over the door. The neighbouring businesses were a car wash and MOT station and a tyre and exhaust fitters. Perfect places to find people who'd notice a vintage Capri. Less perfect now they'd closed up for the night. The only activity in sight was the scrap metal office itself. Seemed Jack Lees or his pals were still in there. I parked outside and watched figures behind the mesh window.

Three duds in a row and a ticking clock. Time for the direct approach. I climbed out and pushed open Jack Lees' door.

'Where the hell is he?' I said

That's an example of the direct approach.

The office was tiny, a grimy hole scattered with junk and rusty tools, cracked tea mugs and discarded food wrappers. An ancient set of golf clubs was bagged up in one corner; an electrical radiant heater was burning in another. The back wall was a gallery of faded girlie pictures pulled from old magazines and a more recent Sun Page 3 calendar. A string of tinsel was suspended across the display. Festive spirit. Expense no object.

The two guys holding the fort wore works overalls. One was bald and bearded and was sliding a box of paperwork onto a shelf. The other had hair but no beard and carried a hundred pounds excess. He was scribbling in a book behind the counter. Both of them looked old and rusty. Both of them opened their mouths and stared at me.

'Has he been in?' I said. The authority in my voice made it clear that I'd come from Tommy Vance or Frank McLeod. The scrap metal guys didn't know me from Santa but they knew I was trouble, knew whom I was talking about.

The guy doing the filing pushed the paperwork box away and gave me a hands-wide shrug. Innocent eyes.

'We've not seen him.' He shook his head and repeated himself. A protest. A defence plea.

'This is a joke,' I said. I let them stew a moment to try to work out where the joke was then clarified things: 'He was seen here today.'

I threw it as an accusation. Watched their faces. Saw fear. But a little indignation too.

'No way,' Beard said. 'That's not true.'

I turned and talked to the wall pics.

'Why don't I believe you?'

'Jesus!' The counter guy's eyes were wide too. 'It's true. We've not seen him. Ray didn't come in.'

'That's your last word? You're still telling us he didn't come in Monday?'

Something they hadn't told me but I guess the discrepancy was lost on them in the general excitement. And I was going with a hunch.

'I think someone's telling lies,' I said. I made it clear who I thought the fibbers were. The two guys picked up the vibes. Both of them shook their heads vigorously. Indignation had taken a back seat. All that was left on their faces was fear. The shit-hole office had a packet of cash to account for, the one Ray was scheduled to hand over, and they hadn't convinced the big guys – me anyway – that they weren't in on the scam.

'He wasn't in, mister,' Beard pleaded. 'Straight. He didn't show up.'

I turned and lifted a finger.

'If I find out different,' I said, 'I'm going to string you both up and beat you with those golf clubs. Do you believe me?'

They believed. They nodded.

'Leave the clubs right there,' I said.

They looked at the clubs. Eyes wide.

I turned and went out.

The direct approach.

Not ideal. Because when the two of them had quit shaking and had time to wonder who the hell I was word would get back to Vance or McLeod. And they'd know who I was. Know that I was still trampling around in this. But I was running out of time.

And I'd got a result.

A positive negative.

Ray hadn't got as far as this drop-off on Monday.

I'd no evidence to tell me whether Ray had shown up at the previous three stops – the negative negatives – but what I knew was that he didn't show up here and he *did* show up at the Rose Hill bookies. So that's where my trail ended. That was my best bet for the crime scene, whatever crime had gone down.

I drove back through Reigate and turned north. Traffic was finally easing. Twenty minutes got me back to the Odds On shop.

I parked behind a residential block and walked up to stand on the main road. It was seven p.m. Businesses were closed, including the bookies. I guess there was no incentive to keep late hours. The shop's main business was transacted Monday mornings. McLeod wasn't competing with William Hill.

The shop was Ray's third stop according to my theory. What my theory didn't tell me was why Ray had waited until here, why he'd handed over three packages before making his move. Why not skip right from his base at Mitcham and save himself thirty K? If he called at the first of his scheduled stops he'd gain a little extra time before the alarm was sounded but wherever he jumped ship he'd be missed as soon as they reported in. If he'd taken his passport it might have made sense to continue his rounds as far as Leatherhead before skipping away down the M23, checking in at Gatwick before anyone noticed he was gone. But he hadn't taken a flight – not on his own passport, at least. So why delay his run? Why hand thirty K over before scarpering?

Unless he didn't scarper.

Maybe he was jumped after he left this shop. Carjacked with the dosh. Taken somewhere where he and the car could be ditched. Was Ray still in the Capri, hidden in a quiet spot? Even a distinctive vintage car could go undiscovered in the right location. But Ray had phoned Lisa on Monday evening, which was well after the event. He was alive and well then. And he'd not mentioned anything to her. Which meant either that the scam was his and that he was keeping Lisa out of it or that whoever had jumped him had forced him to make the call to stall for time, maybe throw McLeod's firm off the scent when they talked to his wife. Either scenario, the Capri had to have been ditched fast. It was too visible.

If this shop was where Ray's round had ended then my real search started here. But nothing was going to jump out. There was no-one around to answer questions. Just passing traffic and a few people scurrying by.

Seven p.m. and no clear way on. I was out of time.

I called Lisa again but she didn't pick up and I began to wonder why. It was almost as if she was hiding from me. Which might imply that she knew something. That I was running round for nothing.

I was out of time. And sweating Ray's trail through the dark for a client who wasn't talking to me had zero appeal. I decided on one last check then I was through.

If Ray wasn't part of it, if he'd been ambushed on his round, then either the Capri was nicked whilst he was in the bookies or he'd been hijacked as he came out. Nicking the car would only be an option if he left the cash in the boot, but that was a possibility. Chances were that Ray just rushed in and out of each place with ten K packets. And snatching the Capri wouldn't be a problem. The car had been a legend amongst car thieves: ten seconds max from hand on the door to driving away.

With the ambush scenarios the plan would be to watch the bookies, waiting for Ray to show up. Then you'd make your move before or after he came out. Snatch the Capri with or without Ray and move it somewhere you could make the switch back to your own vehicle. If this was just Ray acting alone the same would apply: he'd need alternative wheels nearby, ones that wouldn't attract attention.

So one last check: a quick search for a gold Capri parked round the corner or in an alley or on a car park. Somewhere close. If the car had been shifted more than a couple of hundred yards for the swap then I wasn't going to find it.

I walked nearby streets fast. Saw nothing. Crossed to a car park behind a supermarket on the roundabout. The car park was small. Maybe a hundred places. Most of them taken. Evening shoppers beating tomorrow's panic. I walked the rows fast, thinking I'd find nothing. Then ten cars into the third row I stopped by a vintage gold Ford Capri.

Bingo!

The Capri had collected a plastic-sheathed yellow ticket under its wiper. I guess four days was beyond the supermarket's parking allowance.

So.

Theory confirmed.

I'd found the end of the line.

Ray's trip had terminated here. The rest of the cash had not been delivered to McLeod's businesses.

Which said that this was all about the cash.

But the car park was too close to the bookies, too public, for it to be a carjacking. No chance to incapacitate or kill and hide Ray in full sight of the supermarket windows.

So what happened was that someone – either Ray or the car thief – had simply driven the Capri in here and switched cars. If it was Ray then his call to Lisa Monday evening was a ruse as he headed off into the sunset. If someone else had taken the Capri whilst Ray was in the bookies then it wasn't clear why Ray had disappeared or why he'd made the call telling Lisa he'd be away an extra night or so. But it was one of those two things: Ray or someone unknown had driven the Capri round from the bookies and left it here.

Since I was ruling the carjacking theory out then Ray wasn't in the boot but I had to look anyway. Formalities. I checked the car's doors. Locked. I pulled a couple of tools from my coat and looked round. Then opened the boot.

Empty.

I closed it and looked round again. I needed to see the disappearing act. Get a sight of whoever drove the Capri in. Maybe see which vehicle they'd driven out. The supermarket had cameras up on the light poles. They would have caught vehicles in and out on Monday. I went in and pulled the store manager out from the back area. She was a woman in her late fifties feeling the weight of the last Friday before Christmas, perplexed by my request. When her brain got into gear she reeled out references to company policy, suggestions about me taking things up with headquarters, her way of saying get lost, pal. I wondered if she even knew where the camera feeds went – to a control room on the premises? To HQ? To a contractor's offices? Whichever it was, she wasn't going to help this evening. The way she quoted company policy made that clear. I thanked her and went back out to look for other options. Spotted a possibility at the street corner. The corner property was a takeaway called King Kebab. The shop was open but quiet. Inside, two guys had stacks grilling on rotisseries ready for the evening rush, chickens turning on a spit. I'd eaten nothing since my morning rolls and the aroma ambushed me and nearly floored me. Ordering seemed like a good idea on both PR and starvation grounds. I went for a lamb doner in pita, pumped up with tzatziki. A bottle of fizzy water to wash it down. While the guys worked I asked about their camera over the door. A split screen up in the corner of the shop showed that it was operational, and one of the views was a wide angle covering the pavement and the entrance to the supermarket car park. I asked whether the camera had been working on Monday and the guy said sure. I asked how often the recorder sampled and the guy said every few seconds. I asked if there was any way I could take a look at Monday's recording. Told him I was looking for a stolen car that might have come in here. I showed him an agency card. The guy looked doubtful but I was a paying customer, maybe the first tonight, so the fifty quid note I showed along with the card was given careful consideration. Investigators carry fifty quid notes like golden keys. They're the clients' golden keys but they appreciate the results they produce. In this case I wouldn't be billing Lisa Elland further unless she wanted to extend the search, so yesterday's commission was taking another hit.

The kebab guy opted for profit and took me through to a back room whilst my meat was being sliced. He keyed the time on a computer screen. Started just before mid-day Monday and fast-forwarded at twenty times speed until a flash of gold caught my eye. The time was twelve twenty.

I tapped the screen and the guy stepped back and ran the camera at normal speed. The frames were recorded every two seconds but they were played back with a hold and fade that kept things in real time. We watched the Capri go in. It covered the fifty yards in five seconds which gave us two clear frames then a third with its rear end turning out of sight behind the supermarket.

Ray going in. Or someone else. The rear view prevented driver identification.

We let the sequence roll on. Watched the cars coming out. Whoever had driven in wouldn't be hanging around. Nor would they be scarpering on foot with the loaded bag. I was looking for a car coming straight out. Wondering whether I'd see Ray's face behind the windscreen.

Four cars came out but sunlight flashed off their windscreens and obscured the drivers' faces.

Which turned out not to be an issue.

Because I recognised the fourth vehicle.

The car was the black Toyota that had been following me around yesterday.

It was Peter Bonney's.

~~~~~

I showered, rinsed kebab grease from my mouth and drove over the river to park in our spot behind Chase Street. Left the car and walked up to the Podium and grabbed a spare seat at a part-full table in the back. The two others at the table were regulars. We raised glasses and exchanged Christmas cheers.

The club was packed with post-party groups, and a quintet was blasting out bright post-bop seasonal fare that reminded me of Roy Hargrove which I sometimes like. I sat back and relaxed just as I would if I'd clocked off for the vacation. But I hadn't clocked off. I'd missed the office party and I'd be going back in tomorrow. I'd be going in because I had a client who needed protection from something that looked a lot worse than it had two hours ago.

Worse whichever way I looked at things. My mind was turning over the implications of Bonney's involvement and seeing nothing good.

I pulled out my phone and keyed discreetly. If Lisa answered I'd have to go out to be heard. But she didn't answer. The call went to voicemail. I killed the line and supped my beer and wondered. My finger hovered again for a second, ready to call Peter Bonney and ask how *his* day had gone and why he hadn't told me that he was mixed up in this thing, and what the hell he was doing at Rose Hill on Monday?

But I decided against it. Flicked the phone off.

Bonney would tell me tomorrow.

After I'd taken a closer look at him.

CHAPTER NINETEEN
The wrong place at the wrong time

I reached Chase Street just before eight a.m. and diverted into Connie's Greek deli to pick up a coffee. Connie was all Christmas cheer, contemplating a busy day and, when I showed up, contemplating the clearing of my tab. Connie's an optimist that way. Probably imagined that Santa would squeeze down his chimney with the cheque. I promised him I'd be in after the New Year to sort things out. It would be on my list of resolutions. Connie looked unconvinced but he put on a game face and wished me a merry Christmas and threw in a free flapjack with the coffee.

'Give you energy,' he said. 'You flamin' crazy working Christmas Eve.'

'This damn business,' I said. 'It has you by the throat.'

'Take a break, Eddie,' Connie said. 'Enjoy holiday! Come back fresh and wipe the slate. Then we all good in New Year.'

'I'm heading out of town this evening,' I said. 'Taking the break. And good riddance to the whole damn mess.'

'Good riddance,' Connie agreed. 'Come back New Year. Wipe the slate.'

I left him to dream and went into our building. The hallway was cold and empty and stank of spilled alcohol and cigar ash. The stairway echoed as I trudged up. Upstairs I unlocked and flicked the sign to "Open". Habit. The chances of clientele this morning were nil.

The office was freezing. The effect of living under the roof in a building with Stone Age central heating. I went into my room and positioned the electric two-bar by my desk and unwrapped the flapjack. Made a call whilst my computer fired up.

The call connected. Lisa's voicemail again. Still not answering. I began to sense something up. I left a message for her to get back to me, urgently.

But it was her father who interested me first.

Peter Bonney. Ex-job. Fifteen years older than me. Mid-fifties. We'd shared office space back then though we'd never worked a case together and hadn't been close. Just two coppers who lived in the same nick and retired on the same rank, Bonney via an early retirement scheme, me two years earlier without any scheme. I wondered whether Bonney's departure was his choice or whether something had pushed him out.

A shared office space. That was it. Except for one tense episode that I still hadn't fully figured after all these years.

Back in 2003 Peter Bonney had got himself into a scrape and I'd had to make a judgement. He needed me to vouch for his word against the reputation of a slimy character called Lennie Parks whom he'd just killed in self-defence.

I took his word. Backed him up, though I couldn't protect him from the fallout over the fact that he'd ignored procedure and put himself at risk in an incident that produced a fatal shooting. The thing was not for me to judge. Peter Bonney was just a cop with a reputation as a good detective. But my deposition kept him in his job. When I cleared my own desk twelve months later Bonney's two-handed handshake had been warm and his thanks sincere.

'Their loss,' he'd told me. 'Their damn loss, Eddie.'

I'd grinned and patted him on the shoulder. Wished him good luck as I headed for the door. I hadn't seen or heard from him since.

Then suddenly, yesterday, there he was, and even if the fact of his being Lisa's father was a credible explanation for his appearance on my tail it was still a little startling. I'd felt like I'd been caught out. Wrong-footed. Felt as if I was missing something.

And now I knew it.

I needed to know what Peter Bonney had been up to since he left the job.

The only clue was his business card. The card gave him the title "Chief Executive" under the logo of a company called Vista Timeshare.

My desktop stuttered awake with threats of updates and I fought a frustrating twenty minute battle to get something useful out of it. When someone invents a computer with a button marked "Just do the damn work!" they'll make a killing. Mine didn't have the button. It did the work but snail-slow in the spare moments between doing something for the software manufacturer. The trickle of information that did leak out left me with long gaps that I filled with coffee and flapjack, but eventually the info coalesced to tell me that Vista Timeshare was an agency selling apartments in Funchal, Madeira. They had a web page ablaze with sunlit concrete and azure skies, a poetic sales pitch on the delights of condo share ownership along with a listing of available sales and swaps. Seemed Peter Bonney had opted for radical change after he left the Met. Exchanged the disciplined labour of police investigation for the lurid promises of a property salesman. I wondered whether he'd set up Vista Timeshare himself or bought someone out.

I finished the flapjack and drained the coffee. Both excellent. High on flavour. One of them high on calories. I pushed the crumbs away and reclined my Herman Miller executive chair to thirty-five degrees which is the best setting for getting my feet onto the desk. Then I pulled the keyboard into my lap and logged in to a subscription site that executes financial searches. Before I could start my search the computer butted back in with a message that the system had finished sodding around and would I like to restart? I swore and knuckled *Later*. Later I'd be in Norfolk but the AI swallowed the lie and cleared the screen and I keyed Peter Bonney's name into the site and got two hits. The first was a company bankruptcy three years back in which he was a registered director of another property enterprise. This one had invested heavily in a Sheerness Dockyard conversion project that stalled in the post-crash market downturn and hostile planning environment. The second hit was a private security company run by Bonney that was dissolved eighteen months ago. Maybe it had been running alongside the property venture – Bonney keeping multiple irons in the fire as he panned for an income stream to support his retirement. I wondered whether the financial hit from the Sheerness failure had damaged the security business, stopped it getting onto its own feet. Or maybe Bonney had just discovered something better – maybe the Vista Timeshare thing.

The same financial site also told me something else: Bonney had been discharged from the Sheerness Dockyard bankruptcy two years ago but his credit rating was still rock bottom. Maybe continued fall-out from the bankruptcy or maybe other factors, but the result would be the same: Peter would have no access to financing, either personal or business. For a guy trying to build income to ease him through a long retirement Bonney would not find the going easy. I wondered where he'd got the cash to set up or buy Vista Timeshare. Even if he'd set the business up from scratch it would cost money. And if Vista Timeshare actually owned some of the condos it was promoting then the set-up costs would be sky high. Way beyond the levels of a Met retirement package.

I planted the keyboard back onto the desk. Thought about it.

The picture fitted.

Bonney was driving an old Avensis and wearing dull, practical clothes that had seen a few winters. You might have mistaken him for an insurance rep. or a council clerk. His move into self-employment hadn't delivered the entrepreneur lifestyle. Even our Chase Street agency supported a little style, even if we counted the pennies each month. When I'd known him in the job Bonney had been focused on snaring the bad guys. But the failed companies, the timeshare thing, hinted at loftier ambitions nowadays. Were those ambitions in need of a cash infusion? Was Bonney involved in something with his son-in-law?

Had the two of them gone after McLeod's cash?

A nice, simple explanation except for the fact that it was insane. If Bonney and Ray took on McLeod they'd come off losers and they knew it. Knew that Ray's family – Bonney's daughter – might end up in the firing line. And the two of them working together wouldn't explain why Bonney was racing round looking for Ray.

Things still weren't locking into place.

But there was a connection. Bonney hadn't driven out of that car park by chance on Monday.

I swivelled the Miller to watch the Westway traffic and thought about Peter Bonney, back in the day. Prodded memory fragments for impressions. Came back with nothing much. Bonney was just a dedicated, hard working copper. A little full of himself, but so were half the cops on the force. Nothing else stood out other than that single time our paths had crossed and put me in the funny position of bending the truth to back Bonney away from a career-limiting corner.

It was 2003. A year before my own career jumped the rails. It happened because I was in the wrong place at the wrong time.

CHAPTER TWENTY
Bad, greedy and stupid

I was stooging around in drizzle on a scrap of land down by Bow Creek, finishing up a six month secondment to Bethnal Green with SIO for a killing that had occurred there three days before. An old derelict sleeping rough under a plywood carton on the waste land had been found knifed to death for the pennies in his pocket. We'd already charged a nineteen year old druggie from Canning Town with the murder after circumstantial evidence stacked up to point at him like a neon arrow. What we were missing was the knife and any forensics tying him directly to the scene, and a credible story for how he'd spotted the old guy in there. The waste land was walled off from the road and was surrounded on all other sides by rotting iron fencing and vegetation. The place was hidden from any casual passer-by. Then we pulled in a tip that the suspect was in the habit of hanging about on the river to watch the world go by and service his own gutter-level clients, and the stretch of river in question was right by Bow Creek. The guy claimed not to know the location but he was lying and if I could find the place where he'd got a sight of his victim then we'd not only have the Opportunity leg to prop up the prosecution but we'd comb the site for something to prove the guy was there. Some litter with his prints or DNA, some hair or fibres or footprints, anything we could match to put our suspect somewhere he claimed never to have been. But we couldn't comb three hundred yards of the river. We needed the exact spot.

I took an afternoon and drove across. Pushed through rotted ironwork onto the wasteland and put the plywood crate back up the way it had been when I first walked the scene. The afternoon was one of those foul, soaking, early spring species that give London the attraction of a Siberian ghost town and I was soaked through to my socks before I got the crate up. I pulled my collar up and went out and round to the river and spent an hour walking the path adjacent to the ground, looking for the spot where the derelict's shelter was visible through the fencing. Found nowhere. Just got colder and wetter. The high bushes and rusting corrugated metal fencing and rotting machinery behind it put a curtain right across the site. Our suspect didn't spot the old guy from the river path. End of theory.

I walked back onto the waste ground and took another look. The rain was in my face and my feet were filthy with river mud but I stared across the land and saw another possibility.

The ground was bordered on its eastern side by an abandoned works, a brick and corrugated iron shed two hundred feet long that was a remnant of the creek's boat building days. The last firm had died in the early sixties but the shed had been rented out after that to a double-glazing manufacturer before they went bust in turn in the nineties. After that there were no more takers. The building was left to rot, boarded up and forgotten, awaiting the developer's bulldozer. I looked across the land and wondered whether our killer and his druggie clients ever went in there, whether our suspect frequented the upper floor from where he'd get a clear sight over the waste ground through the broken window boards or the open rents where ventilation stacks had rotted and parted from the ironwork. I walked across and climbed the dividing wall and got muck on my pants and jacket to match my shoes.

Police work: the glamour could kill you.

I trudged up an old slipway on the river side of the building to its sliding barn doors which were rusted solid but were inset with a collapsing iron access door that let me through. Inside I flicked on my torch and walked the empty concrete floor to the street end where a brick structure housed the works' offices. Found stairs up to a gallery that ran along the waste ground side of the building, servicing upper floor workrooms. I went up and walked its length. My torch illuminated a mess of litter and drugs paraphernalia in the side rooms, of which there were eight, some with gaps in the window boarding and wall. Gaps that gave a great view of the waste land and anyone moving about on it.

This was the place.

I reached the last room and stepped over the mess to look out through a rent in a window board. Got a clear view of the old guy's plywood crate propped against a line of shrubs near the waste ground's street wall. The thing stood out even on a miserable afternoon that all but hid the grey canvas of the City a mile away. But our killer had been here. He'd been in one of these rooms and he'd spotted the old guy and decided that he was an easy target even if it was only for a few bob. So we'd got a credible location and a fifty-fifty chance that if we swept the rooms we'd pick up something to prove that our suspect had spent time here, though laying out a grid and combing it inch by inch, shifting a ton of junk, was going to take a couple of weeks. But for a fifty-fifty chance it was worth the fire we'd draw over costs. For the opportunity to stitch our killer up before we walked him into court the bitching was bearable.

I left the room and turned to walk the gallery back to the stairs. That's when someone came in through the river doors downstairs. My first guess was that it was some of our druggie's pals, in for a social gathering. I waited for them to come up thinking that maybe I'd grab them and pressure them for corroborating stories. But they didn't come up and I decided I'd get to them later. Continued checking the rooms, planning out the grid. Found that we could discard three of the rooms whose views weren't good. Revised my estimate. Five or six days of forensics support would do it.

The ironwork rattled downstairs and someone else came in from the river and I heard footsteps on the concrete, voices talking, words short and urgent.

Then all hell broke loose.

Two gunshots shattered the air, amplified and echoed by the ironwork. The shots were a second apart and I was already stumbling my way back along the gallery to get to the stairs before the echoes died. Fifteen seconds later I was taking the steps down at the double when a third shot rang out. I kept moving. Ten seconds more and I sprinted out into the main space and saw a guy holding a gun looking down at a body. When he heard me come out of the stairwell he stepped back, tensing and lifting his gun hand, and I was just about to yell at him to drop his weapon when I recognised Peter Bonney, a DI from my own nick, way off his territory and looking shocked as hell. I thought the shock was at seeing me, but I guess it was just the reaction from having killed a man.

I yelled his name, wondering how many more guns were in the building.

'It's just him,' Bonney said. He held up his hands to calm things.

I walked across. Looked at the body. Kept my eyes skinned, my ears open despite Bonney's assurance.

Then I looked at Bonney and waited for him to explain.

What his explanation amounted to was that he'd come in here to talk to one of his informants. This was the dead guy on the concrete. It seemed their conversation hadn't gone as planned. The nark's name was Lennie Parks and he'd been a valuable source of saleable intel over the years on drugs consignments coming up from the south coast ports. The guy was Bonney's prize source, an insider, working for a Russian operation who delivered snippets that only an insider would catch. Most of the snippets concerned other firms but he'd given Bonney information on the Russians too, chewed at the hand that was feeding him.

Bad, greedy and stupid.

Because his game couldn't last. Grasses who get greedy get caught. And it seemed that Parks had been caught blabbing and given a choice by his Russian bosses: take Peter Bonney out of the game or be buried. Bonney had picked up a reputation and wasn't a popular guy with the gangs. Had an unsurpassed record for putting bad guys away, for taking unconventional lines, for going the extra mile to get his man, a reputation for never stopping. Even off the clock Bonney worked the job as a hobby. His reputation was considerable.

So Lennie Parks got caught and was given the choice: kill or be killed. Stupid to the end, though, because once he'd shot Peter Bonney the Russians would put Parks into the ground anyway. They weren't going leave a liability around who'd been grassing on them for years.

Bonney's line of work gave him a firearm when he needed it, when he might bust in on people who carried guns. But solo armed operations weren't part of his remit. If he'd been wary of talking to Lennie, if he'd got wind that something was up and that Lennie might be carrying a weapon, he should have taken a partner and called up an armed unit. Going in alone was his first mistake.

But his second was the big one. His second had put him in a corner. Because even if Parks had pulled a gun on him Bonney should have drawn his weapon and shouted a warning.

And I'd heard no warning.

I was upstairs and everything I heard down on the concrete was mumbles but what I *didn't* hear was Peter Bonney shout to Parks to drop his weapon.

Then Parks had fired and missed. And Bonney fired back and wounded him. Those were the first two shots, a second apart.

Parks had been hit in his gun arm and his weapon had dropped to the floor but he was still standing and Bonney claimed he yelled at him again to stand clear of his weapon, and my ears again didn't pick up the warning since they were still ringing from the shots and my whole focus was on getting down the stairs. But Lennie Parks was desperate. Realised that he had no choice but to finish the job. Because if Bonney walked out of the building alive then Parks would be a dead man. So he didn't stand clear. He stooped and grabbed his gun with his other hand and if Bonney yelled a third warning then I didn't hear that either because I was sprinting down the stairs and his voice was muffled by the brickwork and the sound of my feet. So Parks raised his weapon again and Bonney fired and finished the job.

And now Bonney was walking towards me across the concrete and he was telling me not who the guy was, not what had happened, just the key fact that he'd warned the guy.

'The bastard didn't listen,' he said.

'Okay,' I said. 'Take it easy. Let's talk outside.'

Bonney got it. Lowered his gun and stopped himself walking right across the spot where Lennie Parks was pooling blood. Someone needed to check whether Parks was alive but it shouldn't be Bonney. Bonney needed to keep clear. So I beckoned him away and walked over to check, but Bonney's second shot had been good. Parks was dead. I stood and shook my head and we walked out through the derelict offices onto the road to make the call.

While we waited Bonney gave me the story. I listened, but it wasn't me he needed to talk to. All I was thinking was how this was going to snarl me up in the inquiry, and what a terrific prospect that was. Bonney shouldn't have been telling me anything. I was a witness. And when I was asked about whether Bonney had warned Parks before firing his weapon there was going to be a problem. I'd heard no call, and that fact was going to sit with all the other irregularities in this thing and Bonney was going to have an uphill fight to save his job. So he shouldn't have been talking to me and I shouldn't have been listening but I did and I asked whether he was sure about the warning and he told me yes, *hell* he was sure. We stood on the road below the bridge and Bonney talked until he ran out of steam and reality started to seep in. He pushed his hands into his pockets and stamped his feet as the rain came down.

'Jesus, Eddie,' he said. 'This is a frigging scrape. I got too confident. Forgot that Parks is a double-dealing piece of shit. I got greedy for the intel. I should have brought someone with me and we should have been watching for trouble. I'm looking at a damn problem here. But I warned the bastard. He didn't have to take that shot at me. I'll need you to back me up on that, Eddie.'

His eyes had the glint of desperation. He needed to hear the words but I couldn't say the words. Peter had waded in with his maverick approach one time too often. He'd forgotten that rule books are there to protect the good guys. And no matter how good a cop Peter Bonney was this was not Siberia and it wasn't clear how I could help him. So I couldn't say the words.

We heard sirens. Bonney turned and looked up at the bridge and started talking again about how he needed a solid witness. Needed back-up. How he was in a scrape and all I had to do was tell it like it was. Only how it was wasn't the way he was saying. He turned to me, finally.

'Shit,' he said. 'I shouldn't have trusted Parks further than I could spit.'

His face had lost some of the shock. Picked up anger. He was back to the hard copper, happy it was Parks and not him lying on the concrete, knowing that the world wouldn't give a damn for the loss of another evil little bastard. But he was watching me as the sirens screamed and the vehicles came down off the crossing and there were worry lines round his eyes.

I gave my statement to Professional Standards in an interview booth off the incident room at Limehouse with the aircon blowing and fluorescents spitting, and I told the truth and nothing but the truth, but the truth was camouflaged behind gaps in my statement. I'd heard voices down below in the old building but they'd been muffled, unintelligible. So I had no worthwhile comment on what Bonney had or had not said to Lennie Parks. I didn't mention that if Bonney *had* shouted to Parks to drop his weapon then I'd have heard it, even if I couldn't tell the precise words. I'd have heard the shout.

The whole truth and nothing but, and the DCI who interviewed me asked only what I'd heard and not what I *hadn't* heard. He didn't ask my opinion on Peter Bonney's story.

So the inquiry ran its course and Bonney scraped through with a reprimand and moved on. Got back to what he was good at, which was putting the bad guys away. From time to time he nodded at me in the corridor and I nodded back but I'd gone back to what *I* was good at, which turned to be not so good because eight months later a serial killer got the better of me and another inquiry didn't go so well and delivered a handshake and an open door.

Bonney stayed on for two more years then left the force for reasons that he so far hadn't explained.

Now here he was, involved in Ray Elland's disappearance, and involved somehow with Frank McLeod's people.

And scared for his daughter.

He was in another mess.

CHAPTER TWENTY-ONE
Something like that can sink you.

I called Zach Finch. Asked how the party went.

'Same old,' he said. 'Too much booze, too much phoney backslapping. They'll be back to mud-slinging the third of Jan. How half the bastards got home I don't know.'

I got to the point.

'I didn't spot John Platt's face. He still in the job?'

'He turned up at three. Was rat-arsed by four.'

'He was Peter Bonney's mate. I'm wondering whether he's kept in touch.'

'Pete Bonney?' Zach said. 'Now there's a name! What's up with Peter?'

'Peter's snarled up in my McLeod thing,' I said. 'I'm trying to figure how and why. But he's had an interesting career since he quit the job. I'm thinking John Platt might have some background.'

Zach let out a whistle.

'Well there's one for the books, Eddie. Bonney mixing with the bad guys! But I don't know whether John keeps in touch. And we certainly never hear sight nor sound of Peter.'

I didn't correct Zach on the mixing. I hadn't a clue what Bonney was up to.

'You got John's number?'

'Not on me. I'm out with the strife chasing Christmas turkeys. You could try calling round. John lives in Bayswater.'

Zach described an apartment building off Westbourne. I thanked him and told him to have a good one and we agreed to meet up right after the New Year.

I killed the line and shut down the computer. Unplugged the electric fire and dropped the blinds. Out in reception I flicked the lights off and turned the sign on the door. BACK SOMETIME SOON. No-one would know different until the New Year. I went down and locked the building.

Credit searches only get you so far. I needed to know how Bonney had held up under the pressure of his business problems, whether there was any hint of him getting involved in something that brought him into conflict with Frank McLeod. John Platt had been thick with Peter Bonney back in the day. The two of them worked together and liked to share the odd pint. Maybe John was still in touch.

Zach's info took me to a four storey brick and concrete shoebox tacked onto a corner Edwardian off Westbourne Grove. The building had gone up in the fifties and was bland enough and showing enough wear and tear to peg the apartment prices well below the million mark despite the location. The ground floor housed the offices of a couple of small businesses, closed up and dark. The floors above were residential. I found John Platt's name on the bell plate. Top floor. I knuckled the bell and Platt answered and let me in.

Platt lived alone in a bachelor apartment decked out in chrome furnishings and bright wall colours hung with modern prints and brown and black abstracts. The only major items of furniture were a bookcase stacked with magazines and junk, and a drinks cabinet stacked with drink. Platt looked way older than when I'd last seen him. He'd lost his lean physique to middle age fat. He shook my hand and said helluva surprise, mate, missed you yesterday, then offered me a drink, which I declined. The way Platt had stocked his cabinet it would take the rest of the day just to make my choice. I stood at his window and took in the street view then turned back and caught his puzzled look.

'I'm looking for a bit of info on Pete Bonney,' I said.

The puzzle intensified until I explained that I was doing a job for Bonney's girl, how a straying husband gig had evolved into a missing person hunt. I explained that the husband was a player, that he might be mixed up in something that would set McLeod's firm on him. Platt's face lost its puzzled look. The description of Ray, at least, made sense to him.

'I know about the guy from Peter,' he said. 'Peter wasn't ecstatic when Lisa married the character. Some kind of hoodlum from the East End. Peter was utterly depressed at the idea of his daughter's future involving regular visits to the Scrubs.'

'There's a few different stories,' I said. 'Ray's either in with the bad guys or he's a low ranking employee. Depends who I talk to. I've not picked up anything myself to prove he's into the bad stuff.'

'Maybe not,' Platt said. 'Peter was unhappy though. And he knows the field.'

'The concern now is that something has happened to the guy. Maybe something to do with McLeod.'

Platt joined me at the window. Puffed his cheeks and rocked on his feet while he thought about it. I turned and we both watched the street. Traffic and people trickling down from the main road.

'Is Peter helping you?' Platt asked.

'He's out looking for Ray right now. I guess wrapping Christmas presents is on hold until he figures out whether his daughter still has a family.'

Platted nodded. Lifted his gaze to watch the rooftops. 'If the guy's around then Peter will find him,' he said. He worked up a wry grin. 'Assuming you don't beat him to it, Eddie. I seem to be reading about you every day.'

An exaggeration. We'd had two cases this year that hit the headlines. Both ended badly.

'So why the hell do you need info on Peter?' Platt said.

'Are you still in touch with him?'

'Off and on. It's a couple of years since we met regularly. You didn't answer my question.'

'He may be involved in whatever Ray's up to.'

Platt quit watching the sky and turned to look at me. I kept watching the traffic.

'You're saying Peter's crossed Frank McLeod?' he said. 'That's not him. He's far more sense.'

'He's involved with whatever Ray's in, which might involve McLeod's firm.'

'Something dirty?'

'Hard to see any affair involving McLeod being clean.'

I noted that Platt hadn't given me a shocked denial. The idea of Peter Bonney getting his hands dirty wasn't entirely alien to him.

'Have you picked up anything?' I said. 'Hints, rumours?'

Platt shook his head.

'Nothing,' he said. 'We've not been in touch for a while. But he's never mentioned anything to me. Peter's a straight guy, Eddie. It's the reason he dislikes Ray. Opposite ends of the field.'

'I hear he's had problems,' I said. 'His business affairs haven't been smooth sailing.'

'That's true,' Platt said. 'Peter's had his ups and downs. He was a good copper. In a job for life. And that's where he should have stayed.'

'Any particular reason he got out?'

'He'd had all he could stomach. Being a good copper isn't enough nowadays. You've not forgotten, Eddie: you spend more time playing politics and looking over your shoulder than chasing villains. Peter decided to get out before he sank into the mire and became an institutionalised fraud, good for nothing else. You know how it goes, Eddie. A copper chasing the bad guys across their own turf will work it as he sees fit. But when he's answering to a posse of commissioners and politicos it can get so it's no longer clear who the bad guys are. Peter's dust-up over Lennie Parks wasn't the first but it was nearly the last. But I guess you remember that one.'

I let it go.

'He get a handshake?'

'He got a package he was happy with.'

'A package big enough to buy into that apartment conversion business in Sheerness?' I asked.

'Enough to lose in eighteen months when the investment went bad,' Platt said. 'But Met handshakes aren't of the golden variety – not for working coppers. I doubt if it was much of a pot. I understood that Peter financed most of the venture through loans. The banks certainly demanded blood when their repayments stalled.' Platt paused. 'I'm still not sure where you're going with this, Eddie. I don't see Peter getting into bed with the villains.'

'The Madeira thing. The timeshare business. Is that bringing money in?'

'He's never said. Like I say, we're not close any more. But who knows?'

'You think he might not be doing so well?'

Platt sighed and turned back to the window. Looked up and down the street. Thought about it.

'He's not making a killing,' he said. 'I got the impression Peter was struggling twelve months ago. We'd met up for a drink and a natter but Peter spent most of the time pushing a timeshare slot at me. A condo in Funchal. Here I was, haemorrhaging alimony, working all

God's hours to pay off *this* shithole, and Peter wanted me to take a two-week share on an apartment in Funchal at five grand up front. Made out he was doing me a favour. Fifteen percent discount. I told him I don't go abroad. And if I did, who the hell wants to commit to a single location, a fixed slot each year for the next twenty years? I'd probably go there twice and spend the rest of the time negotiating swaps or renting the place out, paying damn fees every time. But Peter persisted like he was desperate. It got so it was embarrassing, like I was letting him down by not taking on a millstone.'

He shook his head. 'He'd purchased two apartments outright. Set up a website that made it look like he owned the whole complex and lumbered himself chasing sales and rentals. I don't know how successful he's been but any unsold time slots will be bleeding him dry. So it's possible he's struggling. Probably be tits-up in twelve months.'

'He's got his pension,' I said. 'Maybe some of the retirement pot. So he shouldn't be dependent on the timeshare business to live. I'd have thought that kind of investment was pretty safe long term even if it's a squeeze for a few years.'

Platt shrugged. 'I don't know. We don't talk any more. Actually, we've not got together since that night he badgered me. But he did have another thing. A bit of a problem. Maybe that's what's stinging him.'

'What thing?'

Platt jabbed his hands into his pockets. Watched the street.

'I shouldn't be telling you any of this,' he said. 'Peter was a good copper.'

'What thing?'

Platt hesitated. Cranked the cogs as he tracked a black cab crawling between double-parked cars and cyclists. Eventually spoke.

'Peter was gambling,' he said. 'He picked up the habit back in the job. Liked to piss away money he couldn't afford. When your finances are fragile a habit like that can sink you. If Peter's still gambling he'll be struggling. But I don't know what he's up to.'

The taxi struggled with another car coming the other way. No passing room. Neither driver giving ground. Horns started up.

Driving out of car parks where his son-in-law's wheels have just been ditched is what Peter Bonney was up to. Something that involved both Ray and the villains. Peter had chased me down to offer help finding Ray but he knew more than me. Far more than he was saying.

A regular guy, maybe, but my bet was that Bonney was in a financial hole, and money problems can change a person. Maybe Peter was not above playing dirty to find a solution. And maybe he'd been playing me.

Time to ask him.

~~~~~

I called Bonney as I walked back up to the main road. He was out of town but agreed to meet me in Wandsworth. I named a pub near Lisa's boutique. Then I called Lisa again. The off chance drew a negative. She still wasn't answering. Maybe if she did answer at some point she'd be able to tell me what was going on too. Because my client was suddenly as inaccessible as her husband.

Traffic was solid. Thwarted my attempts to cross the High Street. I continued on the south side, dodging shoppers and smartphone ostriches, and was just passing the travel shop where I'd helped with the muggers last night when a brindle and white streak shot out of the alley and skittered about my feet, huffing and growling.

It was Herbie. William's mutt.

I looked up the alley. It was a dead end between the buildings, featureless except for emergency exits and ventilation ducts. At the far end a figure was half sitting, half lying in the corner by a duct. A blanket was wrapped round him and a rucksack sagged on the ground beside him.

William.

Herbie skittered and growled and dropped heavy hints that I was due a trip up the alley. I obliged. Wondered why William was not out selling magazines. Why he was still sleeping at ten in the morning.

Herbie shuffled ahead and sat down beside the old guy, panting like a steam engine. His tongue flopped in nervous tension. He eyed me as if I might have some answers.

I squatted by William and shook his shoulder and the old guy didn't move and I realised that he hadn't headed off to spend the night at his ex-services pal's yesterday evening.

His skin was cold.

I felt his neck. Got nothing.

Herbie panted and whined.

Then my fingers picked up a faint, slow pulse. Alive but barely. Ten in the morning and no-one had noticed the old guy in here, frozen from a night on the pavement. I slid my coat off and added it to William's blanket to conserve what little warmth he still had then called emergency services.

An ambulance rolled up five minutes later and the previously blind crowd started to gather. The paramedics jogged down the alley and asked questions I couldn't answer. They moved urgently. Got William onto the trolley and stretchered him out.

'His stuff...' I pointed to the rucksack.

'Comes with him,' the guy said. 'Not the dog.'

Herbie was unfamiliar with regulations. He trotted out and got his front paws up onto the ambulance steps but the paramedic pushed at him with his boot. Herbie growled and lunged upwards but I made a grab for his collar and steadied him. He turned and looked at me. Panted and whined, muscles tense.

'Good boy,' I said. 'Nice dog. Attaboy.' I eased him away and the paramedic started to pull the doors shut as the ambulance's siren came on. I asked where they were taking the old guy and he told me St Mary's, which was right round the corner. That was good. William had survived twelve hours in the cold but minutes might matter now.

The doors closed and the ambulance rolled away towards Bishops Bridge and the crowd dispersed. I stood with Herbie, watching. Herbie looked up at me and grinned uncertainly.

'Tell me about it,' I said.

Then my phone rang and an unknown voice asked if I wanted to know where Ray Elland was.

CHAPTER TWENTY-TWO

It had sounded too good to be true

Herbie was tugging like a damn mule, pointing up the street to where the ambulance had disappeared into the traffic. I tugged back and clamped the phone to my ear.

'Who is this?' I said.

'You're looking for Ray. What's it worth?'

'How did you get my number?'

'What's it worth?'

'Depends how good the information is. On whether I catch sight of Ray.'

'Okay. Then it's five hundred. Up front.'

'I haven't decided whether you're credible,' I said.

'Don't play games. Do you want Ray or not?'

I thought about it.

'Two fifty up front,' I said. 'Two fifty once I've set eyes on him.'

A short pause. Then:

'Aberdeen Place. Down on the canal. Thirty minutes.'

'How did you get my number?'

The line went dead.

I looked down. The mule had stopped pulling. Herbie was sitting facing me. A grin with a message split his face.

'You want breakfast?' I said.

The grin stretched.

~~~~~

We dodged traffic and found a sandwich bar that sold me four sausages – bread rolls and relish discounted – for six quid. Herbie confirmed that they were edible and we went round to retrieve the car.

I had business that wouldn't wait and a homeless Staffie in tow who'd probably never seen the inside of a car. Might object to being bundled into one the size of a kennel. I reached in and opened the passenger door. Herbie leapt in and sat glaring out of the windscreen like Frogeyes ran on telepathy. Just as I'd thought: didn't know a thing.

'Okay,' I said. 'But don't chew the perspex.'

I went round and slid in beside him and fired up. Herbie racked up the telekinesis and the car moved forwards. Easy.

I guess word had got about from my last couple of days' footwork. Someone had spotted an opportunity. Maybe his info would be good. As good as my money, anyway. The cash in my pocket didn't amount to half the half instalment we'd agreed so when we met there was going to be a re-negotiation. A hundred quid up front. One-time offer. Face to face my informant would see the benefit of going with pragmatic.

We rolled up the main street under a sky that showed no sign of brightening. Solid grey cloud, a dirty quilt hanging over the city. Display windows flashed *Sale!* signs either side. The first signs of unease at the season's takings. Retailers stealing a march on the Boxing Day sales. Traffic flowed around and across us. Bargain hunters made suicide dashes. The afternoon would be worse. If I got clear of this thing by evening I'd be in solid traffic until I got out past Stanstead. And dependent on what this canal guy knew I might not be clear.

'Damn,' I said.

Herbie looked. Grinned.

We worked our way onto the Edgware Road and turned north, and just over the canal I swung right towards the Aberdeen Place electricity plant. I parked up under its walls and told Herbie to sit tight. He misunderstood. Licked his chops. The Frogeye would probably be an empty shell when I returned. I climbed out and walked a narrow alley to the top of the steps down to the canal. Descended onto the towpath. Looked left and right. To my right the canal emerged from a tunnel behind a wide metal duct that routed the substation's high voltage cables underground. To my left was a hundred and fifty yards of empty path running below cutting walls to the Lisson Grove bridge. In front of me, thirty feet of black water slopping against the concrete walls of the cutting's far side. I checked my watch. Ten minutes early. Then I turned to look at the tunnel and saw that the towpath there was no longer empty. Two figures had just stepped from behind the ducting tower and were standing at the foot of the steps, blocking my way back to the street. One was Spud, the guy who'd tried to slug me in the back of Odds-On yesterday. The other was Franco, his sidekick from Lisa's boutique.

McLeod's people.

I backed up along the path to open up space but the two walked towards me. When I stopped they stopped.

'Bet you don't know where Ray is at all,' I said.

They stood facing me, legs akimbo.

'Funny guy,' Franco said, though his expression said not *so* funny. His own voice was still that high pitch from Lisa's shop. He was still chewing gum.

Spud's expression was the same as yesterday, though his face seemed bigger, more misshapen every time I saw it. His hairdo was standing up prouder than the bristles on a wire brush and his muscles were still threatening to rip the sweat-top under his jacket, and he was still wearing boots to make Frankenstein's jaw drop. He worked his own jaw and said:

'This is a final warning, Flynn.'

I'd heard more final warnings than I could remember, going right back to school days. They'd never worked. Too much like red rags. Too hard to resist the bully pushing his face into yours.

'Let me guess,' I said. 'It's about Ray.'

Franco said nothing. The "funny guy" comment had been his full repertoire. But Spud nodded.

'That's right,' he said. 'We're here about Ray.'

'If you've got information,' I said, 'we need to talk about the instalment.'

We faced each other, three yards apart.

'Keep the instalment,' Spud said. 'Put it towards medical expenses.'

Then they moved in, opening a gap between them as they stepped forward. Not much of a gap because the canal path wasn't wide. Ivy-covered stonework on one side and water on the other. If they'd had more space they could have come at me from both sides. But the location was their choice. Bad tactics. But these two weren't going on Mastermind anytime soon.

I took another step back while I decided that Spud would be the first to go down. He had wrecking balls for fists and I didn't fancy taking pile drivers in the kidneys whilst I tussled with Franco.

Then Franco pulled out a flick knife and I recomputed. Fists you can survive. Cold steel is another matter. Spud's "medical expenses" quip started to make sense.

So: change of order. Franco first. The guy was an evil little bastard with a psyche tuned to preying on the helpless, backed by a cold temper and unfamiliarity with fear. But his fondness for the knife – the quick solution – had denied him tactical training. I stepped forwards fast whilst they were both walking towards me and got myself onto the edge of the path between Franco and the water. Total disadvantage. If Franco had puffed a breath he could have put me in the drink, but his fixation on the knife clouded his judgement. He wanted me bleeding, not soaked, so the move caught him out. He turned and stepped back and sliced the blade upwards, aiming for the gap in my coat, the flesh below the ribs. Predictable. I stepped sideways and caught the wrist and swung his arm out and across me and butted him in the face. As his reflex kicked in I wrenched the arm up and spun him round to face Spud and propelled him forward to bounce him off the big guy, who should have stepped back and made his body compliant to damp down the action. But Spud's untrained instinct was to stand solid and Franco bounced off him like a cricket ball off a rebound net and I used the momentum to twist him across my thigh and palm his chin as he passed me, and his momentum carried him into the water. I turned back before he'd splashed down and landed an elbow in Spud's gut. The elbow struck steel but even steel gives a little and the big guy felt it sufficiently to disturb the right-hander that was swinging towards my head. I ducked, came up and landed my own left and right and Spud felt both of them. Not much – it's hard to damage a sack of rubble – but he stepped back all the same and I put my head down and threw my shoulder into his mass and it was enough to topple him backwards and crack the back of his head on the stonework by the steps. The stones were hard and the winter ivy didn't much cushion the impact. Spud's legs took a break and dropped him to the floor.

I turned and stepped back to the canal where Franco was palming the edge stones as he tried to heave himself from the water. My foot connected with his chin and inspired a spectacular back-flip that sent him out and diving below the surface like a beluga. Water churned. Arms and legs thrashed. I turned again and stepped across to land a kick on Spud's head as he scrabbled to get up. Spud's head was harder than Franco's chin. It was like kicking a boulder. Almost left me with a broken ankle fifty steps down from the street. But Spud felt the impact too, which was what mattered. He grunted and sat back, rolled onto his hands and knees. When I turned, Franco was fooling around in the water, standing a yard out, up to his chest, and the temptation was there to wrestle Spud across the path to see how big *that* splash would be. But staying around to play games with these two goons would be tactics as bad as their own.

I opted for sense. Left them to it and jogged up the steps.

I reached the street and walked to the car, a little breathless and with feet soaked from Franco's splashing. I opened the door and checked inside. Found the seats intact. Herbie was curled on the passenger side snoring. Didn't stir as I slid in. Used to waiting around. I pressed the starter and made a turn and eased back up the road and into the traffic.

Ray's location, gift-wrapped, had sounded too good to be true. Half a P.I.'s life comprises things that are too good to be true and never are. But I'd got something, at least, down on the canal. I'd got confirmation that Ray was in serious trouble with McLeod's people. Serious enough that it needed sorting without the interference of a private investigator.

The other thing I'd learned was that McLeod hadn't caught up with Ray. It they had, the affair would be closed and there'd be nothing for me to interfere in. So McLeod was still hunting. And I'd bet my hat that the hunt was about missing money.

And if that's what we were looking at then Ray was in deep trouble.

The clarification was good but I still had nothing to point me towards him, no clue where he'd gone after he'd become separated from his Capri on Monday.

And I had Peter Bonney running round pulling the wool over my eyes, and somehow mixed up in the affair himself.

And now a client who wasn't answering her phone.

It was mid-day, Christmas Eve, and I needed to be out of town by mid-evening and this thing wasn't moving. If all I took back to Lisa was the fact that her husband's disappearance was more than a simple extra-marital adventure I'd be leaving all her fears intact and with something much bigger to worry about.

I turned towards the river. It was time to have a heart-to-heart with Peter Bonney. Start to pull in some answers.

I left Herbie snoring in the car on West Hill while I walked round to a pub called the Red Lion. The Lion's lounge was buzzing with Christmas cheer but felt like a foreign country. Bonney wasn't in yet. I perched myself at the bar and ordered a roast ham sandwich and fizzy water.

Both were served up. The water looked better than the sandwich. I'd taken my second bite of the latter when Peter Bonney arrived and grabbed the stool beside me and shrugged off his coat. Ordered another of his double whiskies and rested his arms on the bar. He studied his knuckles for a moment then rapped on the wood and I wondered why he looked so nervous, what it was that had aged him since Thursday.

CHAPTER TWENTY-THREE
He didn't think it through

I put my sandwich down and waited for Bonney to explain. He took a moment and pulled himself together.

'Lisa's gone,' he said.

I filed the information. Said nothing. The news went with everything else that was happening. Client hires you to snare her husband who's supposedly playing around but turns out to be AWOL. A husband who could be anywhere or nowhere or safe back home. Client not answering her phone to let you know either way. Detective racing round chasing his tail *pro bono* whilst client's father plays his own game. Then client disappears. It all made sense. I just didn't know what sense. I lifted my water and sipped, watching Peter Bonney, who'd been lying to me the last few days and was probably here to feed me more lies.

'What happened?' I said.

'Lisa turned up at the house Thursday night and dropped Jessica off with us. She said she had some urgent business but she wouldn't explain what. Then she headed out. She's not come back.'

His whisky turned up and he grabbed the glass and drained half in one sip and snapped the tumbler onto the bar.

'There's no way Lisa would just walk out,' he said. 'They've taken her.'

'Okay,' I said.

I waited for him to tell me who "they" were. Tell me that this was about Frank McLeod. Maybe pass on a little truth about the game he and Ray had been playing. The reason Lisa had been taken.

Twenty-five years as a Met detective steels a guy against displays of fear but there was something wringing Bonney out from the inside. His grip on his whisky glass threatened to have shards flying.

'Relax,' I said.

Bonney looked at me. Sensed that he was showing too much. He relaxed his fingers and forced himself to sit back, away from the bar. He worked up a grim smile.

'Jesus,' he said. 'Merry fucking Christmas.'

I grinned back. Stayed silent.

Bonney leaned forward again. Toyed with the whisky. Pushed the glass around on the bar.

'Sheryl's no idea what's going on,' he said. 'But she's sick with worry. Wants the police in on it.'

'But unless you've evidence that Lisa has been taken...'

'...the police won't be interested,' Bonney said. 'I explained that to her. For all intents, Lisa has gone off on her own. The police won't do anything.'

'Unless you explain to them about Ray,' I said. 'They might be interested then.'

Bonney breathed out. Long. Slow. Sat back and braced himself away from the bar, gripping its edge, arms locked.

'What can we tell them?' he said. 'That Ray's a petty criminal playing around with the big boys? That he might have trodden on someone's toes but that we've no evidence for it. No evidence that anything has happened to him that isn't explained by his normal behaviour? They're going to laugh in our faces.'

I couldn't argue. I'd laugh all right.

'But we're agreed,' I said. 'Ray *is* in trouble with McLeod?'

I studied his face. Twenty-five years as a copper. The mask was there but it was cracking. Bonney couldn't hide his fear. I watched him weigh options, struggling with a decision on whether to tell me the truth. Then he breathed out again and his shoulders sagged and he sat forward. Decision made. He lifted his drink back up. Turned it in his fingers.

'Yes,' he said. 'The bastard's in trouble with McLeod. And we both know what kind of trouble. It's the kind you bring down when you double-cross villains. Ray's been running round with their cash all this time trying to act the trusty gangster but every time he's done the rounds his eyes have been popping at the weight of the envelopes. And finally he couldn't resist putting his hand in the till.'

I said nothing. Waited as the strategy inside Bonney continued to shape itself. He was an ex copper. He knew that I knew about McLeod but that he knew more. And even though he needed to bring me in he was still holding back. He still wasn't mentioning his own part in Ray's game, still navigating the waters of dangerous facts, ones he didn't feel inclined to share. When he'd finished working through the pros and cons he spoke.

'He took his chance,' Bonney said. 'Ran with the cash. But dumb little Ray didn't think it through. You don't steal from people like McLeod.'

I picked up my bottle of fizz and took a swig. Bonney's theory was so spookily similar to mine that I'd be sure we were closing in on the truth if I didn't know that he was still pitching me bullshit. Because he was involved. Up to his neck. And even with his daughter missing, consequential on their caper, he was still playing me. I was still puzzling over the fact that he'd tagged along to help me the last couple of days. It didn't make sense. Neither did coming to me now, because I couldn't help if I didn't know what the hell was going on. Bottom line, we were both wasting time with this act. I had six, maybe eight hours left and then I was out, whichever way the thing fell, and Peter Bonney didn't look like he had a clue how to make things come right. I sipped my water and wondered whether I should take another bite of the sandwich. Decided against. The bread was stale and the ham was curling at the edges. I pushed the plate away.

'Okay,' I said. 'So Ray's played games with McLeod and it's backfired.'

BS works both ways. I took the same in-job training course as Bonney and the training told me to go along with his story because I needed to see where he was going *with* it. I watched the mirror behind the bar. Bonney's image sighed and his knuckles rapped the counter again. He turned, and he looked more nervous than ever.

'McLeod lured Lisa away last night,' he said. 'Snatched her to get leverage over Ray. To bring him in.'

Well now.

Another theory that matched my own. And Lisa in McLeod's hands explained Bonney's fear. He couldn't give two hoots about what happened to his son-in-law but if Ray refused to come in, Lisa was going to get hurt.

No doubt. Because people like McLeod don't get double-crossed. They don't lose. People like McLeod will wreak as much collateral damage as necessary to make sure they never lose. And Lisa was now the key pawn. Whoever had started the game with McLeod had put her right into the firing line.

Bonney knew it and he was clear about the danger but he was still hiding the fact that he was in on it.

'So what do we do?' I asked.

'We still need to find Ray,' Bonney said. 'Get the cash back. But I'm going to track McLeod down. Pay a visit. Confirm that he has Lisa. And if he does then I may need some help with negotiations.'

He looked at me.

I folded my arms on the bar. Grinned into the mirror. Bonney's reflection was watching me and his face had the same tension as eight years ago when he last needed my help, needed me to be certain of something I wasn't certain of. The same desperation was there in his eyes. The hard copper with his future hanging on a thread. If the thread holds, his future is one thing. If it snaps it's the other.

Eight years ago it had been just the simple decision. My call. I'd recognised a good copper and made the call and kept doubt out of my mind and Bonney's name intact.

This time I could make the call but I couldn't guarantee it would fix things. Moving against a professional like McLeod, getting Lisa safely away from him, would be tricky and possibly lethal. The result would be a toss of a coin.

And this time I was helping a guy who I *knew* was lying. I thought about it. Decided to let the lie sit. I stood to leave.

'Dig out McLeod,' I said. 'Then we'll talk.'

Bonney lifted his whisky. Finished the shot and clamped his lips to nod his thanks in the mirror. Stayed sitting.

'Again, Eddie,' he acknowledged. He tried to work up a smile but it didn't make it.

I walked out with an eight year doubt surfacing in my mind, exposing the question of whether I was seeing the light for the first time or had seen it back then but pretended not to. Sometimes you see things all along but only slowly open your eyes to what's there.

CHAPTER TWENTY-FOUR
Where Magwitch stalked the kid

I backed the Frogeye in behind a van to watch the pub door. Herbie had woken and sat up to give a second pair of eyes. Grinned like he knew what was happening. Maybe he did. I wondered how long Staffies went without feeding or watering. Saw no sigh of urgency in the grin. Just the thrill of riding into the unknown at exhaust level, which was what chasing round after Ray amounted to. Time to change tactics. I wanted to see what Bonney was up to, where he took me. Maybe he'd take me to McLeod. Maybe to Ray. Somewhere. Ten minutes later Bonney came out of the pub and drove off in the Toyota and I followed. We moved east through Dulwich through the grey noon. Picked up the A2. Bonney kept a steady pace, easing through the traffic like he knew his destination. No detours or stops. I stayed three cars back and let him take us. Herbie got bored and curled back onto the seat, nose-to-tail, but his eyes stayed locked on me, looking for clues. I didn't have any. I flicked on LBC. More talk of snow. They were back to fifty percent for this evening. I had a long drive lined up if I ever got clear of this job. The snow I could do without.

Bonney reached the Orbital but skimmed under it, which started me thinking of Gravesend. But sixty seconds later he exited the carriageway and turned south into a shoebox commuter village. The Toyota slowed to the thirty limit and worked its way through. I'd dropped a hundred yards back and kept my lights off in the deepening gloom. Two minutes beyond the village the Toyota's brake lights flared and Bonney turned into a gravel driveway that ran across a lawn behind a roadside ornamental chain-link fence. The lawn was scattered with apple and pear trees, branches all bare. I rolled to a stop and watched. Fifty yards up the drive the Toyota stopped at a steel gate set into a ten foot brick wall that was the real property boundary protecting the privacy of whoever lived behind it. Bonney leaned out and pressed a button and spoke into an intercom. It was a longish conversation, as if he wasn't expected and possibly wasn't known and maybe wasn't welcome but in the end the gates swung open and the Toyota disappeared into the interior.

Snowflakes materialised on the windscreen. I looked up at the grey unbroken blanket. Precipitation imminent. I found gear and rolled down the road and turned the car. Eased onto the verge fifty yards beyond the driveway and killed the engine. Slotted in a Roy Eldridge collection. Herbie stirred and looked up and saw that nothing was moving. He sighed and curled tighter. I grinned and patted his slab head and he snorted. I watched the gate and tapped my foot to the beat as visibility dropped in suddenly ferocious snow.

I wondered whose house this was. Could think of only one answer.

Bonney had made it sound as if digging out McLeod would be a hunt but he'd driven straight here. I watched the gate and wondered. The ten-foot walls blocked any view but I imagined a big house, a swimming pool, tennis courts. A rich guy's estate.

And call it a wild guess but I sensed that the rich guy was McLeod.

Most villains head for the Canaries or the Caribbean for their winter break but maybe McLeod was the traditional kind. Preferred his turkey and Christmas pud. in front of a crackling fire, snow on the windowsill. Maybe Frank McLeod was behind that wall.

And maybe Lisa was here.

Maybe she was leverage to pull Ray or Bonney in, depending on which of them McLeod really wanted to talk to. If it was Bonney then he was on thin ice going in through the gates. So maybe McLeod didn't know that he was involved and was waiting for Ray. But Bonney showing up might still be a problem.

Thin ice, whichever way. Did Bonney think he could negotiate for his daughter? Peter wasn't naive. He knew the answer. Which left the alternative. That Bonney was here to turn up the heat. To make it clear to McLeod that he was being watched, that things needed to end peacefully. And maybe Bonney was trying to put things right with McLeod. Maybe Bonney was proposing to bring Ray in.

But whichever way this fell there was a problem. Finding the cash wouldn't be sufficient. Villains like McLeod weren't about appeasement. They were about respect, demonstrations, lessons. When all this was settled Ray or Bonney or both might not be coming back.

Bonney was smart. He was an ex-cop. He knew all this. So if this was McLeod's nest what was he doing barging in without backup?

The snow slackened to random flurries. I flicked the wipers and cleared the screen. Wondered whether I'd left it too late to drive up to Norfolk. Wondered whether I'd be driving anywhere tonight. Eldridge's horn work floated soft sparkling registers across the seasonal backdrop and flicked Herbie's ears with its highs. Herbie snored, oblivious. It was probably the warmest he'd been in weeks. The snow stopped completely. I gave the wipers a final flick and spotted the Toyota easing back out of the gate. Bonney had been in there twenty minutes.

I let Bonney get clear then pulled out and followed him back towards the A2. He turned towards the Orbital but didn't cross it this time. Took the slip road and joined it. Drove north towards the tunnel. He drove fast through the steady traffic and used the white lanes at the toll, barely slowing for the barriers. I grabbed a fistful of change and threw it at the basket, which was the wrong height for Frogeyes. I didn't have time to count out the charge but the overkill worked. A few seconds clunking and counting and my donation satisfied the river gods. The barrier lifted and I put my foot down to catch up. Followed Bonney down into the tunnel and regained sight of him as I came out on the north side. Bonney had accelerated to seventy-five and held the pace for five minutes before he signalled and took the next exit and turned east off the Orbital. Then he settled into a steady drive. I held my distance and followed the Toyota for forty minutes, almost all the way to Southend. Then on the outskirts of the town he turned off the main road and rolled down towards the railway and pulled into a lane alongside a closed-up static caravan park. The Toyota stopped and its brake lights died. I coasted on up the top road to a lay-by under trees and killed the engine. Herbie raised his head and looked at me. Grinned.

'Not a damn clue,' I said.

I hopped out and walked down the lane and spotted Bonney climbing the fence into the site carrying an overnight bag. If he was planning on kipping in one of the units he'd be doing so without electrical power or water. Council rules had shut down the site for the winter and the units had all the welcome of concrete bunkers. I shimmied over the fence and followed Bonney across the pitches to an old pale-green unit set up on cinder blocks. He climbed the steps and unlocked the door and went in.

I stood under bare trees and waited. No electricity meant no light. Bonney was stooging around in the gloom inside the caravan and if he was staying the night he'd find it frosty. A southerly blast came off the estuary and caught my neck, and I turned my collar up and tried to tell myself that this was getting me nearer to Lisa and Ray.

Christmas Eve. One thirty in the afternoon. The bleakest spot in Essex. I turned to face the wind coming in across the river and breathed the desolation. I could just make out the distant shore through the winter haze, the Kent marshes where Magwitch stalked the kid. When I turned back Peter Bonney was descending the caravan steps and walking back out.

He moved fast towards the fence without looking left or right and climbed over it back into the lane. A few seconds later I heard the Avensis fire up and move off. I stayed put. Bonney had gone but the overnight bag hadn't, and the bag had looked interesting. The bag had looked important.

I gave the Toyota a moment to get clear then went back over the fence and brought the Frogeye down into the lane. Pulled a small bag of my own from the boot. Herbie watched, hoping for food.

'Next stop,' I promised. 'How about a walk?'

The mutt agreed. He grinned and slobbered. I pulled my stuff clear and tugged his lead and we both crossed to the fence. I climbed over then stooped to wrench at the mesh and Herbie slithered under and followed me across the site then stooged around doing doggie things as I went to work on the caravan door. Found that no work was needed. The door had been forced, splintering the woodwork around the lock. Bonney had used his key only as the simplest option but when I pressed firmly the door opened anyway. I went in and found a lounge with dustsheets heaped on its floor to leave a sofa and two armchairs uncovered. Both were shredded. Someone had been here before Bonney and ripped the place up, looking for something. Herbie came in and snuffled about, measured the place up and selected an undamaged bit of sofa. Climbed up to spectate. I moved through the unit and found that the damage was everywhere. Furniture, fittings, beds, cupboards, all torn or smashed or splintered. Someone with a knife and hammer had been through the place.

In the bedroom a photo was lying face down on a dresser. I lifted it to the light and saw a portrait of Ray and Lisa. A professional job.

Soft focus. Faded oval border. Two lovers. Maybe before they were married.

So the caravan was theirs.

Lisa hadn't mentioned it but maybe it had slipped her mind. She'd listed only places and people around town. And if I'd come out here I'd have found nothing and no-one, the same as the intruder had.

Because what they were looking for had only just arrived.

I found it in a cupboard under the sink and lifted it onto the dining bar. Bonney's overnight bag. Full, but not with overnight stuff. I opened it and spilled fat brown envelopes onto the bar and I knew before I opened the first one that this was the cash that was causing all the turmoil. The envelope in my hand was marked "Lees" which was the name of the Cheam scrap metal business, the one Ray didn't reach on Monday. I opened the envelope and dropped band-wrapped notes onto the table. Fives, tens, twenties. Two or three thousand quid. A good week's takings for the dusty guys in that office with the tinselled girlie posters. A nice week's takings for a place selling scrap. I rummaged further. Counted fifteen envelopes, each ID'd with the name of a stop on Ray's round. Businesses he'd not reached after he or the cash were diverted in Sutton. Most of the day's cash was still in the bag. Say forty or fifty K.

But the cash was not with Ray.

Peter Bonney had it.

Bonney was in this thing right up to his neck.

But why had he dumped the cash here? If his daughter had been snatched by McLeod then hiding the dosh wasn't the obvious route to getting her back safe. And where was Ray? Did Bonney know? What was going on between the two of them?

Bonney seemed to be playing some kind of clever game. But if Frank McLeod was holding his daughter then he couldn't afford to fool around. McLeod was a killer. He wanted his money back, and a dispute over fifty K would leave a trail of bodies.

We went out and I closed the unit up and jogged back to the car. Herbie hopped into his seat and I fired up the engine to get warm air. Then made a call.

'What's happening?'

Bonney's voice.

Road hiss. The Toyota driving back towards town.

'I've found something,' I said. 'We need to talk again.'

'What is it?'

'Better face to face,' I said. 'You know our offices?'

'The address is on your card.'

'An hour and a half.'

'What have you got?'

'Three p.m.' I said. I killed the line.

When we talked this time Peter Bonney would give me the whole truth. And if the truth confirmed the fact that Frank McLeod had Lisa then we had a situation.

Frank McLeod wouldn't play nicely over the missing cash. If he had Lisa we'd need to get her away from him.

Which would be interesting. Because McLeod would have his people nearby, Christmas or not. He'd be co-ordinating the search for his cash and he'd have his troops close by until the thing was settled. And after Bonney's visit an hour ago he'd be on red alert.

But what the hell had he and Bonney talked about?

Bonney would tell me, but when he'd finished telling me I'd be left with the same situation and it wasn't one I could handle alone.

I keyed another call. The line picked up. A voice came on.

'Ho, ho, ho,' Shaughnessy said.

CHAPTER TWENTY-FIVE
The thing was kind of funny

The afternoon had dropped to a cold early dusk. Low cloud reflected
the street lamps as a forlorn, smothering light. I kept my foot down
and stayed north of the river until Chelsea then crossed into
Battersea. Made a lightning stop at a convenience store for a bagful
of dog food. How much did Staffies eat? One tin a day? Ten?
William's mutt was probably unused to regular meals but he looked
in good shape. Must be scoffing a fair bit between sausage hand-outs.
I dropped the bag of tins into the Frogeye's footwell and Herbie
looked down and licked his lips. Grinned.

I'd things to do that didn't suit a co-driver. Time to give Herbie a
break. I drove home and took Herbie into the building and stopped
at the ground floor apartment. The door was answered by my
neighbour, Henrietta Hutt. She peered out and looked down.

'You still finding lost dogs, Eddie? That's so sweet of you.'

I smiled sweetly and held up the bag. The firm had only ever gone
after one lost pet and that wasn't such a sweet episode due to the
psychotic nature of the animal in question. A dog. A miniature breed
loosely modelled on the piranha. We were brought in to find it but it
turned out that it had been given away on the sly by a desperate
husband who could no longer live in the same house as the beast,
which we came to understand. But we'd taken the wife's money and
the deranged furball came back and the husband moved out.
Problem solved. Case closed.

I'd mentioned the affair to Henrietta in passing, on account of her
interest in canines. Herbie was a different scenario.

'He's not lost,' I said. 'Just kind of homeless. We could do with a
sitter for a while.'

Henrietta worked as a canine behaviourist over at the dogs' home.
I figured she could handle a hungry Staffordshire. She looked down
at him and Herbie grinned and pulled like hell to get himself past her
legs. Henrietta grabbed the lead and restrained him.

'Is he with me for Christmas?' she asked.

'No,' I said. 'I'll be back.' I handed over the food.

Herbie sensed I was leaving and backed out again but Henrietta held him tight. He strained and whined. I guess he'd got kind of comfortable in that front seat. Or just liked travel. But I didn't know where I was going this evening or what kind of complications might arise, and babysitting a canine wasn't going to be part of it.

I told him to take it easy and went back out. Drove back over the river and parked at Chase Street. The top floor windows were lit. A shadow moved behind the blinds.

I went up. Found Shaughnessy standing at the glass wearing his biker gear. His helmet was on his desk.

'Did you apologise to Jasmine?' I said.

Shaughnessy watched the street. 'I told her it was an emergency,' he said. 'She said to tell you Merry Christmas.'

Shaughnessy's daughter was a smart girl. She knew her father would never run out on whatever they'd planned for their Christmas Eve unless it was an emergency. And she knew that emergencies tended to have my name on them.

'Tell her I'll call by,' I said. 'Right after the New Year.' Shaughnessy was taking Jasmine skiing for the holiday which was better than indulging in his other hobby, which Jasmine had also taken to. The pistes were a snooze relative to jousting with North Atlantic icebergs, which had been the icing on their Christmas cake last year. Luckily their flight out to Austria wasn't until Wednesday otherwise I'd have been sorting this problem alone.

I flopped behind the spare side of Shaughnessy's partners desk, which was the side Harry Green used when he wasn't in the Canaries, and described the problem. Shaughnessy remained standing with his back to the room, watching the street. When I'd finished he was still watching it.

'He's here,' he said.

We heard feet on the stairs and someone rapped on the outer door. Shaughnessy turned and sat down, and Peter Bonney came through. Bonney's face didn't look any less scared than before.

I introduced the two of them and Bonney threw a formal nod and sat himself in a client chair. He was tense as hell. His whole body language screamed that he didn't want to be here and wasn't planning on staying.

'What happened?' he asked.

I tilted Harry's chair back against the angle of the desk and looked at Shaughnessy. Shaughnessy was watching Bonney. The thing was kind of funny, though on balance it was more sad.

'Why not tell us?' I said.

Bonney looked puzzled.

'Come on, Peter,' I said. 'We know that McLeod has Lisa, which means we don't have much time. You need to come clean on what's happened then maybe we can figure out how to get her back. You can start by telling us what you and McLeod chatted about a couple of hours ago.'

Bonney's mouth opened a touch but he didn't find the words. He looked at me and looked at Shaughnessy. Saw how it was. Made a decision. He nodded his head and gave me a wry grin.

'You followed me,' he said.

I waited. Bonney's lips closed up while he thought about it, then he smiled grimly. Shrugged.

'It's what we thought,' he said. 'Ray took McLeod's cash. The kid's insane. And this time he's really screwed himself.'

He was about to elaborate but I cut him off.

'We've got it that this is about the cash,' I said. That wasn't what I wanted from Bonney. I tilted forward and reached across to hand him a sheet of paper. It was a print of the CCTV picture from the Rose Hill car park. Then I rocked my chair back and watched his face harden.

'Let's start again,' I said, 'remembering the fact that your daughter's life is at risk.'

Bonney studied the picture of him driving out from where Ray Elland's Capri had been ditched. His face muscles were so tight they looked like they'd snap.

'You're involved up to your neck, Peter,' I said. 'If you want your daughter back you need to stop lying.'

Bonney gave the picture a few more seconds then looked at me and then down at his shoes then across at the window, and finally he looked somewhere inside himself and saw just where he was, which was in the middle of a wildfire.

Flames closing in fast.

We gave him a moment.

'Okay,' he said. 'Okay.'

He was looking at his feet again, at a loss how to go on, where to start. I helped him out.

'Kind of stupid,' I said, 'scamming the firm's dosh. Wasn't it you told me that?'

Bonney snapped out of it and lifted his eyes. His face was still tight. 'Yes,' he said, 'it was stupid. Ray's idea but I went along. We set it up to look like a heist. Ray's car gets nicked while he's doing his round and the cash disappears.'

'And you didn't think McLeod would go after his money with everything he had?'

'Of course we did. Ray would take heat. No way to avoid it. But if he stuck to his story that his car had been hijacked then there'd be nothing to point back to him. He's a solid worker. He's been delivering McLeod's money for two years.'

'Unsupervised?'

'The last twelve months. McLeod assumes that no-one would dare to rip him off, including other firms unless they're prepared to start a war. So Ray's been running round every week with fifty K in his bag. Alone.'

'And you and he thought that McLeod wouldn't miss one consignment?'

'We knew he'd go berserk. But as long as nothing pointed to Ray we'd be okay.'

'Are you so desperate for money?'

Bonney clamped his lips. Gave it a moment. Then:

'I needed a bail-out,' he said. 'I've a few financial issues. But Ray needed the money too. I listened to his stupid scheme because I was desperate.'

'So where is Ray?'

'I don't know. When the heat came on he panicked and took off. Stupid! His running convinced McLeod that he'd taken the money. McLeod tried to pick him up but didn't get anywhere so he snatched Lisa, and he's not going to let her go until Ray comes in. That's what we chatted about.'

Shaughnessy and I said nothing.

Peter Bonney. Scared and a decade older. The effect of knowing that your family is in the gunsights of professionals. Peter Bonney's business failings, his gambling habit, had got him into deep water.

He looked at us and pushed out a sad laugh. 'Jesus,' he said. 'What a mess. If Ray had just stayed cool...'

I cut him off.

'So what should we do?'

'I need a couple of hours,' Bonney said. 'I've tracked Ray down. I need to catch up with him and get the cash back to McLeod.'

I sighed.

Shaughnessy stood and went back to the window. His reflection spoke from between the slats.

'Cut the crap, Bonney,' he said. 'We haven't got time. You ditched the cash at Ray's caravan in Southend two hours ago. Ray doesn't have it and never did.'

Bonney couldn't quite control his face this time. Another year or two clocked up. The lines deepened. He sagged a little.

I rocked my chair upright and stood. Leaned back against the desk and folded my arms and watched Bonney as he pulled it together, understood how much we knew. Recomputed, still deciding how much to tell us. Still playing us. But time was running out. We didn't have time for his act.

And his story about he and Ray working together was an act. I'd figured that one out on the drive back from Southend.

'Insane,' I repeated. 'Your words, Peter. But Ray isn't insane. He didn't take the money. This was all you. You knew Ray's routine and knew there was money for the taking right there in the Capri's boot. All you had to do was stake out one of his stops and wait until he dashed into the place then nick the car and the cash.'

Bonney was shaking his head but he knew.

'You needed cash,' I said. 'You were desperate, with your property enterprises going down the pan and your gambling habits haemorrhaging money. So you got an idea: snatch McLeod's cash from Ray and leave him in the lurch. Nothing would point back to you and if McLeod's people didn't swallow Ray's story that he was innocent then that was his tough luck. Two birds with one stone, in fact. Because you don't like Ray. Never liked him or the fact that while things have gone wrong for you Ray has been sailing through life without a care, funded by the bad guys, working in the very business that's leeching off your gambling habit, all the time promising your daughter nothing but a life of shady dealings to keep her afloat. And he's never even kept his promises: he's been running round with other women and wrecking Lisa's dream. So any heat he gets is his problem. But the plan was still insane. Because you knew that McLeod doesn't take losses, that you were playing with fire. That he'd put Ray through the wringer. You just didn't think it through. And you didn't cover the scenario where Ray gets away and drops out of sight. All foreseeable, Peter. By you better then anyone. It was entirely predictable that McLeod would use Lisa as his bargaining chip if things went wrong. So your scheme has put her into the firing line and right now we've no reason to assume that she'll get out of this in one piece.'

Shaughnessy turned and we both watched Bonney's face.

The face said that he knew it.

CHAPTER TWENTY-SIX
He's not going to play this straight

I thought about the mess Bonney was in. The mess he'd pulled Lisa and Ray into. The one he'd pulled me into, three days before Christmas.

'You were playing me from the start,' I said.

Bonney shook his head.

'Not my choice. Lisa ran off half-cock and brought you in.'

'And having a P.I. searching for Ray whilst your game was playing out was inconvenient.'

Shaughnessy turned and came to lean against the mantelpiece. He looked down at Bonney.

'Quite a game,' he said. 'You'd set Ray up like a mouse in a cattery.'

'The guy's a fool,' Bonney said. 'McLeod would have sweated him but he'd no reason to believe he was involved. If he hadn't run everything would have been okay.'

'That's a nice assumption,' Shaughnessy said. 'But there had to be a chance that McLeod would do more than sweat Ray. That he'd make an example of him. Make people think twice before losing his money in future.'

'Ray made his bed,' Bonney said. 'Let him lie in it.'

'That was it?' I said. 'It was okay if your daughter lost her husband? If Ray got put into the ground for something he didn't do?'

I pushed myself off the desk and went round to take Shaughnessy's place at the window. Looked down at the street. Cold and empty. A scattering of light and shadow. Mostly shadow. 'Christ, Peter,' I said, 'how did it come to this?'

Bonney's voice grated behind me. 'Well fuck you, Eddie. What do you know about it? This bastard was hell bent on wrecking my daughter's life. It was going to end badly sooner or later. He'd have ditched Lisa for another woman or got himself caught in his dirty trap by his own dirty people. It was going to happen. I'm not apologising for pre-empting things.'

'Sure,' I said. 'And not forgetting the money aspect. I guess that was a factor too.'

I watched Bonney's reflection in the glass. Made out a shrug. A smile.

'There's always the money,' he said. 'The cash solved a problem. I'd picked up a debt that had got out of hand. But if Ray had been a decent, caring husband I'd never have considered heisting him or his dirty friends. But you've seen it yourself. You've met his dancer tart. And she's not the first. Probably not the only. I told Ray at the start: if he hurt my daughter I'd bury him.'

'And you were okay with the idea of McLeod burying him for you.'

I watched movement in the shadows down below. A couple walking in, heading home for a Christmas Eve TV dinner. It was Saturday. No EastEnders, unless they ran a special. A gust of wind slapped the glass and cold air slid through and ruffled the blinds. The air tasted good. A breather before we faced the consequences of Peter Bonney's clever idea. I jabbed my hands into my pockets and turned back to face him.

'You know how these people tick,' I said. 'There are always repercussions. It's hard to believe you couldn't see the spanners waiting to fall into the works. If McLeod had the least reason to suspect that Ray had his money then Lisa would be right there in his crosshairs. Maybe her bringing a private detective in wasn't predictable but there we are. Just one of the spanners. But when she brought me in you realised there was a risk that I'd find out things that I shouldn't, like the fact that Ray's disappearance was nothing to do with his extra-marital fooling around. That's why you gave me Holly Sharma's details. I was supposed to check her out and take Lisa the proof she was paying for then shut up shop and head off for Christmas before the news got out that Ray wasn't ever coming back.'

Bonney pursed his lips.

'That one's on me,' he said. 'I should have known better. Overlooked your reputation for persistence.'

'Though it damn nearly worked,' I said. 'Two days' footwork had got me nowhere. Suspicions but no direction. Time running out. But then the game changed. Lisa disappeared. You knew that McLeod had taken her to reel Ray back in but Ray didn't have his cash. So you were looking at a disaster. Saw there was only one option: get McLeod's cash back to him but make it look like it was coming from

Ray. The trouble was, you weren't convinced that Lisa would be freed even when McLeod got his hands on his money. So whilst you located McLeod you kept up the pretence that we were all still looking for Ray. Kept in touch in case you needed to ask for backup.'

Bonney smiled. Shrugged.

'Sorry, Eddie,' he said. 'I've got us in a pickle. You're right: I didn't anticipate Ray running. Didn't anticipate McLeod going after Lisa. So yeah, I need to return the cash on the Q.T. so McLeod doesn't know where it's come from. I think he'll let Lisa go but I might be wrong. I might need that backup.'

'You talked to McLeod a couple of hours back.'

'That's his country place out at Hartley,' Bonney said. 'He's got family in there for his festive country squire act but they don't know there's an extra guest locked up in the back. A little business going on in the background whilst they carve the turkey.'

'Did he confirm that Lisa's there?' Shaughnessy said.

'He didn't confirm anything,' Bonney said. 'He didn't confirm that he's missing the money. But he didn't deny anything either. She's there.'

'Must have been an interesting discussion,' I said.

Bonney sat forward and rested his arms on his knees. Looked up. Clamped his lips. Age lines mapped his face but his eyes were steel.

'I told McLeod that if he harmed Lisa then I'd come back,' he said. 'And all his soldiers would not be enough.'

But they probably would. Even if Bonney took a few of McLeod's people with him he'd go down for sure before he got to the big man.

'So he didn't discuss a swap offer?' Shaughnessy said.

'He wouldn't discuss anything. The cash. Lisa. Ray. The bastard just stayed shtum and let me talk. So I told him I'd find Ray. If he gets to Ray he's no need to hold Lisa.'

'How does that work?' Shaughnessy said. 'Ray doesn't know where the cash is.'

'I'm not interested in bringing Ray in,' Bonney said. 'The story's just a cover so that I can hand McLeod a tip that Ray's been seen over at Southend. McLeod knows about the caravan. His people turned the place over right at the start but they'll go back there and this time they'll find the cash.'

'And Ray's story that he wasn't involved,' I said, 'will be dead. As will he.'

'His problem. If he can't keep clear of McLeod he'll go down.'

'Not forgetting that McLeod might already have him. Or that hiding from McLeod would mean he couldn't go home. Ever.'

Bonney grinned. Hard. Cold. 'That's fine with me,' he said. 'Just fine.'

I grinned back. Looked at Shaughnessy.

'All those jokes about mothers-in-law,' I said.

Shaughnessy's face stayed straight. 'Maybe they'll let Lisa go,' he said. 'Maybe not.'

Bonney looked at him. Nodded.

'That's the problem,' he said. 'Releasing her is the rational option. What's the point in making trouble with me or the law? What's the point risking some of his people and bringing heat onto his operation? So I think he'll send Lisa back. But there's a chance he's not rational. In that case I'll need backup.'

I came round the desk and sat back down. Watched Bonney.

'McLeod wants Ray,' I said. 'That's not going to change even if he gets his cash. And his best bet of pulling Ray in is to hang on to Lisa. And if he wants to hurt Ray he might hurt her. These people are zombies, Peter. You know it. They spend their whole lives stumbling towards their next mouthful of flesh. They're not stoppable. Certainly not by their own consciences. Hurting Lisa would be a nice demonstration to McLeod's soldiers: cross me and it's not just your own skin. It's your families I'll hurt. You know it, Peter. Time to stop pretending.'

Bonney's face confirmed that he knew it. But he still wasn't ready to concede.

'Let's get the cash to McLeod,' he said. 'He might just decide to call it quits. Take the easy route. Go after Ray separately.'

'I wouldn't give it good odds,' I said.

'I hear you,' Bonney said. 'But that's the way I'm going to play it. Maybe I'll need your help, maybe not.'

Shaughnessy shook his head.

'A tip-off won't work,' he said. 'The swap needs to be direct. Face-to-face. McLeod gets his cash when he hands over Lisa – and Ray if he has him.'

Bonney looked at him. Sighed. Heaved himself off his chair and pulled his coat about him. 'I hear you,' he repeated. 'But it's my decision. My mess. I'm going to call in the tip and let McLeod find his cash in Ray's caravan. Then I'll talk to him about Lisa.'

'Well, Peter,' I said, 'it's not your decision. This is my client's life we're playing with. So we're going to help. And we'll do it as Sean suggests. Face-to-face.'

'You're not thinking this through,' Bonney said. 'If we turn up with the cash we're going to have to explain how we got hold of it. '

'That's better than setting Ray up to take the fall,' I said. 'That's pretty low, Peter.'

'This is my daughter we're talking about,' Bonney said. 'I don't give a shit about Ray.'

Shaughnessy smiled at Bonney. It was an impatient kind of smile. The kind you get when you've been pulled away from a quiet Christmas Eve with your own daughter. When you're being kept away.

'Peter,' he said, 'your daughter's best interests don't include killing her husband. We need to be objective about this.'

But Bonney shook his head and turned to walk out.

'My decision,' he said. 'I'm going to make the call.'

'You can't,' I said.

Bonney stopped. 'Why not?'

'Because the money's not in the caravan. McLeod's people won't find anything there.'

Bonney's face froze for the second it took to take in what I was saying. Then his eyes widened.

'You're shitting me,' he said. 'You've moved the cash?'

'The door was broken,' I said. 'Didn't seem safe to leave it. The kind of people you get round there.'

Bonney's eyes were dark. His face had lost some of its paleness. A little red was flowing in.

'Eddie,' he said, 'what the hell are you doing?'

'We're keeping Lisa safe,' I said. 'Ray too, if we can. You made this mess, Peter. Don't tell us how to sort it out.'

Bonney closed his mouth. His eyes were dark pits.

~~~~~

Bonney keyed a number and flicked his phone to speaker and planted it on the desk. His face had lost some of the red but the ebbing tide had exposed a few more years. But there was still a spark in the eyes. The old policeman. He didn't like what we were doing but maybe he saw the logic. His call connected.

'What's happening?' A voice like gravel.

Bonney spoke: 'I've got the money.'

A pause. The phone rasped and muffled the background voices, a kids' argument, TV sounds. The sounds faded as Frank McLeod stepped away from the family gathering and walked somewhere quieter. We heard a door close; footsteps; another door; then the gravel came back.

'Why should I believe you?'

'See it and believe it,' Bonney said. 'I want Lisa out of there. As soon as I get her you get the money back.'

'Where did you find it?'

'That will never be told. I'm not starting a war here. I was wrong: it wasn't Ray. That's all that matters.'

Another pause. This one stretched. The phone rasped a little more. Then:

'Okay, Peter. Bring me the money and I'll let you have your daughter. No reason we can't be civilised about this.'

I grinned across at Shaughnessy. Civilised! A polite handshake before the knuckle dusters came out. Shaughnessy shrugged and watched the phone.

'When?' McLeod asked.

'Two hours,' Bonney said.

'Okay. Not here. I've guests.'

'Name a place,' Bonney said.

'The football ground up at Northfleet,' McLeod said. 'By the old power station.'

'Fine.'

'Come in at the roundabout end. The "Away" doors. They'll be unlocked. Wait in the east stand.'

'Seven o'clock,' Bonney said.

'Come alone,' McLeod said.

'Yes.'

'And make sure you have my money.'

162

'I'll want to see Lisa first,' Bonney said. 'I'll drive past. Have her over by the doors. When I've seen her I'll go in.'

'Seven o'clock,' McLeod said. He killed the line.

Bonney picked the phone up and shook his head.

'Your backup had better be good,' he said. 'McLeod's not going to play this straight.'

Shaughnessy looked at him.

'Neither are we,' he said.

CHAPTER TWENTY-SEVEN
He hadn't forgotten the canal thing

I went through to my office and retrieved the bag of cash that was the centre of this mess. Handed it to Bonney and told him we'd see him at seven. He wouldn't see us.

He went out and Shaughnessy and I shut up shop and followed fast down the stairs. Two hours was ample time to get to Northfleet for the meet but we weren't going to Northfleet. Shaughnessy and I had agreed that before Bonney came in.

Shaughnessy's Yamaha was parked on the tiny space fronting the building. He cranked up and rolled away and I walked round to the back of the building and drove out two minutes behind him.

Christmas Eve, five p.m. Traffic frenzy at Marble Arch. Oxford Street up ahead, a choke of busses and cabs, blazing lights, last-minute crowds. The shoppers had three hours before the plug was pulled. The stores would be hell. I swung down towards Hyde Park Corner and rolled east to the river. Flicked on a Parker album and turned up the volume. Ornithology. The Bird squealed a frantic crackly tempo that worked my hands like a clockwork puppet's on the wheel as the Frogeye accelerated and skipped and danced across the city, raced out towards the Orbital.

Two hours gave us time but we needed to be ahead of the thing.

Just before six I was back on the pitch black lane beyond Dartford where Frank McLeod had his estate. I pulled in to the verge three hundred yards beyond his driveway and killed the lights. Walked back beside bare hedgerows and found the cover of a tree across from where the driveway went in. Ten seconds later Shaughnessy materialised and reported all quiet. I looked round for the Yamaha. No sign. Stashed up a tree, perhaps. I shrugged my coat tight and we watched McLeod's property.

The driveway was deserted, barred part way down by the steel gate and the ten-foot walls. The walls hid the house, and the clouds hid the stars and the only light was the faintest sense of distant village lamps reflected in the cloud's belly. We waited in blackness. Two cars skimmed by. Shadows leapt and darted. Brake lights flared for the bend then extinguished, leaving everything dark and quiet again. Just the distant hiss of the Orbital drifting three miles over damp fields.

Six p.m. One hour to the swap. Cash for flesh. The stadium up at Northfleet was a nice isolated spot. Just five minutes drive from here. Maybe somewhere McLeod had used before for business transactions. Did the guy bust locks when he went in or did he have the keys? Who owned the club? Hell if I knew. I'd passed the stadium umpteen times without giving it a thought. Recalled only a corrugated iron wall backing the stands. The sum total of my knowledge about the club was that it had narrowly missed a direct hit when HS1 went through half a decade back. Plus the fact that it was isolated. The perfect place to transact business that might go smoothly or might not.

Lisa was still here at the house. McLeod wouldn't bring her out until just before seven for the short drive up to Northfleet to give Bonney his sight of her. But McLeod would have his people at the location long before Bonney turned up, ready for a counter-strike if Bonney tried any tricks. And some of those people would come from the house. McLeod might be playing the country squire but whilst he was chasing his cash he'd have his troops closer than Santa's elves. This would be the HQ for his recovery operation. We needed the elves out before we went in.

Ten past six. Another car. Brief blinding lights. Then more darkness and silence. Nothing in or out of the steel gate. Shaughnessy a shadow beside me.

Six fifteen. Finally. Movement.

A flash of headlights beyond the gates and a car coming up from the house, turning into the driveway. Shaughnessy and I stayed in the shadows, blinded by the strobing metalwork shadows. Santa's helpers coming out.

Sloppy. Far too late. If you're putting people in to control a meet the first thing you assume is that the other guy will do the same, so you make *your* move an hour earlier; watch him set up. Forty-five minutes was late even if you believed that your opponent was just a lone guy with a bag.

Not that it mattered.

The gate swung open and the car rolled up to the lane and turned towards the estuary. A Merc. The silhouettes of four men behind the glass. No detail. All you could say was that there were four and that they were big.

McLeod would have other troops converging on Northfleet from elsewhere. He'd want eight or ten people in there to put their stamp on the swap. So how many of his people was he keeping back here? A minimum of one, to keep an eye on Lisa and to drive her out at seven. More likely two guys. Enough to handle an emergency.

Of the sort that was about to happen.

I pulled out my phone and made a call. Bonney picked up.

'Steer clear,' I told him. 'The stadium's a set-up. Bring the cash to the house.'

'Where are you?'

'At the house. We're going in now.'

'Are you crazy? You're moving the swap?'

'It was never going to be Northfleet,' I said. 'You know it was a set-up, Peter. McLeod wasn't going to hand Lisa over.'

'Of course I know! This whole face-to-face thing is a bad idea. But it was your bad idea and you're my back-up. That's how we've set it up.'

'No,' I said. 'That's how we told McLeod we'd set it up. But the face-to-face is going to be here with McLeod and his skeleton crew. Shifts the odds in our favour. Maybe helps the guy see reason.'

'He isn't going see reason, Eddie.'

'Just bring the money,' I said. 'We'll take care of the social side.'

Bonney started to say something but I cut the line and looked at Shaughnessy.

'Ready?' I said.

'Ho, ho, ho,' he said.

Festive spirit! The guy's a gas like that.

I left both him and his side-splitting humour under the tree and walked back to the Frogeye.

~~~~~

Gate intercoms are set up so you can lean out of your SUV – the sort of vehicle accessed by airstairs – and press the button. They tend to be out of reach of fifties' vintage cars. I had to hop out to get at the button. Got crackle and a voice I recognised. A hint of surprise when

I identified myself. Then: "Wait".

A long silence. Distinctly longer than that needed for a decision on whether to eject a double glazing rep. Consultations were ongoing. I guessed I was in.

My guess was right. The intercom spat out a gruff invitation and the gates swung open. I folded myself back into the Frogeye and rolled up the driveway to Frank McLeod's house.

I was right about the voice too. As I swung round to park by the entrance steps I spotted McLeod's potato-headed goon walking along the front of the building towards me. I jumped out and waited but Spud beckoned me away from the steps.

Tradesman's entrance.

He watched me as I came up. The bandage round his head and the intensity on his face suggested that he hadn't forgotten the canal thing. He turned and I followed him round the side of the house.

The house was a country manor. A three storey Victorian built by a merchant who'd either made his fortune in the Port of London or inherited it from an earlier generation who'd made their stash in Liverpool or Bristol. A guy with plenty of cash and an image to project. A little like the present occupant. I counted six vehicles on the forecourt. Family, friends and thugs, in for the festivities. Normal security would be one guy, living in a cottage or shed out in the grounds. Stepped up periodically if there was a spat on with the Russians or Albanians or Chinese. In quiet times just the one guy. McLeod's people had homes of their own, families, respectful neighbours. His soldiers were only here tonight because McLeod was fifty K down on the week and no-one was clocking off before the mess was cleared up. Four fewer soldiers now that the Merc had gone out. So who'd be left? Maybe Spud plus one other. Manageable. I wondered whether Spud's pal Franco was around or was he still off sick with pneumonia? London canals are cold in winter.

We rounded the corner and walked back to a brightly lit two-storey annex running off the side of the house. Spud held the door open and invited me through. Having him behind me wasn't a great option but no alternative was on offer so I went ahead and into the building. Spud grunted directions and stayed at my shoulder and we entered a library. The room was large enough for three Chesterfields and matching wing chairs between ceiling-high bookshelves. The

Chesterfields formed a lazy "U" with the open end at the far end of the room where a desk topped in burgundy leather was on display before a grand fireplace. The bookshelves were crammed what were either *faux* book panels or wholesale clearance stock because the guy sitting behind the desk wasn't the kind to read. Neither was he a pencil-pusher. The desk was there to establish his place as the top guy in the room. I guess the room saw a few conferences.

The desktop behind which Frank McLeod was sitting was bare except for tessellated glass lamps at each end, though McLeod would doubtless have a few things handy in the side drawers.

I'd had no direct contact with McLeod in the job but I'd seen his mug shot, and the face in front of me was recognisable even with a decade plastered on. He was middle fifties. Ten years meaner than the photo I'd seen. He watched me walk round the Chesterfields and his hands stayed clasped atop the desk and his eyes stayed cold like an alligator's with toothache. The light from the desk lamps mottled his skin and brought up the grey stubble across his cheeks. The stubble had been there in the old pics.

The other guy in the room, standing quietly in the corner behind McLeod, was Tommy Vance. He was still wearing his aviator shades and his navy blazer, though the checked shirt from yesterday had been replaced by an off-white polo-neck sweater. His arms were crossed over the sweater and his right fist gripped a baseball bat. He looked like a pensioner on parole.

McLeod watched me walk up. When I reached his desk he spoke.

'Are you really as stupid as they say?' he said.

I didn't know who was saying things, though if he was quoting Spud or Franco then they must have worked up an interesting interpretation of what happened this morning.

I smiled and looked round the room. Nodded to Tommy Vance. Spud was lurking somewhere behind me.

'Why have you come here?' McLeod said.

I eased over to the side of the desk so that I could keep all three of them in view. One of the desk lamps came into reach. It had one of those push-bar switches beneath the bulb that gives a satisfying thunk when you light it up. I thumbed the bar. Got the thunk. The lamp went dark. I thunked it again. The lamp illuminated.

'The arrangement at Northfleet,' I said. 'It's off. I thought we'd do

168

the exchange here.'

Tommy Vance stirred. The bat twitched. Frank McLeod sat motionless.

'What arrangement?' he said.

I jabbed my hands back into my coat pockets and turned away to admire the bookshelves and a painting hanging in alcove within them.

'You know what arrangement,' I said. 'We decided that the stadium wasn't a good idea. Too easy for you to take the cash and beat Peter Bonney to a pulp then bring Lisa back. Northfleet didn't really work for us.'

McLeod was staring at me when I turned back. His old photo hadn't really done him justice. The feral set of his eyes was more effective, face to face.

'I don't change my arrangements,' he said. 'I think you *are* stupid, Flynn.'

The eyes continued to hold me, smouldering with evil schemes of pain and power, but his hands stayed calm atop the desktop, even if the knuckles had whitened a little.

'It's a done deal,' I said. 'The exchange is here.'

McLeod thought about it. Shook his head.

'You're playing around with Bonney,' he said. 'That's clear. But for two ex-coppers you're not such a bright pair.'

I shrugged. Kept my hands in my coat pockets. Kept Spud and Vance in my peripheral vision.

'Bright enough,' I said.

McLeod thought about that too and his lips pursed. He nodded briefly.

'Point taken,' he said. 'I've done a little research since yesterday.'

I waited.

'Concerning Nobby Snape,' he clarified.

His research had been good. After all these years he'd finally connected my name to the torpedoing of his onetime-boss's jailbreak attempt a decade back. The torpedo had done its job. The last I heard, Snape was still in his cell browsing the travel brochures. But my name had never been publicly connected to the thing and it had never got out back then. Seemed McLeod had better resources nowadays. So his check on me had pulled up a little surprise.

'How long have you been working with Bonney?' he asked.

'Only met him Thursday.'

'When you were chasing Ray.'

'You got it.'

'And why are you after Ray?'

I shrugged. It was warm under my coat. The fireplace behind McLeod was empty but the central heating was hissing.

'That's a private matter,' I said, 'though I assume my client has given you the details.'

McLeod nodded. 'Lisa has told us everything,' he said. 'So: you're a private dick chasing an unfaithful husband. It beats notice-serving, I suppose.'

'The hours are more dependable with notices.'

'And less hazardous,' McLeod said.

'You'd be surprised,' I said. 'I've stories that would scare you.'

McLeod held the neutral look but his eyes continued to drill into me.

'I doubt it,' he said. 'But that's by the by. You're not easily scared off. That's the main problem. When my men told you to walk you just came right back.'

I grinned. Wondered how much Spud and Franco had reported from their canal escapade. Half-truths at best. Franco's war report must have been impressive as he wrung out his underwear.

'What Lisa didn't know,' McLeod said, 'was that you'd hooked-up with her father.' He unclasped his hands and pointed two index fingers, side by side. Like the gun turret on a ship. 'And that's my problem,' he said. 'You've chosen the wrong time to get under my feet, Flynn.'

'I'm here to help,' I countered. 'You want your cash and we want Lisa. And Ray too, if he's here. If we can sort this out we can all go home.'

McLeod shook his head. 'We're not sorting anything out. In half an hour I'm driving up to Northfleet to do business with Peter Bonney.'

'You'll be disappointed. He won't be there. Nor the cash.'

McLeod stayed quiet a moment. Took it in.

'So,' he said, 'where is it?'

'It'll be here in five minutes.'

McLeod re-clasped his hands. Looked down at his desk. Tried to figure out whether I was bluffing. The hands tightened gradually. The knuckles showed even whiter. His expression when he looked at me again was still feral. Ice cold.

'Who do you think I am?' he said. 'One of your stray dog husbands?

'I can get the cash back to you,' I said. 'That's all that matters.'

I wondered how McLeod handled stray dogs.

CHAPTER TWENTY-EIGHT

There was a whole evening's entertainment there

'We've got the money,' I said, 'but the swap will be here.'

McLeod thought it through then sat forward. His hands were still clasped tight.

'So Bonney's coming here?' he said.

'In five minutes. With the bag.'

'How did you get involved with him?'

'I was looking for Ray,' I said, 'and so was he.'

'Did Bonney tell you what Ray was up to?'

'He told me what he originally told you: that Ray had pinched your cash and that he would help to find him. But his information was wrong. Ray didn't take the money.'

'So who did?'

'Not Ray. That's all you need to know.'

Bonney had told him the same thing an hour ago. McLeod let it go.

'So how did you get your hands on the cash?' he asked.

'Irrelevant,' I said. 'What matters is that we've got it. You get it back in return for Lisa and Ray.'

'I don't have Ray.'

I said nothing.

'Is Bonney coming alone?' McLeod said.

'Yes.'

McLeod turned to look at Tommy Vance and they exchanged some kind of signal. A message, though Vance stayed motionless and his face stayed expressionless and his aviator shades stayed black, which concealed the meaning. McLeod breathed out and sat back and looked at me.

'Okay,' he said. 'We'll wait for Peter and talk to him when he hands over the cash. That leaves us with you, Flynn.'

'When I leave here with Lisa that's the end of it,' I said.

McLeod shook his head. 'That's not going to happen,' he said. 'People don't come barging into my house, disturb my business, my family, and walk away. What kind of man do you think I am?'

I knew exactly what kind of man McLeod was. I'd hoped

pragmatism would prevail though, that he'd opt for the easy solution and get back to his brandy and nuts, count his money and shove it back into the safe. There was a whole evening's entertainment to be had if he took it slow. And maybe McLeod *would* have been more inclined to pragmatism if he hadn't done that research and found out who I was. But that's the flaw with these types. They can't let old affairs lie. There are always scores to settle. I stepped back, watching Vance and Spud.

'Let's be sensible,' I said. 'It's Christmas.'

The appeal didn't cut ice. McLeod's eyes continued to broadcast evil and power and the promise of pain, and very little in the way of sense. But then he relaxed. Sat back and folded his arms across his chest and pinned me with an intense humour.

'Nobby actually put a contract on you,' he said. 'Did you know that?'

Sort of. I'd heard rumours at the time but nothing positive.

'I went in to see him,' McLeod said. 'A couple of weeks after the break. Filth and kangas up my arse all the way from Wandsworth. I took Nobby's brief along so we could get a little privacy. Our conversation wasn't for civilian ears but we told the guy we'd rip his tongue out if he ever opened his mouth and he never did. He was good that way. Anyway, Nobby was unhappy. Very unhappy. He'd come *this* close to going over the wall. He had a villa lined up in Portugal. Booze and girls waiting round the pool. And the helicopter had cost him eighty K. I'd arranged that myself. So this was two weeks after the event and Nobby was feeling annoyed as hell. Do you know how much he put on your head?'

I waited. McLeod was going to tell his story. With any luck he'd be through before Bonney arrived.

'Five hundred,' McLeod said. He was watching me. 'Half a mill. for whoever gave us the copper who'd shafted him. There'd been stories circulating that it was an unauthorised operation. A rogue copper meddling in things he shouldn't. Maybe working with a rival firm. All sorts of rumours. So Nobby stumped up half a mill. and said get me the guy's name. But do you know, we never got the name. Until now. How about that? Were you so far off the books that no-one knew, Flynn? Or did you have better pals than everybody else?'

Neither. The thing had happened and I was there by chance at the wrong place and the wrong time so there was no trail leading back to me, barely a handful who knew I'd been involved, and they weren't the type to gossip. So I got clear and went back to my day job. I'd heard rumours about a bounty but I was busy. This was the first time I'd heard the number. The number was impressive, though a round million would really have been something.

McLeod was still talking.

'And now...' he said. 'Do you know how much it cost to put it all together yesterday, finally get your name?'

I waited.

'Zilch!' he said. 'We got the info through friends of friends with just two broken arms. We've a guy inside the Met now in just the right place. We didn't have him back then.'

He smiled for the first time.

'Life's funny,' he said. 'The thing's none of my business now. Nobby and I parted ways a long time ago. But Nobby's still waiting and he'll be glad of a chance to talk to you – or have his soldiers talk to you – and he'd still stump up the fee to get you gift-wrapped. But I'll offer him the opportunity *gratis*. A goodwill gesture between old friends. And if truth be told I'm still a tad annoyed about the thing myself. We had Nobby out and clear. We had the helicopter right outside the walls. We'd have been clear and away if you hadn't butted in, Flynn.'

'I explained to your guys at the time,' I said. 'Expect the unexpected.'

'Very good! That's good advice. You should listen to it yourself, Flynn. Keep you out of a lot of trouble. So what did you *expect* coming here tonight?'

I replied with a smile. Said nothing.

McLeod sighed. Sat back. Storytelling over. He turned and nodded to Tommy Vance and Vance dropped his arms and moved out of his corner. The bat was hanging loosely. This was Tommy's show now. The old school lieutenant, all ruthless efficiency. The guy who gets things done, handles business when complications arise, doles out lessons when they're needed. Vance's speciality was people who needed to vanish with no fanfare. He was cold, mean and efficient. Nothing personal when he swung the bat.

Over to my left, Spud stepped away from the door. But he was the hired help. The pit bull. All muscle and no brain. I'd already done my calculations. If I went after Spud I'd knock him about, ham fists or not, but in ten seconds I'd feel Tommy Vance's bat in my kidneys and I'd go down for sure. So Vance was the one to handle first. I stepped away from McLeod's desk and walked down the side of the room, behind the sofa, towards the door.

Spud had gone the wrong way round the door Chesterfield, giving me the route through. I could have been out before he turned and reversed his course. And even though Tommy Vance was coming across the room he wasn't going to stop me. He was mean but he was old. You don't leap sofas at that age.

But running wasn't going to get Lisa back. So I walked. Steadily, down the bookshelves behind the nearest sofa and towards the door. I kept it slow enough to let Spud reverse and move back to block me. He reached the door and stopped with a smile. We were both behind the Chesterfield now, with Vance stranded on the other side of it, and Spud still hadn't seen it. He just held the sneer and pressed his back to the door.

I turned and grabbed the back of the Chesterfield and vaulted it and was face-to-face with Tommy Vance in the middle of the room before anyone could react. Just three feet separated us and now it was Spud who was stranded. Vance saw the play and tensed then took a step forward, holding his bat two handed, ready. His lips parted and exposed his intent and a second later he swung at my head in a vicious arc. I ducked and dropped and by the time I came up Vance had lifted the bat to crack it down on my skull and the only way out was a sideways roll to the floor. The bat missed and pounded the sofa. Spud was moving now but the two of them had lost the advantage. I came upright fast and stepped round Vance to draw him away from Spud but he saw my game and took a few steps towards the far wall, then stood quietly and let Spud come through and open the engagement. Spud complied. Barrelled up and swung a ham-fist. The fist was lethal but it was slow. I dodged it and landed my own fist in his throat, which is a Queen's Regulations no-no but very effective. Spud coughed and staggered back.

I moved away and skipped round by the desk to get between the sofa and the far wall, then moved fast along it to reach Vance before Spud got back into gear. Vance turned and swung as I came, and a

175

six-foot standing lamp with a Victorian shade exploded into smithereens. Before Vance could swing the bat again I stepped in and kicked him in the knee then landed a right-hander on his nose. His aviators disintegrated, throwing glass shards and wire. Blood spattered and he staggered sideways on his bad knee. But the old guy was tough. His lips set in a slitted snarl and he gripped the bat and came back to make the next strike count. I stepped away fast and rounded the door sofa just as Spud got himself moving to round it from the opposite side, a little earlier than I'd expected. Then Vance came in behind me, closing the trap, and suddenly my options were reducing. If I repeated the stunt and hurdled the Chesterfield Vance would catch me in full flight. Bones would break. Organs would take damage. So I stood mid-way between them and when Spud rushed in early I turned and swung at him. Connected but couldn't dodge his fist, which caught me on the temple and delivered an explosion of stars. I hit him with a following left-right to his own head but it was like assaulting a sack of turnips. The brick wall at the canal had been a stroke of luck. Behind me Tommy Vance was coming up and Spud stepped back to give him a clear swing, which gave the game away. I ducked down and sideways and the bat crashed into wall plaster and showered me with flakes. I was still seeing double from Spud's contact but I got myself upright and thinking. Decision time. Go for the bat and risk Spud's pile-drivers pounding me from behind or go for Spud and hope I could stop him before the bat connected with my skull.

No choice: option A. The bat. I turned quick and lunged, gripped Vance's wrists to stop his swing and palmed his chin. Vance snarled and fought to pull the bat clear but I pushed him back hard until his feet tangled and left him staggering backwards. But he kept his legs and wrenched the bat clear and I'd lost the advantage. He took another swing. Fast and vicious. I jumped back and a Chinese vase got in the way this time. Porcelain shattered. Shrapnel flew. I launched myself at Tommy before he got himself balanced from the impact which must have hurt his wrists like hell. My momentum took him down this time, and he fell hard against the bookshelves, barking at Spud. Spud closed in and I turned in a crouch and saw that he'd pulled a hammer from his jacket. Probably one he kept handy for collection days in the protection business. A big, ugly thing, useful for settling arguments about above-inflation premium hikes. I crouched, ready. When Spud let fly I'd only get one chance.

Spud grinned and lifted the hammer.

Then the door opened and Shaughnessy walked in.

Spud's potato head turned. He grunted. Tried to make sense of things. Failed, beyond the basic understanding that this guy was enemy. He turned and re-directed the hammer in a vicious arc but Shaughnessy stepped aside and did some kind of move I couldn't quite catch, and I heard a crunch and snap and Spud went down without a sound. The hammer bounced on the floor.

I was already turning to pull the bat away from Tommy Vance before he got up. Vance was scrabbling about, trying to get his feet working, and I wrenched the thing free easily and tossed it to Shaughnessy and calm descended. Tommy finished pulling himself up and leaned against the bookshelves assessing tactics. His lapel was torn and there was blood all over him. He'd need a new blazer along with his shades. Maybe the New Year sales.

Across the room McLeod growled and stood to pull a sawn-off shotgun from his desk drawer. I'd known it wasn't pencils and rubber bands in there. Shaughnessy and I moved simultaneously and stepped across to Tommy Vance's shoulders as McLeod's gun came up. If McLeod loosed off a shot then his man was going to be collateral. I wondered how much Vance was valued. Sufficiently, I figured, though with someone like Frank McLeod you never knew. I held up a cautionary finger.

'Think about it,' I said. 'The deal's still on. Cash for Lisa. Then we all go home.' I was breathing hard. My head was spinning.

McLeod watched us from behind the barrels of the gun and weighed things, and it looked for all the world like the bloodbath option was tempting him. His trigger finger was waiting only for him to complete the balance sheet. Pros and cons. How much did he value Tommy Vance? The calculations seemed to be stalled but the gun was holding rock steady and things were tense.

'Don't do it,' I repeated. 'It'll be hell getting the blood off the walls. And tiresome explaining the body bags to family and friends. Play it sensible, Frank. We'll take Lisa home and you can go and count your cash.'

Then a buzzer sounded. The gate entry phone. McLeod suspended his computations. Angled the gun up and stepped towards a panel with a tiny screen. Stabbed a button. The speaker crackled.

'It's me,' the speaker said. 'Bonney! Open the gate.'

CHAPTER TWENTY-NINE
Our demolitions were better

McLeod thought it through. Weighed the pros. Specifically, his cash, waiting up at the gate. He pressed the button and told Bonney to leave the car outside and come through. Walked to his desk and laid the gun down. Sat.

'Bring him in, Tommy,' he said.

We stood away from Vance to give him room. He was holding a hankie under his broken nose and his cheek was swelling impressively. His lips were parted, taking the air, and his blazer was ripped and his shades were in pieces on McLeod's carpets. The damage was a new experience for him, the first time that the other guy was still alive, anyway. He looked briefly at me and Shaughnessy. The look said "Okay, friends." Across the room McLeod was still screwing the lid on his own bristling fury.

'Bring him in,' he repeated.

The two of them exchanged a message, then Vance stepped over Spud and went out. I nodded to Shaughnessy and he turned and followed Vance out. His exit was fast. He was through the door by the time McLeod yelled at him to stop and got himself up and across the room with his gun. He grabbed the door, pointing the gun my way, and pulled it open to bark at Shaughnessy. Careless tactics. I was still too close. I stepped clear of the barrels and gripped them with my right hand and threw a left-hander that connected with the back of McLeod's neck, and the impact stunned him enough to slacken his grip on the weapon. Enough to let me heave it free as I landed a second left. I got lucky. McLeod's trigger finger came free without discharging the gun. I stepped away and flipped it round and pointed it and we stood there in the doorway with Spud laid out between us whilst McLeod decided whether it was worth jumping me. He had a notion that I wouldn't pull the trigger on him, which was true but I spotted his calculation. I smiled and swivelled the gun towards the bookshelf alcove with the spotlit painting. The painting was a hunting scene in pale colours. A little too stylised for me; like a Ferneley, which it might well have been. McLeod understood the gesture. Knew I'd not hesitate to pull the trigger and annihilate the artwork and maybe he was rather fond of it because things calmed down and he relaxed.

I angled my head towards his desk. 'Let's sit back down, Frank,' I said.

McLeod hesitated a moment longer, wondering how much the Ferneley would cost to restore, but I'd planted the thought about family and guests and peace and quiet, and in the end common sense prevailed. He closed the door and walked back to his desk. He sat down and re-clasped his hands.

'Fine, Flynn,' he said. 'We'll wait.'

I walked over and perched myself on the corner of the desk.

'That's good,' I said. 'We can sort this out like reasonable people.'

I said it for the sake of it. McLeod had never been reasonable in his life. Not since he punched a kid in the face at kindergarten to steal her toffee. But here we were and I had the gun and Peter Bonney was on his way in with a bagful of cash so we waited and were *reasonable*. Somewhere behind the couch over by the door Spud was making coming-round noises but he was in no hurry. Then the door opened and Peter Bonney came in with Tommy Vance behind him, still pressing the hankie to his face. The hankie was crimson. But Vance was still sharp. His eyes flickered at the sight of the gun across my thighs but otherwise he showed no sign. He and McLeod had faced setbacks before. Nothing to make a fuss about.

Bonney's face was a little more expressive. He worked his way between the sofas and lifted the bag onto McLeod's desk. He let it drop with a thump. McLeod ignored it. Watched Bonney. Tommy Vance hung back by the door.

'That's the lot,' I said. 'Every penny. Now if we could just pick up Lisa – and if Ray's here we'll take him too – we can all go home.'

McLeod broke Bonney's stare and looked at me. He shook his head. Faintly and slowly. More an internal thing.

'In your dreams,' he said.

He pulled out his phone and keyed a number that would connect him to his people kicking their heels over in Northfleet and bring them back here at the trot.

I lifted the gun casually and pointed it past Bonney. At the other wall this time. The bookcase on that side had an alcove too and the alcove also had a painting, discreetly lit by a gold-plated fitting. A nicer painting to my taste. A portrait of an eighteenth-century squire holding his horse by its bridle. Too realistic for Ferneley. Maybe a Stubbs, though an original would be pricey even for McLeod's pocket, though less so if it had been nicked from a country house. Whatever the provenance, the artwork wouldn't look the same peppered with shot.

'Kill the call,' I said.

McLeod said nothing. Left the call connecting and watched me with down-turned lips. But he saw my trigger finger tightening, saw there was barely an ounce of pressure separating his work of art from the bin, and he finally held the phone up and disconnected with his thumb. I watched him and held the pressure until he placed the phone back onto his desk.

Then the door opened and Lisa's face appeared.

She looked down at her feet and stepped round Spud and away from Tommy Vance to make room for Ray Elland and Shaughnessy behind her. I recognised Ray's face from the photo, though this was more of a Picasso version, pushed out of place by a mess of cuts and bruises. But at least he was walking, which was more than I'd have expected if Tommy had had his hands on him for the last few hours. But maybe McLeod had believed Ray's story. Believed that he was innocent, had just walked into the Rose Hill shop to make a delivery and found his Capri gone when he came out.

Innocence wouldn't have saved Ray. McLeod had no use for people who screwed up. But maybe his story's credibility had saved him from the more extremes of unpleasantness when he came in. We watched as he walked across the room beside Lisa. The two of them stopped in the centre, unsure where to go. They looked stunned. Regular people caught up in the vicious world Ray had courted. Lisa was staring at Bonney.

'Daddy,' she said. Bonney looked at her and for a moment had no words.

Shaughnessy steered clear of Vance just as Ray and Lisa had. He came to join us at the desk.

I grinned at McLeod.

'How about that,' I said. 'Ray was hiding here all along.' I nodded at the bag. 'Funny what we find when we look.'

McLeod wasn't smiling. He looked at Ray and Lisa then at Vance and more messages passed between them. In five minutes McLeod's soldiers would wonder why no-one had shown up with Lisa at the Northfleet stadium. In ten they'd wonder why Bonney hadn't shown up either. In fifteen they'd phone McLeod, and one minute later they'd be on their way back here. That was what the messages said. McLeod and Vance didn't have their guns and baseball bats any more but they had time. And not just tonight. Tomorrow. Next year. Ten years. They had all the time in the world to sort this out. Tommy Vance came away from the door and walked across to stand at Peter Bonney's shoulder. He looked at each of us in turn then looked at McLeod. You could taste the tension.

Shaughnessy caught my eye and raised an eyebrow. I looked back down at McLeod.

'Frank,' I said, 'you've got your cash. Ray didn't take it. You know that. He and Lisa were not part of it. So lets all go home. You can tell your boys to knock off while the pubs are still open; get back to your family.'

McLeod looked at me.

'I don't give a toss about the pubs,' he said.

I sighed. Tapped the gun barrels on his desktop.

Of course not. This wasn't about the money. This was about people who crossed you. About a message that needed delivering. A message about transgressions. The same message you'd pounded into the kid in kindergarten when she'd protested over her nicked toffee, the message you delivered when you pulped a security driver who'd resisted your attempt to heist his vehicle, the message you broadcast when you burned a shop that had fallen behind with its premiums, or when you buried an opponent who'd stepped onto your territory. This was about fear and respect. If Ray hadn't pinched McLeod's money neither had he looked after it. And when his family brought a private investigator and an ex-cop barging in here, when these people came into your house and smashed up lampshades and vases and put your men down then talked about closing things quietly they were in cuckoo land. So even if McLeod opted for the rational, the pragmatic, here, tonight, with family and guests in the house, there'd always be tomorrow, next week, next year. The message would be sent. Having the cash back in your safe wasn't the issue. The issue was transgression and respect. I watched McLeod and saw it. His kind weren't fuelled by reason.

The room was quiet a moment. The tension stretched. Walking out tonight wasn't going to close anything.

'Frank,' I said. 'You're a businessman. You've got the bag. Go and have a drink. Think it over.'

McLeod ignored me. He was looking at Vance now. Calculations were still running. Best strategies for this evening. Best strategies for next week and for next year. The calculations coalesced finally and formed a plan and McLeod relaxed and opened his fists. He turned to me. Lifted a hand and flicked a finger doorwards. Dismissive.

'Get out,' he said, 'before I come round this desk. If I do then the gun's not going to help you.'

I smiled. The gun was helping quite a lot. Things had certainly calmed down since I'd got my hands on it. But it didn't solve our problem and the problem needed solving. I looked at Shaughnessy. He stepped forward and perched himself on the other end of McLeod's desk and pulled a photo from inside his leathers. He pushed it over to McLeod.

'Think about it,' he said.

McLeod looked at the photo.

'This stops tonight,' Shaughnessy said. 'You've got your money. This stops right here.'

McLeod stared at the photo and looked a little puzzled. I leaned across to get a view and looked puzzled too.

The snap was of a single storey building in adobe brick, somewhere out in the wilds. A few similar buildings further back. Scrubby vegetation. The buildings were the kind with wooden shutters and protruding roof joists up top. Suggestive of Mexico or Central America. McLeod stared and wondered what the hell Shaughnessy was showing him. He looked up. Shaughnessy slid another photo across. I leaned closer.

Same place. Same buildings and vegetation in the background. But the main building was gone. In its place was a charred crater, lots of wood splinters and shattered brick.

Before and after.

We both looked at Shaughnessy.

'A job in the forces,' Shaughnessy said. 'We had issues with some people. The demolition took us fifteen minutes. They teach you good techniques.'

He gave McLeod a moment then retrieved the snaps.

McLeod was still looking at him.

'Listen to what Eddie says,' Shaughnessy said. 'Ray didn't take the money. Eddie didn't take the money. I didn't take the money. All we've done is recover it for you. We've done you a favour. So let it go.'

McLeod stayed silent, still trying to work it out.

Then Bonney butted in. 'Let it go, Frank,' he said. His face had collected a few more lines but they were mostly from anger at being in this house with his daughter. McLeod looked up at him and they stared each other out for a while.

Then Shaughnessy came back in.

'We're going to leave now,' he told McLeod. 'So just think about this: we've done our research. This isn't your only house. We know about the property near Torquay. Nice place. Amazing views. And we know about the condos in Spain and Jamaica. And I really love the ten-acre beach villa in Barbados that the family uses every summer. Let me know if we've missed anything, Frank, but if you decide to follow up on this we'll be ready.' He slid off the desk and stooped to plant his palms. Leaned into McLeod's space. 'Here's a personal assurance,' he said. 'I can get round all the places inside seventy-two hours, air travel included. And every one of them will look like the "after" picture I've just shown you. Seventy-two hours.'

'Listen to the man,' I said. 'Save on rebuilding costs.'

McLeod locked stares with Shaughnessy and said nothing. His fists had bunched tightly again.

I hopped off the desk and flicked the switch to break the gun. Pocketed the cartridges then planted the gun on McLeod's desk. Then Bonney, Shaughnessy and I walked out with Lisa and Ray. McLeod and Vance didn't move. When we stepped across him Spud just rolled over and made hurting sounds. His eyes were starting to open.

We went out and back round to the front of the house and Shaughnessy walked the group down the driveway while I fired up the Frogeye and rolled along behind them. When the gate swung open I drove through and parked on the outer drive behind Bonney's car. Then I climbed out and waited for everyone to come out.

CHAPTER THIRTY
The guy seemed impressed

We congregated at Bonney's car. Lisa was quiet, shaking a little, fighting back tears. Ray was awkward beside her. At some point the dam would burst. Whether Lisa had a husband to turn to when it did was up to Ray. My initial report to Lisa had been low on specifics but I'd confirmed what she'd suspected and maybe she didn't need any more. Case closed. If she didn't ask I wouldn't tell. And if I didn't tell then she'd be spared the ice cold blade of the stark evidence, the detail that would make Ray's betrayal real. And maybe Ray saw his betrayal now. His days of playing with Holly Sharma were over, for sure. The dancer wouldn't forget her bruises, even if they'd come from McLeod's people. She wouldn't forgive Ray for bringing the stain of fear into her life. And maybe Ray had learned something. Maybe he'd lost his taste for the wild side, for associating with people like McLeod. He stood awkwardly, uncertain how to reach his wife, but then something kicked in and the man inside him took over. He put his arm round Lisa's shoulder and pulled her in and that's when the dam broke. Lisa collapsed into him. Peter Bonney looked like he was about to tear the guy apart but I guess he was stopped by the thought that what he'd done to his daughter was far worse.

The dark softened the bruising on Ray's face, though his nose was swollen and his left eye closed tight. He held Lisa for a moment then turned to us, puzzled.

'Where was the money?' he said.

'We got a tip-off,' I said.

He continued holding Lisa. Pulled her face tighter into his chest.

'Who?' he said. His voice gained strength. 'Which bitch took my car? The bastards were going to kill me. Tommy wanted to off me on Monday afternoon.'

'They knew you didn't take the money,' I said. 'If they thought you did have it the last thing they'd do is kill you.'

'I've been handling the cash for two years,' Ray said. 'They can trust me. Frank knows it. Tommy knows it. Why did they come after me?'

'Because you ran,' I said. 'And they couldn't be sure.'

'I didn't run! I came in and told them what happened. I came right here like Frank told me. But Tommy didn't believe me. He slapped me about and called me a thief and said that even if it wasn't me they couldn't know for certain. Tommy scared the hell out of me. Frank knew I wouldn't rip him off but Tommy didn't care. So when I saw a chance I ran.'

But then they'd taken Lisa and hiding was no longer an option. Ray had come back in, just as we'd guessed. But as we'd guessed too, he was never going to get out again, and probably not Lisa, despite Bonney returning the money.

'Who are you people?' Ray said. He looked at me and Shaughnessy through his one open eye.

'It's a long story,' I said. One that Lisa could tell him. Assuming he stuck around. Assuming she allowed him to stick around once her tears had dried. Ray was still hyper, adrenaline-pumped, scared, disoriented. He asked more questions without waiting for answers which was lucky because the only important one – about who had stolen the cash – was best left unanswered. Peter Bonney stirred beside me and fingered his car remote. The Avensis unlocked itself.

'Get in,' he told them.

Ray looked ready to continue our discussion but Lisa unwrapped herself and tugged at him and the two of them got into the car.

Shaughnessy watched them then looked at me. A faint smile, barely visible in the dark. I nodded back.

'Nice pictures,' I said. 'I never knew you carried a résumé pack.'

The smile held.

'Just for this evening,' Shaughnessy said. 'I thought a little pressure might be required. The pics were screen-shots of a spaghetti western we were watching. The demolition was Clint Eastwood.'

'But a little like your old job.'

Shaughnessy shrugged. 'Our demolitions were a little bigger,' he said. 'And we didn't take photos.'

'Well McLeod appreciated the visuals. Could you really drop his properties within seventy-two hours?'

'The first sign of any move from him I'll demolish the Torquay house. If that doesn't calm him I'll drop the others inside seventy-two, yeah. I'd bring in a couple of friends from the regiment. Too dangerous to do the rounds myself with his people waiting. It would have to be one strike. A fifteen minute window. Rubble both sides of the Atlantic.'

I believed him. Shaughnessy can do stuff like that. It must have been cool being in his class at school. And Frank McLeod had sensed it. McLeod understood that he was dealing with an unknown.

'These people don't know fear,' Shaughnessy said. 'There's nothing in their world *to* fear. But a total wipe-out of their properties would not be welcome.'

'Jesus,' Peter Bonney said. 'You people are lunatics. All this for an infidelity case.' He was looking back at the glimmer of lights through the gate.

'We keep a lower profile,' I said, 'when it's actually an infidelity case.'

Shaughnessy coughed. His smile was gone.

'Have a good one,' he said.

I nodded again and told him to apologise to Jasmine. Hoped he'd catch the rest of the Clint Eastwood.

'It's on pause,' Shaughnessy said. 'I just have to press the button.'

The same message he'd left with McLeod.

He turned and disappeared towards the road, to wherever he'd hidden the bike. Bonney watched him go then stamped his feet. His face was shadows. He turned to me.

'This has been a mess,' he said.

The guy was putting a face on it but he couldn't quite hide that he was shaken. That he was looking for therapy, for someone to confirm that it had been a damn mess but now it was over.

But it wasn't over. McLeod's soldiers were rolling back from Northfleet right now and I didn't want to be here when they arrived. Bonney's rhetoric I could do without.

The breeze was getting colder. The cloud was low and thick and black except where the reflected village light bounced back. I jabbed my hands in my coat. We needed to leave. Give McLeod time to think about Shaughnessy's pictures. About charred wood and rubble. I kicked my own feet.

'Yeah,' I said. 'A mess.'

But Bonney was still talking. He looked across the dark fields.

'I guess this goes no further,' he said, 'if Lisa asks questions.'

'She'll ask Ray the questions,' I said. 'There's nothing more I can give her.'

'Appreciated,' Bonney said. 'You were right. It was a stupid move, taking on McLeod's firm. I didn't think it through.'

I looked at him.

'Well,' I said, 'I suspect you did think it through, Peter. As far as Ray being fed to the sharks at least and your bank account being fattened. You just didn't think about the possibility that Lisa might get hurt.'

I looked back at the lights beyond the gate. Listened for the sound of big cars coming down the lane.

'You tried to have your son-in-law killed, Peter,' I said. 'You'd thought it right through.'

'Christ!' Bonney said. 'Ray was bound to get his fingers burned one day, working for these animals. And I'd warned him fair and square. Told him that if he ever hurt my daughter I'd put him in the ground. Lisa deserves better than that punk. So I'm not apologising. I was a fool for endangering Lisa but I won't apologise for Ray.'

I looked at the Toyota. At the shadows huddled in the back.

'That was Lisa's call,' I said. 'Sooner or later she'd have had to confront Ray and deal with her suspicions. But it was her call, not yours. And she certainly wouldn't have wanted Ray dead.'

Bonney had gone back to watching the fields. His face was a silhouette.

'I hear what you say,' he said. 'Different opinion. The bastard deserved it.'

'Did Lennie Parks deserve it?'

Bonney turned.

Lennie Parks. The informant he'd shot eight years ago. Self-defence according to his account. An account I backed up. 'Did it happen that way?' I said.

'What are you saying?'

'Just that I've sometimes wondered. You were a good copper, Peter, and your story made a kind of sense but I always wondered.'

'You think I set it up? Killed my own informant? Why would I do that?'

'A million reasons. Maybe it was like you said, that Parks had been turned by the Russians and was there to kill you. That's why I kept things vague about the warning I didn't hear. I told them the truth:

that all I heard was muffled voices. But I've always wondered whether I'd have heard you clearly if you'd actually called out to the guy. And there's a million reasons a cop might decide that an informant is a liability. If the informant's about to inform on the cop, for example. But I gave you the benefit of the doubt. You were a good cop and I didn't see you as a killer. But this...' I said, 'makes me wonder.'

Bonney's eyes were blacker than the night. His voice was low and hard.

'Leave it, Eddie,' he said. 'You got me out of a fix back then. Saved my skin. And again tonight. I'm grateful. What can I say?'

I watched his silhouette.

'Take them home,' I said. 'And if Lisa or Ray ever start to wonder how their Capri got snatched so quickly, maybe wonder if someone had access to Ray's spare keys, then you'll have some questions to answer. Take them home and hope that McLeod sees sense.'

The dark hid Bonney's expression. He clamped my shoulder briefly then turned away.

'Have a good Christmas, Eddie,' he said.

I said nothing.

He got into the Avensis. I watched the car drive out and turn into the road.

CHAPTER THIRTY-ONE
I thought I'd surprise you

I drove back through light, mid-evening traffic with Charlie Parker improvising frantically over the purr of the Sprite's engine. As I hit Blackheath the snow came back. It started as a flurry then came on thick, smashed silently against the windscreen and transformed the world into a disorienting light show. I thought about what had just happened and whether it was over. Pictured the McLeod family get-together back there in the mansion. A crackling fire, chestnuts roasting, McLeod popping back in from the library to top up the drinks and offer apologies all round. These damn business affairs! Can't get away from them. In the New Year someone else would be carrying McLeod's bag round the shops and this week's scare would have started to fade. But grudges don't, so I guess we were dependent on Shaughnessy's message to see an end to the thing. Even psychopaths like McLeod can recognise danger.

I'd eaten nothing since the abandoned lunchtime sandwich and hunger was vicious but I'd packing to do then a long drive out and there was time only for one quick detour. I hit Vauxhall and swung towards the bridge and drove up to Paddington.

I didn't know William's second name and neither did the hospital, which did the trick. They gave me a ward number and I chased my tail round an NHS maze for ten minutes then landed at an eight-bed ward with an old guy, a tiny husk, bedded down at the far end and more comfortable than he'd been for a couple of decades. William was hooked up to tubes and looked like he was sleeping but when my shadow crossed his face his eyes opened and the face cracked into a smile.

'Good evening my fren'!' he said. His voice was quiet but it was steady. 'Wasn' expecting visitors.'

'How are they treating you?' I said.

'Oh, plenty fine,' William said. He was so deep in pillows you'd think he'd never get out. 'They've got me in luxury. The doctors couldn't locate a cardboard box so I'm in clover.'

'Better in than out,' I said.

'Better by far. I nearly popped me clogs las' night. The damn cold. Caught me short.'

'So you didn't make it to your pal's?'

He lifted a tired hand.

'A long way to go. A lot of trouble. Maybe tomorrow night.'

I grinned. William was going nowhere for a few nights. He'd be scoffing his turkey right here – whatever species might flap out of the hospital catering system – and when the old guy was discharged he'd be put into sheltered social housing until the authorities decided that they could in good conscience wash their hands of him. If William played it smart he'd stay in the system. London streets are unforgiving in January.

'They treating you okay?'

The old guy's face lost its peace.

'They won't let Herbie in. He'll be needin' his dinner.'

I doubted it. Herbie would have eaten his dinner in Henrietta's kitchen. I told William that his dog was in good hands. A personal sitter from Battersea Dogs Home. His mutt was sleeping in a warm bed with his toes singeing on the radiator. The image lifted William's spirit to a new contentment. I didn't tell him that when they moved him into his new accommodation there'd be no room for dogs. Council rules. The same everywhere.

'Herbie's fine,' I said. 'We'll take care of him until you're up and running.'

'Tomorrow,' William said. 'I'll pick him up then.'

I grinned.

'Anything you need until then?'

'A tumbler for me whisky and a stick to fight off the nurses,' he said. 'And mebbe a couple of ciggies.'

I grinned. 'I'll see what I can do. The ciggies will be tough.'

William tensed. His tubes danced. 'None of this vaping stuff!' he said. 'Ciggies or nothing.'

'Got it. Lie back. Rest a little.'

'I'll lie back when I'm dead,' William said. 'Life's too short to idle away.'

But he didn't look inclined to go anywhere soon.

'Got it,' I repeated. 'Take care, mister. Merry Christmas.'

'And the marryest of Chrissmases t'*yer*,' William said. 'You see the tree over there? Tree and lights! All we need is for Santa Claus to come through the winder.'

I threw him a wink.

'I'll let you know about Herbie,' I promised.

I left him to it and went out. Hit Battersea at eight thirty, which was a day and four hours later than I'd been planning to do my packing. The snow had eased off again but the street shone in the ghostly luminescence of its cover. I went in and knocked on Henrietta's door. She opened it and a wide panting face stared up and threw a gruff bark. Herbie pushed out and planted his paws on my thighs. I stooped to pat his wide head.

'He's fed and watered,' Henrietta said. 'Is he staying with me?'

I looked down. Herbie's grin stretched.

'His owner won't be taking him for a while,' I said. 'I guess that would be tricky for you.'

'I could manage,' Henrietta said. 'I'm in and out though, rushing round a little. Be good if someone had more time.'

'I'm taking a trip out of town,' I said. 'I guess Herbie wouldn't mind a few days in the country.'

I looked down. Herbie's grin extended to his ears. His tail whipped. Henrietta reached behind the door and passed his leash out along with the bag of food.

'All yours,' she said. 'Just tell me when you need a sitter.'

'I'll do that,' I said.

All mine.

Until William was on his feet and independent again. Which could be a while. I stooped and clipped the leash. Herbie still had his feet on my legs which facilitated things, though moving about was going to be difficult.

'Down!' I said.

He dropped back to the floor and I wished Henrietta a Merry Christmas and we went up.

It took fifteen minutes to pack. Then I grabbed an extra duffel and threw in an old blanket for Herbie on top of his food and we were ready.

We went out; trod snow. I opened the Frogeye and Herbie leapt into place and grinned at the windscreen, panting for the car to start. I went round the other side and pushed the bags into the boot then squeeze in beside him.

My phone rang.

Amber. Wondering where the hell I was. I told her I'd see her in three and she asked if I'd eaten. I told her the truth.

'Jesus, Eddie! What the hell are you doing working Christmas Eve? Do your clients never sleep?'

'This business...' I said.

'We'll have something on the table for you. Bill's got a bottle of Macallan warming. Be here in three hours or it's history.'

'Three hours,' I said. 'And I've a guest with me.'

A second's silence. Then:

'That's great, Eddie. I thought it might take a little longer... You didn't mention there was someone new.'

Barely a hint of disappointment that she'd not be meeting Arabel, the girlfriend who'd split three months ago due to catastrophic complications with a job. But life is a carousel of change, not all of it for the better.

'I thought I'd surprise you,' I said.

I killed the line and grinned at my passenger. Pressed the starter.

Herbie grinned too, bursting to inflict his surprise. When I flicked on the lights they illuminated snowflakes melting on the glass, the street disappearing in a fast-thickening flurry. The main storm coming in.

I slotted in some music to see us through then hit the wipers and let the wheels roll onto crisp, fresh snow.

THE END

ACKNOWLEDGEMENTS

I wrote this story as a short breather during a six month interlude between publishing *The Watching,* a stand alone story that demanded a good deal of research and validation – work, in other words – and the fifth Eddie Flynn story which will involve a more complex plot and therefore may also feel like work. *Slow Light* is a short and simple tale that didn't demand too much in the way of research and correction. I've hoped, by this means, to get the book to the reader a little faster without compromising on quality. The little research that has been needed has been gathered in snippets from my reference library and from the internet, involving too many sources to make their mention worthwhile.

Most of the incidental detail that colours the narrative is true to the supposed time of this case (December 2011), though the British government's sagacious "Go Home" advertising campaign exhorting undesirables to leave the country didn't start until two years later. Sean Shaughnessy's movie demolition snaps are fiction, unless I've missed a good Clint Eastwood film.

Thanks once again to my wife, Odette, for reading the draft and pointing out the rough edges, to which I have applied chisel and sandpaper. I hope the result is an enjoyable read. Errors always get through, factual and typographical, no matter how careful the proofreading, and for these I apologise and hope they haven't intruded.

BEHIND CLOSED DOORS
Michael Donovan

Family feuds, booze and bad company. Teenager Rebecca Slater's walk on the wild side has taken a downward spiral. And now she's disappeared.

But her family don't seem to have noticed. Wealthy, private, dysfunctional, the Slaters deny that their daughter is missing – even as they block all attempts by Rebecca's friends to contact her.

So the friends contact a private investigator.

Eddie Flynn is good at finding people. And he's good at spotting lies. It doesn't take him long to see through the Slaters' denials. So he digs around, and isn't too surprised when some unpleasant people come scuttling out of the cracks in the Slaters' perfect world.

But for these people the teenager's disappearance is part of a plan. One that's too important to be threatened by an investigator with more persistence than sense. So it's time for the investigator to disappear...

Winner of the **Northern Crime 2012** award, *Behind Closed Doors* has been acclaimed for its departure from the norm for British crime fiction...

'Donovan refreshingly breaks [the tradition] with remarkable success'
Cuckoo Review

'Eddie Flynn is part Philip Marlowe, part Eddie Gumshoe, a likeable wisecracking guy but with a temper when roused ... humour ... violent confrontations ... well recommended.'
eurocrime

www.michaeldonovancrime.com

THE DEVIL'S SNARE
Michael Donovan

They call them the "Killer Couple". Accused of killing their daughter the Barbers have been on the run from public opinion for two years.

But the Barbers are still fighting. And if their high profile campaign to clear their name and get their baby back has made them rich that was never their intention.

Meanwhile a failed prosecution hasn't dampened the media's hunger for revelations. Their investigators are on the job, moving towards an exposure that will spotlight the Barbers as the killers they are. And now a dangerous vigilante has joined the fray: if the system can't bring justice he'll mete out his own.

P.I. Eddie Flynn doesn't read the tabloids. Shuns limelight. Trusts only in facts. But can't resist challenges. When the Barbers come to him for help he pushes judgement aside and signs up. His mission: keep them safe and find their child.

Sounds like nice, solid detective work. Until Flynn realises that his clients are hiding something...

'A slick, dynamic mystery.'
Kirkus Reviews

'Escapism at its best'
Postcard Reviews

'... complicated ... wonderful ... brilliant. I recommend anyone ... to try this book. [It] will haunt your days and nights.'
Georgia Cuthbertson, Cuckoo Review

www.michaeldonovancrime.com

COLD CALL
Michael Donovan

In the black of night the intruder breaks into the victim's house armed with a knife and garrotte. Her body is found thirty hours later, a mass of stab wounds, a deadly laceration round her neck.

Is this the Diceman, killing again after seven years lying low? Or does London have a copycat killer?

P.I. Eddie Flynn has been out of that world since his failed hunt for the Diceman let the killer go free and cost him his job in the Metropolitan Police.

Now, with the new killer on the rampage a bizarre phone call from his dead victim drags Flynn right back to centre stage and a new hunt. But this killer – copycat or not – takes a P.I.'s interference personally.

So now he has a new focus for his madness.

"Chilling ... crafted with style...
wild nightmarish scenes."
Bookpleasures

"Masterful... If you haven't been
introduced to Eddie Flynn yet, be prepared"
Red City Review

www.michaeldonovancrime.com

Printed in Great Britain
by Amazon

86274346R00120